W9-BZJ-904

THE SOFTWIRE

THE SOFTWIRE
AWAKENING ON ORBIS 4

PJ HAARSMA

CANDLEWICK PRESS

Copyright © 2010 by PJ Haarsma

First edition 2010

Library of Congress Cataloging-in-Publication Data
Haarsma, PJ.
The softwire : awakening on Orbis 4 / PJ Haarsma. — 1st ed.
p. cm. — (The softwire)
Summary: As the Scion's guardian, Johnny Turnbull is expected to
begin training as a Space Jumper, a role he promised his girlfriend
Max he would never take on, and which might not be enough
to save his sister and friends when Orbis is threatened.
ISBN 978-0-7636-2712-6
[1. Computers — Fiction.   2. Space and time — Fiction.   3. Mercenary
troops — Fiction.   4. Science fiction.]   I. Title.   II. Title: Awakening
on Orbis 4.   III. Title: Awakening on Orbis four.   IV. Series.
PZ7.H111325Soi 2010
[Fic] — dc22   2009032482

10 11 12 13 14 15 MVP 10 9 8 7 6 5 4 3 2 1

Printed in York, PA, U.S.A.

This book was typeset in Utopia.

Candlewick Press
99 Dover Street
Somerville, Massachusetts 02144

visit us at www.candlewick.com

For my family

"Stop it!" I begged.

"I can't," Theylor whispered. "Ketheria *must* suffer this."

"When will it be over?"

My sister's body convulsed while suspended over a thick block of chrome deep within the Keepers' lair on Orbis 1. I turned away.

"This is one of the fourteen steps of the awakening," Theylor reminded me. "We have discussed this."

"But look at her. Her eyes are going to pop out of her head!"

"The *glow* is doing that. Her eyes will remain firmly inside their sockets," he assured me. "That is nothing more than an illusion."

Glow was a clumsy description of what was happening to Ketheria. Her skin was shining with a lustrous golden light that pulsed brighter, not with each heartbeat but with some other-worldly measure that I was not privy to. I stood by, helpless, and watched as the metal block she floated above refused to absorb the glow, tossing it back while her body deflated with each throb of light. During one convulsion, Ketheria's head lobbed sideways and her eyes seemed to focus on mine.

"Ketheria!" I called out, but her vacant stare just bore straight through me. I don't think she had a clue that I was even in the room with her.

I felt Theylor place his slender hand on my shoulder. I turned and looked into the eyes of his left head. I had grown to trust Theylor over the last three rotations on the Rings of Orbis, and I searched his bluish face now to find any justification for my sister's suffering.

"The Nagools have been waiting their whole lives for this moment," he said. "They will do everything to make the Scion's —"

"*My sister*, Theylor. She's my *sister*, nothing more," I corrected him. "We traveled from Earth to work on these rings just like the zillions of other aliens who come here every rotation to do the exact same thing. Once our debt is paid, we get to start a new life of our own — as *Citizens*. That was the deal. Not this! The *Scion*? The *Tonat*? None of it makes sense to me, Theylor. I don't want any of it, and I'm certain Ketheria doesn't, either. You guys are the ones calling her the Scion. That word doesn't mean anything to me."

Theylor bowed his head before he continued. "Even if you do not want this to happen, you cannot deny that it *is* happening. This is self-evident." Theylor motioned toward Ketheria. "Yet for some reason, you resist believing what you see right before your very eyes. Your sister *is* the Scion, Johnny Turnbull. I assure you that the Nagools will do everything possible to make her awakening a painless experience. I do not understand your anger."

"I'm not angry," I whispered. "I'm confused."

"Some things are easier to accept if you simply trust the Universe."

That was easy for him to say. He wasn't a knudnik.

"Come now," he added. "I must get you to the spaceport. There is not much time before the Orbis 4 shuttle launches. Your new work rule has already started."

Despite the fact that everyone believed Ketheria was the new Scion, the Trading Council insisted that we finish our fourth rotation of indentured service, and the Keepers and the Nagools did not argue. They believed that the Scion had to awaken along the path that the Universe had predicted for him or her, no matter how dangerous that path may be. It was a small miracle that they even let me follow Ketheria to Orbis 1 once she got sick. I had hoped she might come out of her awakening and we could travel to Orbis 4 together, but that did not seem likely now.

"Please," I begged. "I was hoping for a little more time."

"I am sorry. I have done everything I could just to let you stay this phase."

"I've been here a whole phase?"

Theylor nodded, and I remembered the moment when I had found Ketheria in the middle of one of her spells. It was right before we were all about to leave to meet our new Guarantor on Orbis 4. Ketheria had started doodling those little spirals on the walls while everyone else was packing. Soon afterward she slipped into the catatonic state that now consumed her. Usually Ketheria came out of one of her spells by the end of a cycle, but this time she hadn't. Instead, the glow had started. I told Vairocina, my friend inside the central computer, the moment it began, and she contacted Theylor immediately. Soon Theylor and an army of Nagool masters converged upon Ketheria. As they shuttled both her and me to Magna on Orbis 1, Theylor informed me that the glow was the Source working through her, making connections with the rest of the universe. Max, Theodore, and everyone else were shipped off to Orbis 4.

"Johnny," Theylor called. "I'm sorry, but it is time."

Reluctantly, I turned from my frozen vigil and followed Theylor out of the room, entrusting my sister to the Nagools. When I thought about waking up the next cycle not knowing a thing about my sister's condition, I felt as if a Neewalker had clamped his hands around my throat, trapping the air inside me. It scared me and I hated it.

Theylor paused next to one of the many treelike pillars that supported the largest cavern of the Keepers' lair located beneath the city of Magna and waited for me. I looked up to where the deep blue stone pillars made contact with the roof. Bands of yellowish light oscillated from the top of the support with a beat that was oddly reminiscent of the glow. I then followed Theylor as he navigated around huge pools of black water that glittered from deep below the surface.

A small domed craft waited on a rail of shorter pillars next to a platform. I followed Theylor aboard, and we sat in silence during the short trip to the surface. It gave me time to think. What had happened? Why Ketheria? No one had any answers for me, but that didn't mean no one knew. I had heard stories of other Scions and the horrible fates they met. No matter what part of the universe they came from, new Scions were always persecuted by one group or another, tested until they broke. I had also heard tales of the Tonat, the guardian entrusted to protect the Scion once the awakening was complete. That's who they wanted me to be. But if the Tonat was so important, why was I leaving my sister behind? It didn't make sense, but then when had my life on the rings ever made sense? No one ever explained anything here. Three rotations had taught me that most people on the Rings of Orbis protected their knowledge more than they did an Orodi Orb.

Once we disembarked from the small craft, I followed Theylor up a wide staircase that led to two metal doors, scuffed and marred by eons of use. At the top of the stairs, Theylor paused and turned to me. "Others may have come to see the Scion," he said, as if it were a warning.

"I thought no one knew where Magna was located."

"Idolatry has a unique way of bringing light to the blind," he replied.

When Theylor pushed back the thick doors, the glassy glow from a distant star burnished my eyes, and faster than my pupils could contract, a throng of aliens burst upon us.

"Who are these people, Theylor?"

"Worshippers," he replied, holding up his hand to the crowd.

The effect seemed to push the people back, which allowed us to move forward. "I did not expect to see so many. I am afraid news of the Scion has spread quickly. This is not good."

"Why is the Scion so important to them?"

"It has been a very long time since a Scion has been discovered. In fact, most people thought it was no longer possible. Your sister is their last hope."

There must have been thousands of people gathered there. Every one of them seemed to be whispering something at me. Hushed pleas called to me from every side as we pushed through the crowds.

"They worship my sister?"

"They worship the Scion," he said, as if Ketheria was a separate entity entirely. "And some even worship the Tonat."

"I'm not the Tonat, Theylor. The Trust said *I* have to make that choice, and I don't want to be a Space Jumper. In order to be the Tonat, I have to be a Space Jumper."

"I believe the Trust merely presented you with that choice as a gesture."

"A gesture of what?"

"To appease your fierce need to control your own existence. I wonder how much choice you actually have in this matter."

"What does that mean, Theylor? It *is* my choice."

But Theylor did not respond. It frustrated me to be fed these cryptic answers all the time.

"If this is so important, why won't you tell me anything else?" I shouted as more people pushed in on us, but Theylor did not answer. His attention was now on the crowd. More and more people rushed toward us, and the crush was beginning to smother me. One alien tugged at my vest, another simply rubbed her hands over me, while another squawked in my face. Theylor tried to force them back, but that only created an opening for more to pour into.

"Theylor!"

"I'm trying," he grunted.

The crowd now engulfed me. I could no longer see the sky and had lost sight of Theylor in a sea of wanting hands.

"I have nothing to give you!" I shouted. "I can't help you."

Then someone struck me. It was a quick blow to my forehead, but still painful.

"Death to the Tonat!" the alien screamed, but the crowd turned on the assailant. At least a dozen worshippers descended on my attacker and delivered blows much worse than the one he had given me.

"Stop!" I screamed at them, but the crowd swallowed the brawling aliens. Then I saw the flash of a Zinovian Claw, a nasty little weapon that was often equipped with a poison cartridge. "Look out!" I screamed, pointing at the weapon. The effect was instant. The same punishment dealt to the first detractor was unleashed on the claw-toting alien. Fights were now breaking out between different groups, and my body flowed helplessly with the energy of the crowd.

"Theylor! Help me!"

Suddenly the crowd blew apart. Bodies wrenched away from me like metal shavings pulled helplessly toward a huge magnet. Theylor stood in the opening, flanked by two Space Jumpers, who immediately descended upon me. Theylor moved calmly, but I can't say the same for the mass of worshippers.

"Do you wish for war, Keeper?" a shocked Citizen shouted.

"We will crush you!" another added as the effect of seeing the heavily armed mercenaries rippled through the crowd.

"This is a taste of your life now, whether you accept your fate or not," Theylor whispered to me. "Just imagine what this is going to be like for Ketheria. She is going to need you."

"I won't do it, Theylor. This is not our battle. I don't know how any of this happened. I'm just a kid from Earth."

One of the Space Jumpers grunted.

"But she is your *sister*," Theylor pleaded.

"And I will protect her, but it has to be in my own way."

Theylor breathed deeply. I knew he didn't like my answer. "You are naive. Your actions risk your life, they risk your sister's life, and they might even risk every life in this universe. We will talk of this again," he said, motioning to the Space Jumpers at my side. And then I was gone.

A moment later, I was standing in a field, rubbing the smell of sweat-soaked socks out of my nose. The Space Jumper to my left had released me. I looked up and saw the city of Nacreo gleaming in the distance.

"Hello, Johnny Turnbull. Or do you prefer JT?" a voice called out.

I turned; a tall, strong-looking humanoid was standing next to one of the Keepers' fliers. He was wearing a heavy-looking over-coat flung back to expose his tall black boots. When I noticed the small stalactites of flesh that hung from his jawline, I suddenly realized that I had seen this alien before. At Odran's! The dinner party! This alien was a Trading Council member.

"You're the-the—" I stammered.

"Hach. I believe we've met once before. I am your new Guarantor."

My first Guarantor was a weaselley little rat named Weegin. The Keepers replaced him with Odran, a vile creature whose scruples were worse than his appearance (and trust me, his appearance was disgusting). My third Guarantor was my friend, a human named Charlie Norton. A cycle never passed when I did not think about him. But Hach was nothing like my previous Guarantors, even Charlie. I'd never forget the way he had confronted his fellow Trading Council member for insulting us at Odran's party. Hach stood confidently, with his hands cupped, waiting patiently for my reply.

"Hello. Yeah—JT. That's what my friends call me," I told him.

"I look forward to being your friend, then, JT. If you'll follow me, the Keepers have arranged transportation to the spaceport." Hach motioned toward the flier. It was nothing more than a wheel with a cockpit near the center. "Normally I have a driver, but I couldn't resist flying one of these things."

The Space Jumper to my right pushed me toward my new Guarantor. The unexpected force tripped me up, and I fell to my knees. Hach spun around and unleashed a small staff from beneath his cloak. I had the keen sense to duck as he thrust his right arm in front of him, unfolding the device like a double-sided whip. In one complete motion, Hach caught the Space Jumper around the ankles and pulled. The Space Jumper toppled to the ground.

"What's it like from down there?" Hach hissed at the fallen Space Jumper.

"Wow," I mumbled. I had never seen anyone take out a Space Jumper before. I didn't think it was even possible.

"Come, JT," Hach ordered, and turned toward the flier. Both Space Jumpers glared at me as I walked past. The air around them seemed to ripple as the light folded in on them, and then they were gone, jumping back to wherever they had come from.

I had seen one of the Keepers' fliers on Orbis 3. It was basically a large wheel piloted from a cockpit positioned off center and lower to the ground. This cockpit remained in its position as the wheel spun around. Hach took his seat at the controls while I climbed in and sat up behind him. I snuggled in, and the seat conformed to my body.

Hach uplinked to the control panel using the neural port embedded behind his left ear, and the cockpit closed in around us. The clouded glass slowly became transparent. I was seated slightly higher than Hach, so I had an unobstructed view of what was in front of me. The craft rolled forward and then lifted into the air, picking up speed as the huge wheel spun faster and faster. Soon it was spinning so fast that I could barely see it except for the slight distortion it made in my vision.

"Comfortable?" Hach asked, his voice soft in my ears, amplified through the smart material behind my head.

"Um, yes," I said. "Thank you." I was not used to having a Guarantor care about my well-being. (Except for Charlie, of course, but that was different.) Most of the Citizens on the Rings of Orbis treated knudniks with the same respect they gave the dirt between their toes, if they had toes. I wasn't going to let Hach's seemingly open manners go to waste.

"Hach, may I ask you something?" I said.

"You may."

"How did you become our Guarantor?"

There was a pause before Hach answered. History had taught me that this sort of pause was usually followed by a lie.

"You were given to me."

"By whom?"

"Your last Guarantor."

"Charlie?"

"Yes."

I didn't know what to say. When could Charlie have entrusted us to anyone? The attack had left him unconscious and he'd never come out of it. During our first rotation back on Orbis 1, Madame Lee had murdered Max's first Guarantor, Boohral, and since he had not willed his knudniks to anyone in time, the Keepers redistributed Max and the others (much to the anger of Boohral's brood). I could only assume the same would have happened after Charlie died.

"When?" I said. "How?"

"I am not at liberty to say," he replied. "Policy of the Trading Council."

And there it was again, the same nonanswer to my most important questions. Why couldn't anyone on these stupid rings just tell the truth? Every response was a diversion.

"Can I ask another one?"

"How many do you plan on asking?"

"I—I . . . don't know."

"You may ask me three more questions. I'm sure that's all we'll have time for before we reach the city of Nacreo."

Three questions? I had a million, and Hach was a Trading Council member. Didn't they know everything? I watched the city growing in front of me as the flier sped toward the space-port. Three questions. Better start now.

"Do you know what's happening to my sister?"

"Of course. Everyone does. That's an odd waste of a question since I'm sure you, too, are aware of that answer."

But that's not what I meant! I knew about the awakening. I knew it was some sort of transformation. That's how the Keepers explained it, but I didn't believe it. There was no way my sister or I had anything to do with the salvation of the universe.

"No, I meant what does it *mean*?"

"It means your sister is the Scion and you are the Tonat."

"I know that, too." I resisted the urge to call him a split-screen. "You don't understand. No one knew I was coming to Orbis. I can't possibly have anything to do with all of this. Our parents smuggled us onto the *Renaissance* in hopes of a better life, away from Earth. That's all. Did *you* know that?"

"I did."

"So then I don't get it. I don't understand how my sister is the Scion or how I'm supposed to be the Tonat. What's going to happen to us if what they say is true?"

"Oh, it *is* true, but that, I'm afraid, is question number four, and we've arrived at the spaceport. Get ready for a jolt. I can't land these things as well as the Keepers can."

Once inside the spaceport, I gazed at the starships nestled in their docking bays as I waited for Hach on a crystal bench. *Is this their first time to the Rings of Orbis?* I wondered. *Are they here to do business with the Trading Council, or are their bellies filled with aliens looking for a better life?*

"Keep going if *that's* what you're looking for," I whispered to them.

I tried to remember what the *Renaissance* had looked like sitting in the same spot after its one-way journey from Earth, but I could not recall ever seeing our ship docked in the spaceport. What would have happened if we had never arrived? I suddenly wondered. Where would I be right now if I had listened to Switzer and helped him escape with the *Renaissance*? Would I have been able to pull it off? I didn't even know I was a softwire back then.

I watched the largest ship unhook and push back, moving like a Samiran in the crystal-cooling tank. The nose of the starcraft pushed away from me as if sniffing out the open space behind it. Suddenly I sprang from the bench and rushed to the window. I wanted to be on that ship! At that very moment, as I pressed against the glass, I wanted nothing more than to feel the thrust of the engines against my chest. I couldn't explain why, but my stomach surged with a huge gulp of regret as the starship disappeared into deep space. Then Hach called for me, and I followed him to our ship.

Inside the shuttle to Orbis 4, the drill was familiar. I was placed in a lower cabin while Hach sat in an area reserved for Citizens. *Where would the Scion sit?* I wondered as I glanced at the empty plastic benches. *If I had chosen to be the Tonat, would I still be sitting here?*

"Your actions risk your life, they risk your sister's life . . ."

I shook Theylor's dire words from my head and tried to focus on the activity visible through the portal that lined the shuttle's cabin, but the huge passenger shuttles tethered to the spaceport only reminded me of my friend Toll. Would he have approved of my choice? Of course not. He would have insisted I follow in my father's footsteps — a Space Jumper whom I had never met and whose origin was still a mystery to me. Argh! So many things pointed to a conclusion that I was simply not willing to accept. I was *not* just some kid from Earth. Neither was Ketheria, *but why*? How did this happen?

Even if it was true, I still refused to become a Space Jumper. I had my reasons, and the most important one was waiting for me on Orbis 4. I had made a promise to Max that I would *never* become a Space Jumper. I knew full well how much she detested Space Jumpers, and it would kill me to have her think of *me* like that. I *was* going to watch over my sister, but I would protect Ketheria in my own way, no matter how difficult that proved to be.

After the shuttle pulled away, I must have fallen asleep with my face pressed against the glass. I woke to find Hach standing over me.

"Get up," he ordered. "We're here."

I wiped the drool off the window and looked out at the space-port of Orbis 4. The ring was in shadow, and the inky darkness was pierced by a multitude of lights that glittered throughout the port. Red beacons flashed across the sky, alerting incoming ships to the tallest buildings inside the port, while glaring white spotlights interrogated the docked spaceships, exposing the fatigue of deep-space travel. Gold, orange, and green lights advertised the locations of the different trading chambers within the port, while frosted blue lights wove their way through the different levels, one after another, like a stream of frozen water. The spaceport on Orbis 4 was a busy place.

My temples throbbed and I felt nauseous as I jogged to keep up with Hach. Then it dawned on me that this was the farthest I had ever been from Ketheria. Ever since we were young, I had never liked being apart from her for long periods of time, and whenever we were separated, I became distracted by a weird empty feeling that I had always assumed was simply anxiety. I never really paid much attention to it, but after the awakening started, it had become more noticeable. This was the worst I had felt since the start of her awakening, and it was also the farthest I had been from her — a fact that was not lost on me.

I followed Hach as he marched across the spaceport and through one of the many exits. Once outside, we descended a broad set of stone steps that led into a city. When I caught sight of the city, I gasped. Hach turned and saw me gawking.

"Welcome to the dumping ring," he said.

"Who calls it that?"

"I do. They call it Murat. I believe it was named after some Nagool. Now, come, we have people waiting for us."

I followed my Guarantor into the city. Murat looked like a way station, a shantytown constructed from used materials fastened to anything that was standing. Metal and glass structures like you might find on the other rings were buried under an erratic framework of multilevel trading chambers that sold what looked like the worthless trinkets Switzer and Dalton had scavenged on Orbis 2. The ones that sold useful items, like food or tools, were the busiest, but most of the action seemed to come from customers haggling over prices.

As I was walked deeper into Murat, I noticed that a lot of the signs were painted on boards or scratched right into the concrete and that the central computer did not translate half of them. Along the cramped streets, I also witnessed small fires burning in the open, where aliens roasted small creatures — skin, fur, and all. The smell was disgusting, as if you had burned the hair on your arm.

"This is where you work?" I said.

"Of course not," Hach replied. "My industries are off-ring, mostly on Ki and Ta. This is where *you* will work."

What could I possible do here? my mind cried.

I stepped to the side as an alien with a narrow chin and a hunched back scurried toward Hach and offered him what I thought was a chemical analyzer, though the tool was too mangled to be certain. Hach took the used item from him and tossed the alien a tiny crystal in return. Two other aliens emerged from the shadows and pawed at the alien's new bounty. Farther down the path, Hach gave the broken device to another alien, sitting alone in the street.

"Sad, isn't it?" he remarked. "This is what they risked their lives for. They've traded rotation after rotation of indentured service for this meager existence."

"I don't get it," I said. "How do they end up like this?"

"It's simple, really. The First Families like what they have, and they work diligently to keep it for themselves. When knudniks complete their work rules, most of them don't have the finances or the skill set required to live as proper Citizens. Do you know what it costs to live on Orbis 3? Even if half the people here pooled their resources, they couldn't afford a dwelling on the ring. Here lies the Rings of Orbis's dirty little secret. And it could be even worse."

"Worse?"

"Orbis 4 would be overflowing with refugees if these aliens weren't offered passage through the wormhole after their work rule ended. If I were them, I wouldn't stay here, either."

"But don't the Keepers know about this? I can't imagine them allowing it."

"But that's the genius of the Citizens, especially the Trading Council. You see, the Trading Council controls the wealth. The Keepers do not have to do anything; the Citizens pay for everything, but that leaves the Keepers without any hard currency. Don't get me wrong: the Keepers are wealthier than you can imagine, but they waste their money here. They try to do what they can, but it's a futile effort. There are too many forces working against them."

"But you're on the Council. You sound like you hate this. Why can't you do anything?"

"I *was* on the Trading Council, but I'm not anymore. That is why *you* are here," he said.

Hach was no longer a council member! When had that happened? And more important, why?

I must have been gawking. "Don't worry," he said. "I left the Trading Council of my own accord."

Then Hach stopped in front of a private flier. I looked back down the street toward the spaceport. I knew it was rude and dangerous to question my Guarantor, but I had to ask.

"Why didn't we just—" I pointed back toward the spaceport.

Hach cut me off. "I wanted you to see Murat. I wanted you to experience the city for yourself. I felt it was important for you to know. You'll understand my motives later."

An alien with thick legs and muscular arms emerged from the ruby-red craft.

"I trust your trip was satisfactory," the alien said.

"Yes, I believe it was," Hach replied, motioning toward me.

The alien looked at me and smiled. *Another knudnik*, I thought. It was undeniable. The hopeless look in his eyes gave him away. Did I look like that?

Then the alien reached for the door. I thought he was opening it for Hach, but another alien with taut, glowing-white skin, stepped out of the flier and strode toward me. As he stood up, the skin at the edges of his collar and sleeves seemed to ripple before settling.

"It's good to see you again, Queykay," Hach said, but the candescent alien stepped around my Guarantor without even a glance. Queykay was the same height as Hach but walked with his chin raised, forcing him to look down upon anyone he spoke to. Hach ignored the snub and continued. "Queykay ba Torel, meet JT. JT, meet your new liaison with the Trading Council. It was not possible for me to be your Guarantor and sit on the Council, but the Trading Co —"

"The Trading Council feels the pulse of its Citizens," Queykay interrupted him. "And we feel it is necessary that a member of our elite supervise the arrival of a Scion, independent of your Guarantor's responsibilities. Besides the honor her presence bestows on the multitude of Citizens on Orbis 4, your sibling's existence creates many security risks. The Tonat cannot be in all places at once."

"I'm not the Tonat," I informed him.

"I thought this was taken care of," he said as he turned to Hach.

"It will be," Hach assured him. "I am aware of the arrangement, and I will deliver as promised."

What arrangement?

Queykay stared at me, sizing me up before speaking. "So if you are not the Tonat, then who are you?" he asked. I could hear the sarcasm in his voice.

"I'm. . . . I—" I stumbled for an answer. "I'm the Softwire."

What a stupid answer, I thought. I didn't want to do this. I saw the other knudnik get into the flier and took it as my cue to get away from this guy. I tried to step around Queykay, but his hand darted out from his burgundy cape and pressed against my face. His skin felt damp and sickly except where a large crystal ring encircled his finger. Repulsed, I pulled away from him, glancing up his sleeve.

"But you are still a knudnik," he hissed. "It would be healthy if you remembered that."

I didn't like Queykay. It was one of those instant feelings you get. His entire demeanor seemed polished to make me feel inferior. And he was creepy. When I had pulled away from him just then, something rattled my senses. It wasn't even possible, my mind reasoned. For the tiniest moment of time, I swear that I saw a hundred tiny red eyes blink at me from the depth of his black silk shirt. I shook it off. Weird. I hoped I didn't have to be around this guy too much. I did not see a long-lasting friendship in our future.

Hach leaned in and mumbled something to Queykay. Then he motioned for me to get in the flier. I slipped into a seat at the back, glad to be out from under Queykay's glare, as the flier lifted above the crowds and then turned toward the ring's edge on my right. After a short trip across the tattered city, the flier settled down atop the only building I could see that appeared to be constructed from a set of plans rather than the wire and guesswork that seemed to hold the rest of the city together.

When the flier settled, I waited for my Guarantor to exit first, but he turned to Queykay. He was about to speak when Queykay raised his finger and focused on me. They were both staring when Hach motioned for me to get out.

My pleasure.

I scrambled out of the flier and moved as far away as possible. While I waited for their conversation to finish, I surveyed what I assumed was my new home. The ship was resting on the lower roof of a multilevel structure, some sort of landing pad, I figured. Behind the flier, about a hundred meters away, I spotted an entrance to the second level—a curved structure comprised of nothing but tall black windows. I looked for some sign of life but saw none. *Is Max inside?* I wondered. I hoped so.

I turned away from the black windows and moved to the edge of the lower roof. I glanced below and spotted a long, walled walkway that led away from the front of the building. The concrete path ended at a huge open square. *What does Hach do here?* I wondered. Or rather, what was *I* going to do here?

"It's impressive, isn't it?" Hach called out.

I turned and saw him walking toward me. Queykay and the flier were nowhere to be seen.

"Don't worry—he's gone."

"Would I be punished if I said that I hoped he was gone for good?"

"I won't punish you, but don't let *him* hear that. Just stay out of his way, all right? The Trading Council needs to appear to be in control despite the fact that they were caught completely off guard. They need the Citizens to believe that the Scion is in *their* pocket. They don't want the Keepers taking all of the credit."

"She's not in their pocket," I told him.

"That doesn't matter. Appearances can have just as much influence as fact."

"It sounds like more politics to me," I said. "What is this place?"

"For you? This is home. For me, this is a unique partnership. I hope it does us both some good." Then he let out a deep breath and turned away. "Come, there are some people eager to see you, I'm sure."

"Excuse me, Hach?"

He turned back toward me. No Citizen I ever met liked to be addressed by a knudnik. Inside I cringed, waiting for his punishment, but none came. "Yes?" was all that he said.

"I was hoping that the work I have to perform, you know, what you want me to do, could keep me close to my sister. I've always looked out for her and —"

Hach interrupted me. "Don't worry, Softwire. I'm counting on that."

I wasn't used to getting my way with a Citizen, but I knew when to keep my mouth shut. If Hach was expecting me to stay close to my sister, then that could only mean that he was counting on me to play the Tonat. Even Queykay seemed to expect it. The way those two had confided in each other made me think they were planning something. *But what?*

I followed Hach toward the wall of black glass. As he neared the middle, he waved something in the air and the glass plates parted in response. When I stepped through the door, I was greeted by a digi three times my height, hanging in a hallway that ran parallel to the curve of the glass. I could see at least twenty digis, lit with pinks lights that appeared to float above the polished floor. Some digis showed images of aliens I had never seen while others displayed places I had never visited.

Hach had turned right and was marching down the hall. "This way," he called over the echo of his boots striking the glasslike floor.

Past the last of the enormous digis, Hach stopped under the center of an arched doorway, where cooler light spilled out from the room beyond, along with a familiar chatter. I knew instantly who was in there. I rushed past Hach.

"JT!" Theodore shouted as I entered the room. He sprang from the floor. Theodore was as tall as I was now, and he had let his hair grow into a shaggy mop. It reminded me of the mane on a Garin, the knudniks that served the Trading Council. Everyone rushed toward me — all of the eighteen kids who had lived together with Ketheria and me as knudniks on the Rings of Orbis, though we were only a small fraction of the total number of kids from the *Renaissance.*

I scanned the room for Max. When I saw her, my stomach

tightened and sent a jolt to my heart. She looked up, tucked her hair behind her ear, and smiled. She was so pretty—I couldn't take my eyes off her. Some of the other kids gathered around me and created a barrier between me and Max before she slipped out of sight entirely.

"How's Ketheria?" Grace asked.

"Where is she?" asked someone else.

My replies were quick but friendly. I didn't have the nerve to break through the crowd and go over to Max. Something inside me still hesitated when it came to showing my affection toward her in front of the others.

"Is the awakening finished?" Theodore asked.

"No," I answered. "Ketheria is still with the Nagools."

That's when I noticed Theodore's clothes. He should have been wearing his vest and the tattered clothes he had owned since the *Renaissance,* but he wasn't.

"What are you wearing?" I asked him.

"This?" he said pulling at the burlaplike robe wrapped around his body. "It's actually quite comfortable. Don't laugh. You have to wear one, too."

I looked around. Everyone was wearing these dull robes; some had different-colored cords tied around the middle or scarves draped around their necks.

"I'm not wearing that," I told him.

"Actually, you won't," Hach remarked. "The Tonat requires something a little different."

I looked around and found Max standing behind Grace. I saw her frown when Hach mentioned the word *Tonat.*

"I'm not the Tonat," I insisted. "I have no intention of becoming a Space Jumper." I looked directly at Max when I said it.

"But the others on the ring don't need to know that," Hach argued. "Remember what I said about the power of appearance? I simply need you to *pretend* to be the Tonat. Will you at least agree to that?"

"Pretend? Why would I would I pretend to be something I don't want to be?"

"Because that's our new job," Max said, now standing to my left and looking at Hach. "Well, yours, anyway. This whole building has been designed for it. Once Ketheria is finished with the awakening, this building will become a shrine and fees will be charged so others may visit her."

"Correct," Hach exclaimed. "Humans are so much more observant than they give you credit for. Personally, I have no need for these fables. OIO and its teachings have no room in my life, but that doesn't mean there aren't plenty of individuals on the rings who feel differently."

"And will pay a lot for the privilege to see the Scion," Max added.

"As well as the Tonat," Hach reminded her. "The Trading Council sees a great profit in this little charade."

I didn't know what to say. I just stared at Hach. Could it be true? Were we going to be put on display like animals in a zoo?

"What about everyone else?" I asked.

"Every deity needs her disciples," Hach replied.

"Ketheria won't go for it."

"I would not count on that. When your sister is delivered to me, she will be well on her path to becoming the Scion."

With that, Hach turned and headed out of the room. "Queykay will return later with instructions on preparing for the Scion's arrival."

"Queykay?" I cried.

"I take it you've met him," Max commented.

"Although I am your Guarantor, the Trading Council's needs supersede any authority I may have over you. They, along with the Keepers, are an integral part of this arrangement. I know you will not like to hear this, but when I am not around, Queykay is in charge. He is to be treated with the same respect you would afford me, if not more."

"You're leaving?" I called after him. "But I don't understand. I thought we were working for you."

Hach stopped at the doorway. "My new contracts require my presence on Ta. I have simply provided the building to house the Scion. You are in capable hands with Queykay. This is what's best for everyone, you included. Please trust me when I tell you that this arrangement is far too complicated to explain."

Hach looked at me, waiting for a response, but I said nothing. Anything that I wanted to say would only make matters worse for everyone else.

"Remember," he added, "you could be sleeping in Murat this cycle, and eating one of those things you saw grilling in the street." Then he left. I turned away, grinding the palm of my hand into my forehead.

"I don't understand what's wrong, JT," Grace said. "I think

it's wonderful. One more rotation, and then we're free, with Ketheria as the Scion. I can't think of a better scenario."

"I can think of a few," I muttered, glancing at everyone in the room, dressed in those stupid robes. Max caught me looking.

"What? You don't like them?" she said, smiling and smoothing out the material on her stomach. "They're really quite comfortable." She came over to me and took my hand. I instantly felt better. "C'mon, you have to admit this place is better than the trash belts at Weegin's. Remember that radiation gel?"

I followed Max away from everyone else and out of the back of the room into another glassed hallway. She led me past small pools of water cut into the stone floor and stopped at a crystal bench under a yellow tree that grew right inside the building. The black windows, despite their color, provided an ocean of light, as if a beaming sun were hanging right outside.

"Are the windows lights?" I asked, pointing toward them.

She didn't answer. Instead she grabbed my arm, pulled me close, and kissed me.

"I've been waiting a long time to do that," she said.

"You can do it again if you like."

Max leaned toward me, and this time I kissed her.

"How long is this going to go on for?" Theodore interrupted as he walked toward us. Max pulled away.

"Not long *now*," I complained.

"Good, because there are some things we need to discuss," he said, and thrust something in my face. It looked like the taps we used to get at the Illuminate on Orbis 3.

"What is it?" I asked him.

"Queykay has us handing them out all over Murat," Max said.

"No one refuses them," Theodore added. "Some people even try to resell them."

I poked into the tap with my softwire. Accessing something like a tap was almost as easy as breathing for me now. I no longer thought about the mechanics; I simply concentrated on the outcome, and the contents of the device filled my thoughts. The tap contained moving images of Ketheria with the glow all about her. She was smiling and touching people softly, people who were kneeling in front of her. Some were crying, some rejoicing. It was all strangely eerie, as if Ketheria were some sort of god. This was followed by more images of crowds streaming up the walkway that led to this building. The fictitious events played out inside my head stronger than my most vivid memories.

"I don't get it. Ketheria has never been here before," I said.

"It's an advertisement," Max informed me.

"The Trading Council is going to have Ketheria hold sermons or something," Theodore said.

"Hach knows about this?"

Max nodded.

"What does it mean? They're using *us* to start a religion?"

"OIO is not a religion," she argued.

"But some aliens distort it for their own gain," Theodore said. "They prey on those who worship the Ancients."

"He's right," Max said. "I think that's what the Trading Council is attempting to do here, but OIO is actually a philosophy. It's the art and science of cosmic energy. It helps you to interpret the events in your life so you might gain control. They believe that everything, even your thoughts, goes out into the cosmic soup and has the potential to affect everyone else. Through this energy, we are connected with everything in the universe, no matter how close or how far. Nagools try to master this energy, releasing only constructive energy while avoiding deconstructive energy. But even they look at the arrival of Ketheria as a messiah, as if she's going to help them tip the scales of the deconstructive energy they claim plagues our universe."

"They think it's that bad?" I asked.

Theodore scoffed. "Have you seen it out there? This place is a hellhole."

"And Hach is trying to capitalize on this?" I said.

"The Trading Council is. I'm certain of it," Theodore whispered.

"Queykay has been the one making us hand out the taps," Max reminded him. "I think most of Hach's work is with mining or something."

"You just wander around the city handing out taps? Isn't Queykay afraid we're going to try to escape?"

"Where would we go? This is by far the best place on the ring. Besides, our staining would make it easy for them to find us."

I shook my head. "It doesn't make sense."

"Yes, it does. Hach is a Citizen," Theodore reminded me.

"I know, but you remember him, don't you? Remember how he acted toward that other Citizen at Odran's party?"

Max was nodding. "The one who didn't like knudniks much? I think her name was Pheitt."

"Hach was golden." Theodore smiled.

"I can't picture him doing this. Why would he want to start a religion? You said he was into mining? This doesn't make sense."

"Well, he's doing it," Theodore insisted.

"Vairocina?" I called out. "You can show yourself. It's just us."

Particles of light pooled in front of us, and a figure began to form. Vairocina had started changing her appearance ever since she had begun projecting her holograph for us. Each time it seemed as if she was trying to look a little older. Her new look was not lost on Theodore, who always straightened up when-ever Vairocina appeared.

"Hi, V!" Theodore gushed.

"Hello, Theodore. Hello, everyone."

I looked at Theodore and mouthed, "V?" He only shrugged.

"Hi, Vairocina," I said. "I know I'm always asking for your help, but . . . well, I need your help again."

"You know I will always help you in any way I can."

"Thank you. This time I was wondering if you could help us with our new Guarantor. Hach told me earlier that he gained possession of us from Charlie."

"He did?" Max interrupted, and I nodded to her.

"Can you check and see how that happened? I can't figure out when Charlie had any interactions with Hach. Charlie never mentioned him. It just seems strange that he would leave us to Hach. Will you see if you can dig anything up?"

"Certainly," she replied.

"Did you ever find out how Charlie got all that wealth when he became a Citizen?" Max asked her.

"After his demise, I was certain you wouldn't be interested anymore. I did find a trail, but it ended at the Keepers."

"The Keepers?" I said.

"Do you wish me to look further?"

"No. You're right. It's not important anymore, but I would appreciate any information about Hach and how we came into his possession."

"I'm on it already," she said, smiling and blinking.

"Bye, V!" Theodore said.

"Good-bye, Theodore."

Vairocina's image mixed with the light in the room, and then she was gone.

"You *like* her," Max squealed.

"I do not," Theodore said.

"Yes, you do!"

Theodore shot me a look. "Don't look at me," I argued. "I mean, you do act a little . . . weird whenever she's around."

"Me? *I'm* weird? Maybe I should leave so you guys can get back to sucking on each other's faces."

"Theodore!" Max exclaimed, but I was nodding (hoping my friend would leave quickly).

3

Another entire phase passed and still there was no sign of Ketheria. I was nervous, and to make matters worse, Theylor had not sent me a single screen scroll updating me on my sister's condition. *How long does this step of the awakening take?* I worried.

I was lying in my sleeper, squeezing my temples with the palms of my hands, when Theodore barged into my room. The pain in my head had been coming in waves ever since I woke.

"Come on, malf!" Theodore cried, but then stopped short. "What's wrong with you?" he said.

"Don't get too close," I groaned. "I just might throw up on you."

"We have a lot of these taps to deliver," he complained while hoisting up a large blue sack. "How are you going to help if you look like that?"

"I can't. You go. Queykay's not here, is he?"

"I don't know. He might have left already. He did ask for you, though. Max covered. She'll be here in a sec."

I sat up, making the pain worse, as if my brain was trying to squeeze out around my eyes. I couldn't help but think of Ketheria and the glow.

"No," I said. "I can't. Tell Max I'm not feeling well or something. Tell her I'll catch up with you guys later."

"She thinks you're avoiding her, you know."

"Did she say that?"

"Not exactly."

"I'm not doing this on purpose. I can't control it. I go from zero to puke in a nanosecond. Can you imagine if I tossed in front of Max? Not to mention while I was kissing her!"

Theodore cringed. "No. I don't want to imagine that." He squeezed his eyes shut and shook his head. "Argh! Too late. All right, I'll cover for you again. Get some sleep, but you'll have to do them *all* next cycle."

I nodded as Theodore left. Then I lay down, careful to place my head on the sleeper as gently as possible. I was aching to see Max, but not like this. I tried to avoid her whenever I felt this way. I knew it wasn't right, but I couldn't face the alternative. After a few moments on my back, another wave of nausea crested in my throat and I jumped off my sleeper despite the cries from my splitting head. I made it to the bathroom just before I threw up.

Satisfied that my stomach was empty and hoping that the others had already left to flood Murat with more propaganda, I set off to find the chow synth. I still hadn't adjusted to the layout of the building, so every stroll was an adventure. The place was enormous. I swear it was as big as a space station, but I needed some water. Outside my room I saw a knudnik pulling a train of double-shelved carts filled with bowls and flowers. The alien deftly maneuvered the six or seven linked carts around the corner; none of them even came close to scraping the wall. It had been like this for the whole phase. Knudniks and construction-bots were everywhere. Queykay was building some sort of shrine in preparation for Ketheria's arrival, but I didn't care. It just meant that Ketheria would be here soon.

I was following the train-pulling knudnik down an enormous hallway when I heard Max and Theodore coming toward me.

"This is ridiculous. If he's this sick, then he needs to see a doctor, Theodore," I heard Max say.

I was trapped. If I headed back in the direction of my room, I was certain she would see me. What would I say to her?

"Trust me, Max. I saw him. He's in no condition to see anyone," Theodore said.

The knudnik with the carts stopped, as if he, too, were reacting to their voices. For a moment I thought about crawling into the cart, but I didn't see anything that could hide me.

"This is stupid," I muttered. *Just deal with it*, I thought.

Then the wall to my right seemed to split apart as two seamless stone doors swung open. A couple of Argandians, squat knudniks with yellow, scaled bellies, waddled through the opening. The alien pulling the carts greeted them, and they continued down the hall in the direction of Max and Theodore.

I dove inside the room before the doors swung closed.

I waited for my eyes to adjust to the light, or the lack of it. A soft blue glow arched around the perimeter, but it was not enough for me to see anything. I groped the wall, looking for some sort of control panel that I might push into, but I found only smooth stone, cold and indifferent under my fingertips. *What is this place?* I wondered. I walked slowly toward the blue glow. *That light has to be controlled by something,* I thought. I reached out in front of me, swiping at the air for any obstacles lurking in the dark, when *BAM!* I hit my shin on something hard and sharp. The pain bolted up my leg, and when I reached down, expecting to find blood, I struck my forehead on another stupid barrier.

"Of all the—!" I yelled, and then I was gone.

At first I didn't know what had happened, but the rancid smell of feet gave it away. I had *jumped.* I hadn't tried to jump; I just did. *But how?*

The smell of feet was too much for my weak stomach, and I unloaded the meager contents of my stomach onto my boots. Embarrassed, I wiped my mouth and looked around. Thankfully, there was no one watching. I was alone in an alley, except for a bunch of garbage and busted shipping crates that gave no clue to my whereabouts. As I moved away from the smell of my own vomit, the space rippled while the light closed in, forming a single point. It meant only one thing to me.

Space Jumpers.

Two of them surfaced on either side of me—tall, imposing figures clad in silvery chest plates and thick leather boots. One wore a helmet that covered half of his face. Him I recognized, from my encounter last phase on Orbis 1, but the other I had never seen before.

"You again," the familiar one grunted.

"For a group of individuals who are supposed to be banished from the Rings of Orbis, you sure do show up a lot," I remarked.

"Here, take this," the masked Jumper ordered. "Keep it with you at all times."

"What is it?" I asked, holding up the smooth disc he'd handed me.

"That device informs us that it's just you trouncing through space," he replied.

"So we don't have to babysit you anymore," the other spat.

The new Space Jumper glared at him before telling me, "What you're doing is illegal, and we have no way of telling who you are without a belt. This is for your own safety."

"We should arrest the *popper*," the surly one complained. "Let him spend a few rotations in slow-time."

"Take it up with the Trust," the other Space Jumper snapped at him. "You have your orders."

"How do I get back?" I asked him.

"You're smart; figure it out," one of them replied, and then they were gone.

"Wait!" But there was no one left to answer. The Space Jumpers had left me there, and I had no idea where *there* was. I tried to jump back home, but nothing happened. I closed my eyes and concentrated on my new home, but still — nothing. I simply remained there as motionless as the metal crates that surrounded me, only feeling a little more stupid.

"Great. Now what?"

I stepped away from the crates and found myself behind a small group of trading chambers. *Is this Murat?* I wondered. I had no idea. I could be anywhere, couldn't I? I mean, I had no clue how I was jumping, let alone where. *Spontaneous space jumping? This is great,* I thought. I knew everything about my softwire abilities but nothing about this new, uncontrollable ability to move through space. I knew that Space Jumpers were softwires, but they all used belts to jump. I also knew that the Trust trained softwires to jump, but I had no training. So how was I jumping without a belt?

Suddenly I wished Charlie were there. He never answered much, either, but at least he had a way of making me feel better about not knowing anything.

The streets were clogged with aliens as scruffy-looking as the tiny trading chambers wedged together, some even built right on top of one another. I saw stuff for sale that wasn't much better than the scraps we used to throw out at Weegin's World. Max was right. If this *was* Murat, Murat was a dump. *How do these aliens even survive?* I wondered. I was waiting for an opening in the traffic of well-worn trams and smoking cargo hovers when I heard my name.

"Johnny Turnbull!"

I spun around and saw a Keeper disembarking from one of those circular fliers.

"Drapling?"

"How are you, child?" Drapling said, rushing toward me.

Drapling was my least favorite Keeper. From the moment I met him on Orbis 1, he had treated us humans with such contempt that I had always tried to avoid him. But then he had changed. It started after the staining on Orbis 2. Now Drapling was . . . well, nice. Almost too nice. I wondered if he'd known about Ketheria and me back then. Did he *have* to be nice to us now for some reason? I didn't know, and I knew he would never tell me. Drapling was just like everyone else. Despite his new friendly attitude, he still had that look on his face and that slight pause before he spoke, as if he were going over some list of rules in his head, deciding what information he could divulge without really telling me anything.

"Hi, Drapling," I said. "What are you doing here?"

"Someone informed me of your misfortune," he said as his left head smiled.

"Someone? How did you find me?"

Drapling held up a small device, cradling it in his long bluish fingers. "I told you the staining would help us protect you."

"From whom?" I mumbled.

"Excuse me?"

"Drapling, I'm sure you must have better things to do than chase an errant knudnik around the rings. Besides, what are you doing on Orbis 4, anyway?"

Drapling was next to me now. He was trying to shake his left head, but it just sort of wobbled. He wasn't that good at Earth gestures. "Keepers spend most of their time on this ring," he said. "You have no idea about our work on this ring, do you?"

"So we're on Orbis 4?"

"Yes. Let me show you what we do."

I felt awkward walking through the streets with Drapling, almost as if we were friends. He informed me that I was somewhere on the far side of Murat. He asked if I was hungry and how I'd gotten here. They were simple questions, nothing too probing, since I didn't know myself. I asked him when Ketheria was coming.

"Soon," he replied.

"That's all you know?"

"No one can say for sure. Remember, this is only the beginning of her awakening. It will take your sister a while to adjust to her new responsibilities. The Nagools will help her through each step. Ketheria will know when she is ready."

How my sister even had a clue about what was happening to her was beyond me.

"Why here?" I said.

"What do you mean?" Drapling replied.

"Why this place? I mean, if Ketheria is going to be so important, why are they bringing her to a dump like Murat? Is it because of our work rule? Somehow I think Ketheria would be better served on a different ring."

"That is where you are wrong," Drapling said. "Murat needs her the most, and it is here she will find her strongest advocates."

"You mean, this is the place with the most knudniks who

are willing to give up what little they own to have an audience with her?"

Drapling stopped and turned toward me. Both his heads were focused on me, and they were both frowning. "You know so little," he whispered. "You have much to learn."

"I couldn't agree more, but the funny thing is that no ones ever tells me the truth."

"Let us try to change that. Shall we start here?" Drapling said, gesturing toward a slanted glass building flanked by several impressive spires.

"What happens here?"

"I'll show you," he said, and stepped toward the building.

The doors disappeared, and I followed Drapling inside. I noticed that the air in the building was much cooler, like in the Keepers' home below Magna. Even the glass walls changed the light to a bluish color similar to the tone down in the caverns. I saw dozens of Keepers strolling across the atrium and even more knudniks waiting on narrow benches that lined the long room.

"When their work rules are completed, many former knudniks are unable to adapt to the Citizens' way of life. We help arrange passage for them through the wormhole. This allows them to find another planet more suited to their needs."

"So you just get rid of them?"

"The Descendants of Light struggle every cycle to improve the living conditions of new Citizens. Some don't want to leave, and we help them as well."

I looked at the aliens sitting, waiting. Would that be me at the end of the rotation? Assuming the Citizens declare my work rule finished, that is. Each alien looked either worried or just plain exhausted. Had they failed? Was their dream to live as Citizens on the Rings of Orbis simply a bust?

"So if I understand this correctly, the Trading Council makes promises of a better life to lure knudniks here, but it's a promise they never plan to keep. When these individuals learn they've been lied to, you ship them off to another world. Problem solved." I turned to Drapling. "Do you like doing the Council's dirty work?"

"Your judgment is too harsh. It is quite expensive to live on the Rings of Orbis, despite our best efforts. Many Citizens are descendants of the First Families, and their wealth is, well, unimaginable. It makes it impossible for the newcomers to compete."

"Or maybe the Citizens just like it that way. Isn't it true that when you become a Citizen, you receive a percentage of the proceeds from the crystals harvested from the moon?" I said.

"That is correct, but before you can receive your share, you must first establish a place of residence and prove to the Trading Council that you are a stable and contributing member of this society."

"So then the other Citizens aren't too big on sharing what they have with these new Citizens, especially the ones who used to slave for them."

Drapling looked at me but said nothing. Then he leaned in and whispered to me, "Some observations are better kept to oneself. Especially since there is a new Scion on the horizon."

He nudged me toward the door and then in a louder tone said, "You know, many of those who want to stay on the rings reapply for work rule. I admit the circumstances are slightly different, but it does give the new Citizens more time to establish their residency."

"You mean they volunteer to be knudniks again?" I was astonished.

"Queykay is one such alien," Drapling informed me. "The rules become a little blurred at times, but look at Queykay. He is a very respected Citizen on the rings now. He even sits on the Trading Council, and he was once a knudnik, just like you."

I still didn't like him any better.

"But despite the success of a few individuals like Queykay, many do struggle. I cannot deny that, but Ketheria will change everything." Drapling was whispering again. "She will give us hope. She can restore the dream that was the Rings of Orbis. This is where she belongs."

"You mean *them*," I corrected him.

"Excuse me?"

"You said she would give *us* hope. Don't you mean *them*?" I said, pointing to the aliens on the benches. "I think the Keepers already have it pretty good around here. How can the Scion help the Keepers?"

"I believe I was referring to the work class here on the rings. You must be mistaken."

He said *us*. I was sure of it.

He lifted his hand toward the exit. I took this as my cue to leave.

"If you ever find yourself lost, I want you to know that you can come here," he said. "And if you are ever in trouble, please tell your friend in the computer to find me. I will come immediately."

I looked at Drapling as he walked ahead of me back onto the streets of Murat. He was up to something.

"Drapling?"

He stopped and turned. "Yes?"

"What are you up to? What do you want?"

"What do you mean?"

"Let's face it. When we first met, you were not this nice to me, or to any of us, for that matter. Does this have anything to do with Ketheria?"

"How can you say that? I remember several instances where my actions displayed nothing but kindness toward you."

"Yeah, ever since the staining. Is that when you realized Ketheria was the Scion? What are you trying to get from us?"

"You are forgetting Odran's. Do you not remember my concern for your well-being when Odran forced you into the crystal-cooling tank? That was well before your staining."

"But you still let me get inside," I reminded him.

"The sanctity of the rings was at stake. Everyone was at risk, not just you."

Boy, he was good at lying.

"JT!"

I turned and saw Max waving at me from across the street. I was glad that I was feeling better. Theodore and the others were marching down a narrow path that separated the stacks of trading chambers. I must admit that they were an imposing group dressed in their matching robes.

"Your friends can show you the way home, JT," Drapling said.

"Thanks for your help, Drapling."

"Remember, do not hesitate to contact me if you need anything," he said, and then he slipped away.

"What are you doing here?" Theodore asked. "And was that Drapling?"

"It's a long story. What are you guys doing?"

"We're all done," Max exclaimed, holding up an empty sack. "Let's get something to eat."

"We don't have any money," I said.

"Wait until you see what these robes can get us."

Max led us to a narrow eating-house a few streets away. Tables were constructed from scraps of metal that looked like they were torn right off one of the shuttles.

"Far cry from the Earth News Café, huh?" Theodore whispered.

"Yeah, but the food's good," one of the other kids remarked.

"I still don't know how we're going to pay," I said.

"Watch and learn," Max boasted.

After we entered the café, an alien leaped out from behind the tiled counter. "You're back! I'm honored," he shouted, throwing his hands up in the air. "Do you see who my café attracts?" he added, addressing the other patrons. "Sit, sit! I will bring you my finest dish. No charge. Nothing but the best for those who share their existence with the Scion."

I was attempting to decipher the café's odd odor — pungent spices mixed with a strong detergent — when the round little alien spotted me. His mouth hung open and he pushed past the other kids. The alien dropped to his knees and began rubbing my feet with his thick hands. He was mumbling something, but I couldn't understand a word.

"Please don't do that," I whispered.

The alien bolted upright and said, "Whatever you ask me, I will do. Please sit. I, Kasha, will serve you personally."

He led me to a seat near the front and shoved a patron off one of the short stools. He cleared the table with the sweep of his hand. Everyone in the café turned and looked.

"Dodu! Clean this mess!" he shouted, and an alien appeared at his side, snatching the broken dishes off the floor.

"Is this comfortable for you?" Kasha asked me.

"Please don't do this," I told him. "Please don't make a fuss." He saw me looking at the other patrons.

"I understand. The Tonat wishes to have privacy. I will respect this." Kasha stood up and clapped his hands. Four aliens rushed from the back, dragging metal stands, each draped with purple cloth. Kasha directed them to place the dividers around my table. I only groaned and shook my head.

"You're coming out with us more often," Theodore gushed, stepping around the cloth dividers with the others.

I looked at Max. Her pained expression rattled me more than the café's odor.

"I'm sorry," I said to her.

"It's not your fault," she mumbled.

"Are you crazy?" one of the kids said, eavesdropping on our conversation. "You've got it made here, JT."

"Shut up," I told him.

Max sat to my right while Theodore sat across from me. Grace dragged a stool across the floor and squeezed next to Max. She and Max had grown closer, ever since Grace started hanging out with the tall boy with black hair. I couldn't remember his name because he was always changing it. Even on the *Renaissance* he was always trying different names, the same way Ketheria would rummage through other people's clothes and try on different shirts.

The other kids were also trying to squeeze through the dividers, and the table was getting a little crowded.

"This is ridiculous," I said, standing up and pushing back the dividers.

Kasha flew to my side, wringing his hands. "Is something wrong?" he gasped.

"We don't need these, Kasha. Thank you, but we can eat without them," I told him.

"As you wish." Kasha clapped his hands once more. The aliens returned and dragged the barriers away, scraping the metal against the concrete floor. Some of the other patrons were staring now. Not my favorite feeling in the world, that's for sure.

I sat back down. "A lot of people on Murat act like him," Theodore pointed out.

"It's weird. I don't like it," I told him.

"Better get used to it," Grace said. "Especially when Ketheria gets here."

That worried me even more.

"Forget Kasha. I'm just glad you were feeling well enough to join us," Max said, slipping her hand onto my knee. My mind became focused on her warm touch. "How did you find us?"

"I jumped here. Can you believe it?"

"What?" she said, pulling her hand off my knee. The empty space now felt like a hole in my leg.

"Wait, it's not like that. It was an accident."

"Well, you're acting like it's golden to be one of those vile mercenaries."

"No, I'm not," I pleaded. "You know I don't want to be a Space Jumper. I told them, no way. You have to believe me. I told the Keepers. I told Hach. I told everyone. I didn't *try* to jump. I couldn't control it."

"I believe you, but do you really think the Citizens on the rings will? Do you think they're just going to let you pop around the rings as you please? You know how they feel about Space Jumpers around here. If someone sees you and complains, you'll be banished for sure, whether you *say* you're a Space Jumper or not."

I never thought about that. "I guess you're right," I mumbled. I was staring at my feet. How could I have been so stupid? If I were banished, I would never see Max again.

"You have to start thinking like that, JT. We're still knudniks."

"I'm the last person you have to remind."

"Really?"

I looked up at Max, but she was already talking to Grace as if the two of them had been in conversation the entire spoke. Max hated anything to do with space jumping, especially when it involved me.

"What do you mean by 'an accident'?" Theodore asked.

I turned to Theodore and sighed. "It was weird," I said. "I was roaming around in the dark, trying to find some sort of control panel, when I bumped into something and the next thing I knew I was at the back of some trading chamber in Murat."

"How did you do that?"

"I don't know. I didn't *try* to jump, it just happened," I whispered.

"You better get that looked at."

"Get what looked at? It's not like I have some sort of switch that I turn on and off. I don't even have a belt."

I sat back as Kasha and the others arrived with bowls of steaming liquid and placed them in front of us. I could see chunks of meat and vegetables bobbing in the brown stew. It smelled like cinnamon and apples.

"This is the dish my father served to me as a boy. An ancient recipe my people share during the Hudshuka. Now I make it for you. Please, enjoy!" Kasha exclaimed.

Kasha passed out an assortment of mismatched spoons, one to each of us, and then crowded in next to me. He was grinning wildly, waiting for me to try his dish. I only asked the Universe that it would taste as good as it smelled.

I dipped the spoon into the bowl and scooped up the broth,

trying to avoid the chunks of meat until I knew what they were. I lifted the spoon to my lips, blowing on it gently. Kasha leaned in even closer as I tasted it. It was sweet with a meaty thickness. I liked it. I smiled and nodded to Kasha. "It's good," I told him. "Really good. Thank you."

Kasha bolted upright and clapped his hands. "He likes it! He *really* likes it! The Tonat likes my *hudspa*. The Tonat is eating at my café. I will rename this dish after the Tonat," he cried, turning back toward me.

"I am not the Tonat," I seethed through clenched teeth.

"I don't understand. You *are* the Tonat. You will be the greatest Space Jumper ever to step on these rings, and *you* ate my food."

"I am not the Tonat!" I yelled. I felt my face flush with rage. Kasha was staring at me. "Stop looking at me!" I slammed my fists on the table.

And then I was gone — again.

I tumbled backward onto a soft patch of grass and leaves, my hands still ringing from the contact with Kasha's table.

"This is ridiculous!" I screamed, and fell back onto the ground. It was darker here, wherever *here* was. I looked up at the lights sparkling on the far side of the ring. Was that Murat? There were more patches of twinkling lights spread across the ring but none in the vicinity of where I landed. Where was I now?

"Vairocina!"

Drapling sent a small shuttle to pick me up. By the time I arrived back home, everyone was already sleeping.

"That's a nasty tic you've picked up. I hope you don't make it a habit," said Queykay, stepping out from the shadows.

"Tell me about it," I replied. I tried to slip past him, but he reached out and caught me by the shoulder. I turned and looked at him. *What now?* I thought, but Queykay didn't say anything. He just stared at me, studying my face. It was creeping me out.

"It's not my fault, Queykay."

He pulled his lips back, sucking in air as if charging his lungs to speak. His teeth were narrow and pointed and just as white as his skin.

"What!" I asked.

"The Scion arrives next cycle. You may not be the Tonat, but I'm certain she will ask for you. Do not mess this up."

"Ketheria? Ketheria is coming?"

The alien let go of my shoulder and turned away without a word.

"Queykay!" I called after him. "Mess what up?" But he was already gone.

4

I woke the next cycle to the hum of cart-bots. I stepped outside my room and saw a dozen motorized baskets writhing through the corridors like the jointed tail of a sea dragon. The only other time I had seen this much commotion was during the preparations for the Harvest of Life back on Orbis 2, and that only happened once every seventy rotations. I reached out and snatched a peachlike item from a bowl of fruit. It was one of the few items I could actually recognize on the carts, besides the enormous bouquets of flowers.

I stopped a Honine carrying three bolts of silk and asked him, "What's all this for?"

"The Scion is coming," he gushed, and hurried past me.

"When?" I yelled after him in vain.

I turned to go back into my room and found Max standing in the doorway.

"Hi," I said softly.

"Can we talk?" she said.

"Sure."

Once we were inside my room, the door closed behind us. The building was big enough that each of us had our own room, but they weren't really more than large closets with a sleeper. Max found a spot on the floor and leaned back on a pillow against the wall.

"I'm sorry about last cycle," she said. "I didn't realize how bad it was."

"Me neither. That's what I tried to explain to you."

"You don't have to, JT. As much as I don't want to accept it, you *are* a Space Jumper."

"I'm *not* a Space Jumper. Being a Space Jumper requires training. It's something I have to choose, and I haven't chosen it."

"Why not?"

"You know why not."

"Say it again anyway."

"Max!"

Max stood up and wrapped her arms around me. "Say it," she whispered.

When Max was this close to me, I usually wasted most of my time worrying about when it was going to end. This time I forced myself to focus on Max.

"It's because of you. I'm doing it for you. You know that."

Max pushed me away.

"For *us*!" she said.

"That's what I meant. I made you a promise."

"But you understand *why*, don't you? I don't want you to do this just for me."

"But Max, I don't really understand."

"Space Jumpers are horrible, JT. They're trained for one purpose — to destroy things. They're hired killers, just like Nee-walkers. They have no life outside of the Trust, and they certainly don't get to make any choices for themselves. I know that's not you, JT. If you choose that path, there will never be an *us*!"

I slumped on her pillow.

"I don't know who I am anymore, Max. When I came to the Rings of Orbis, I just wanted a home. A place to belong, to grow up. A place to have some *fun*. But I don't get to have any of that."

"Me neither, but we still *can*. We simply need to stay out of their way. The Keepers, the Space Jumpers, the Citizens, the Neewalkers, they've been fighting since the beginning of time. They're not going to stop whether you're a Space Jumper or not."

"Then what *am* I, Max? I'm certainly not normal."

"You're mine," she said, and climbed into my lap. "That's all I care about."

"I know *that*."

Max frowned.

"I mean, c'mon, Max. They're not telling us everything. First the softwire thing, then Ketheria becomes the Scion, now I'm bouncing through space if I sneeze. I don't get it. It has to mean *something*. I'm really beginning to believe we're here for some other purpose."

Max didn't say anything. She just stared at me for an uncomfortably long time.

"What?" I said.

"No, we're not. We're a bunch of kids from Earth. You've said that a million times. It's just a freak coincidence what happened to you and Ketheria. How come no one else from the *Renaissance* has any of these abilities or powers? Don't you find *that* strange? If someone had planned this, then why aren't we all softwires, or Scions, or Space Jumpers? Why just you guys? Look, we have one rotation left, and then we can go do what we want. They'll forget about us, pin their hopes on some new knudnik, and we can live life the way you always said we would."

"That's another thing. What's *that* going to be like? I don't think I can live like those other knudniks in Murat. It's horrible."

Max sat back. "I know," she mumbled. "And it's so sad. Do you know some of them become knudniks again?"

"Drapling told me. I'm certainly not going to make that choice."

Max kissed me. "We'll figure it out together, all right? Nothing's changed. Everything is still the same. Nothing will come between us."

There was the sound of a chime in the room, and then the door opened. Queykay was standing there. I thought I noticed him grimace slightly when he saw Max in my lap.

"Your sister is here," he said. "She's asking for you."

Before I realized what I was doing, I had pushed Max away from me and rushed toward the door.

"JT!" Max complained.

I turned and found her on the ground. Had I pushed her that hard?

"I'm sorry," I said, and helped her off the floor. I made a mental note to make it up to her later.

"I want to see her, too," Max said, pushing me out of the room.

It was easy to tell where Ketheria was. All the knudniks who had been working in the building were now crowded around the open door of the room where I'd made my first unwanted jump. Max and I tried to nudge our way through the crowd, but they were having none of that. I looked at Queykay, and he rolled his eyes.

"Move back!" he demanded, and the crowd parted. Then he turned to me and said, "The Citizens should be thankful that you're not the Tonat. I doubt you could make the Scion's enemies very nervous."

I ignored Queykay and examined the circular room. It was filled with Citizens and bathed in a soft blue light from huge crystals lodged in the ceiling. Some aliens were draped in clothes that sparkled under the godly light, while others wore fitted suits with their Citizen's emblem displayed prominently, as if their arrogance wasn't enough to announce their status. I found Ketheria engulfed in some sort of ceremonial chair at the center of the room under the brightest crystal. I could swear the air around her seemed to sparkle. She was dressed in a pure white version of the robes we all wore.

"Wow," Max whispered.

I hung back, watching the crowd watch Ketheria. With each delicate move she made, an anxious shiver rippled through the crowd. Ketheria's hair seemed fuller and longer, covering most of the silver band that was still wrapped around her head. The amber crystal at the center glowed brighter than I remembered.

"She looks different," Max said.

"It's scary," I said.

"These people worship her."

"That's even scarier."

Aliens dressed in navy jumpsuits and masked in ashen helmets that extended beyond their chins to form narrow chest plates kept the perimeter of the room clear. Queykay strode along the open passage, and Max and I followed. When we stepped onto the riser supporting Ketheria and her chair, she saw us.

"JT!" she exclaimed. She stood up and glided over to hug me. I swear her feet never touched the ground.

Over her shoulder, I watched the crowd react to her affection. Their admiration now seemed to consume me as well.

"Are you all right?" I whispered. "The last time I saw you, you didn't look too good. I was worried."

"I'm wonderful," she said, squeezing me tighter. "I feel fantastic."

She pulled away and then hugged Max. "I've missed you so much," she gushed.

"Me, too," Max replied.

Then Ketheria took Max's hand and placed it in mine. She smiled at Max, and I felt my skin flush. Then I saw them. Her eyes. Ketheria's pupils were gone. Well, they were still there, but they were strange-looking. As if the glow was still circulating through her eyes, weaving through her irises, surfacing occasionally, and then settling back where her pupils once were. I caught Max staring.

"There's so much to do," Ketheria exclaimed. "So much."

"What?" I asked. "What do you have to do?"

"We! *We* get to do it."

Just then Queykay began to address the crowd. "The Trading Council is pleased with your presence. The honorable Citizen Hach Ba Fay and myself welcome you, our closest friends, to this privileged viewing, but as you are aware, the Scion will not receive guests until the next phase," Queykay announced. "The Scion must begin her work. Believe me when I tell you how excited I am that the Universe has chosen a Scion from among us. It echoes our belief that the Rings of Orbis are truly an important place. Again, the Trading Council thanks you for your patronage, and we are looking forward to a long and special relationship with the Scion. I am personally handling her security for the Trading Council, so everyone can leave here knowing that she is safe. You are all welcome to return to hear the Scion speak at the Cycle of Witnessing. Admission to this rare and distinguished event will be available for a nominal fee."

Many in the crowd moaned, but most turned for the door. No complaining, no pushing or shoving, just an orderly reaction to Queykay's announcement. As the visitors streamed out, six Nagool masters squeezed in and waited patiently in the wings.

Ketheria acknowledged them and then whispered to us, "We'll talk more later. I have so much to tell you."

She turned away and moved toward the Nagools.

"Ketheria?" I said, but the Nagools had swallowed her up. I felt cheated. Where was my little sister? Who was this diplomat they had replaced her with? Queykay nudged me toward the door.

"Don't touch me," I spat, not caring whether he'd punish me for my rudeness.

Queykay squeezed my shoulder, digging his fingers into my skin.

"Do as you're told, knudnik," he sneered.

"But why do I have to leave? She's my sister."

"That is irrelevant. She is far more important than that label. Now, do as you're told and run along, knudnik."

I reached across with my robotic arm and grabbed Queykay's wrist. I applied just enough pressure to make him grimace and his fingers retract from my skin.

"Do not underestimate me," I warned him.

"JT, what's gotten into you?" Max cried. "Stop it!"

Then I felt a stinging sensation run up my arm as if something bit me. I pulled away, and Max grabbed my wrist, dragging me toward the door. I looked back and caught Queykay smirking.

Outside the room, Max continued to drag me away from

everyone else. When we were alone, she pushed me up against the wall.

"What are you doing?" she hissed.

"What am *I* doing?

"Yes! That's a Trading Council member you just assaulted. Do you want to get thrown into one those blue cells again, or worse? What's wrong with you?"

"With *me*? There's nothing wrong with me. I want to see Ketheria! If that even is Ketheria. Did you see her eyes?"

"Yes, her eyes seemed a little strange, but she said it herself: she feels fantastic. You should be happy right now."

"Well, I'm not. That's not my sister in there. She's changed."

"You're the one who's changed, JT. You avoid me for a whole phase — I have no idea why. You freak out at the slightest thing and then disappear into thin air."

"It has to do with her. I'm sure of it."

"Then what happened at Kasha's? Ketheria wasn't there. It was just you getting angry again. Soon you'll be jumping who-knows-where around the ring."

"If I could just talk with —"

"I don't have time for this. Figure it out and let me know." With that, she turned and stormed away.

"Max! Wait!"

I stood frozen, my brain unhinged, waiting for any part of my consciousness to take control. My body ached as the sound of Max's boots against the hard floor faded. *Go after her!* But I turned to find Ketheria instead.

I returned to the hall where I had left my sister. I didn't feel completely in control. I was relieved to not feel the nausea and headaches I had been experiencing for phases, but still I felt different. I had an overwhelming urge to be near my sister. I only hoped nothing was wrong. I found the room still lit, but empty. I spotted another door at the back of the room behind Ketheria's chair. I slipped through it and moved quietly, hoping Ketheria was still inside with the Nagools.

"Ketheria?" I whispered. The room was so still that I could hear my own heartbeat.

I moved into another room, hoping to find Ketheria, but instead I found two Space Jumpers guarding an archway. I knew my sister was through there.

When they saw me, the Jumpers stiffened and closed the space between them. I hesitated but tried to act as if I was supposed to be there. As I moved toward them, the Space Jumper on my left said, "She's not seeing anyone right now."

"I'm . . . I'm the Tonat," I lied, hoping it would work.

"The Tonat? Really?" the other one said. "As far as I understand, you've chosen *not* to be one of us. Instead, you let the insects who run the Council do what you were born to do. Where is the courage in that? Now, get out of here before you get hurt." His words hissed through a face mask that covered the lower part of his face.

"Well, then, tell my *sister* that her *brother* wants to see her."

"Go home, *popper*," scoffed the first one.

"What does that mean?"

The other one gave a knowing grunt.

I moved forward, trying to squeeze between them. They both reached for their weapons and pressed their shoulders together. The clacking of metal and the hum of their plasma rifles changed my mind.

"Ketheria!" I shouted. "Ketheria!"

It felt childish, but what else could I do? It was my *sister* back there. Why couldn't I see her? *They would let you pass if accepted your destiny. You are the Tonat,* someone whispered inside my head. It wasn't Vairocina — that's for sure. The voice rattled me. I stumbled back, waiting to hear it again.

"Go home," one of them growled.

"I don't have a home!"

"JT?" I heard Ketheria's voice from inside the room.

"Ketheria! These space monkeys won't let me through!"

My sister squeezed between the Space Jumpers. "It's all right," she told them. "We're finished."

Three Nagool masters slid out from behind her and slipped away. My skin prickled as their robes brushed against me. One glanced back at Ketheria, and she nodded, smiling. All I could do was stand there and stare. I was not part of Ketheria's world anymore.

"I'm glad you came," she whispered to me. "Come. There's lots I want to tell you."

"Finally," I said under my breath.

"Popper," one of the Space Jumpers muttered as I elbowed my way past them.

Inside Ketheria's room, I stepped around bowls of fruit and

flowers. The same ones I had seen delivered earlier that cycle. Long silks clung to the pale stone walls, and lights seemed to sparkle through pinholes in the rock. The floor was padded with a thick carpet that swallowed up the soft tones that resonated off metallic bowls of water placed about the room like sculptures.

I spotted Nugget sitting in the corner. He saw me as well and jumped to his feet.

"Nugget! What are you doing here?"

"I take care of Ketheria," he proclaimed, standing in front of me with his fists on his waist and his feet planted shoulder-width apart. The bald little beast had hardly changed. His pink skin seemed a little more burgundy, but he still sported the same thick, protruding lower jaw, and he had it raised proudly (as usual).

"Good for you," I said.

"Someone has to do it," he grunted.

I chuckled. "You, too, huh?"

"Let him be," Ketheria said. "He makes a good bodyguard."

"Do you need a bodyguard now?" I asked.

"So they tell me."

I didn't want to get into an argument with my sister, so I turned away to admire the room.

"What is this place?" I asked.

"It's my place," she replied.

"You mean you're not staying with us?" I knew it was a dumb question.

Ketheria shook her head, smiling and resting herself on

a long cushion on the floor near a shallow metal pan. A blue flame flickered from is center. Ketheria tapped the cushion, inviting me to sit, which I did. I couldn't help but think how much older she seemed.

"Isn't it amazing?" she gushed.

"Isn't *what* amazing?"

"All of this," she replied, stretching her arms out.

"Is it? I wouldn't know."

Ketheria frowned. "Why do you have to be like that? Aren't you the one who always talked about having some sort of purpose on Orbis, something to do? That's all you ever talked about. I loved listening to your stories about the rings when we were on the *Renaissance*. Now we have everything you ever wanted. Why is this so hard for you to accept?"

"Because I don't see it that way at all."

"What do you mean?"

I stood up, feeling an argument coming on again. I inspected the room once more and noticed several antechambers that led from this main room, each with the same sparkling walls. The place was so still, I could hear myself breathe.

"We didn't get to pick this," I said, turning back to her. "You didn't choose to be the Scion. I don't even know what you are, really."

"Some things choose us, JT."

I shook my head. "It doesn't make sense. Why us? I think they know more and they're not telling us. That scares me, Ketheria, and it should scare you as well. You know their history, their greed. This doesn't feel right."

"Who? Who are you talking about?"

"*Them*, Ketheria. All of *them*. The Trading Council, the Citizens, the Trust, even the Keepers. This is their world, not ours."

"I'm not the one who has changed, JT. Listen to yourself. This is not the brother I know. You couldn't wait to get to the Rings of Orbis and start a new life, and now you're going to be the Tonat."

"No, I'm not!"

Ketheria cocked her head at me. The swirling in her eyes intensified, and I looked away. It was freaking me out. When I turned back, Ketheria had a large book opened on her lap and she was reading something. The book's pages were yellowed, and its edges looked tattered.

"What's that?" I asked.

"It's a book," she replied.

"I know that, but why do you have it?"

"The Nagools gave it to me." Ketheria closed the book and slipped it partly under the cushion. It was too thick to go willingly.

"Don't do that, Ketheria."

"Do what?"

"Be like them," I said. "Toy with your answers when you know the truth. I'm your brother. I deserve the truth."

"Sit down," she said. It was an order, and I obeyed.

"You must stop this. It's only a book. It helps me understand the reactions of those around me. The awakening is not finished yet. There are fourteen stages in all, and there is much

I have to learn. That's why I have this book. That is all, nothing more."

"What do you have to learn?"

Then Ketheria reached up to the metal band that wrapped around her head and removed it with a click.

"I didn't know you could do that," I said.

"The Nagools showed me how."

Ketheria turned it over and pointed at the underside. "See that?" she said.

I leaned in and saw an OIO symbol carved into the metal behind the amber crystal. "Yeah. What does it mean?"

"The person who made this knew he was making it for me."

"That's impossible."

"That's the first thing you have to change, JT. Anything is possible. Learn that now. You are so bound to a false vision of how you *think* your life should be that your eyes are closed to everything around you. Don't feel bad, though. Most of the universe is like that."

Ketheria pushed the metal crown toward me. "Take it," she urged.

The metal was warm in my hands. I rolled it around and ran my fingers over the OIO symbol. "So what does it mean, then?" I asked, trying to sound open to her ideas.

"The person who made that—"

"I thought that guy Tinker made it."

"He did. He knew the Scion would be forced to wear it some cycle. Tinker is a believer, and he worked with the Nagools to create something that would enhance the Scion's abilities while allowing the Citizens to believe that he or she was under its control. That's why Tinker was so freaked out when he met us. He recognized his work and knew who I was. Who *we* were."

"But what does that mean?"

"There are many, many forces at work here, JT. This is bigger than me; this is bigger than *you*."

I stood up again. "You make me sound like some self-centered fool."

Ketheria didn't reply.

"I'm not just thinking about myself, Ketheria," I argued. "Did you ever think that we might just be tokens, meaningless gambits for them to use?"

"Pawns in their game?"

"Yes!"

"Now *you* are a cliché. This *is* our game, JT. That's what I'm trying to tell you. You *are* the Tonat. There is no choice. This is your life now whether you accept it or not."

"Well, I won't."

"Max will understand," she said. "Would you like me to talk to her?"

"Max! Are you reading my mind right now, Ketheria? That's not fair. Get out of my head."

"Max is worried about losing you."

"Stop it, Ketheria. I don't want to talk about Max."

"She's smart. More than you give her credit for. She knows what the life of a Space Jumper will be like, and there is no way that life can include her. It's Max that's being selfish here, JT."

"Don't say that!"

"I'm sorry, but it is true."

"I'm leaving," I announced.

"Will you come and visit again?" Ketheria asked me as if my being upset had little relevance. She opened her book again, and this time she made a mark in it.

"What's that for? Why are you doing that now?"

"I explained that to you already," she said. "Are you going to come back?"

"I doubt it," I snapped. "Your goons here won't let me in, and why do you have Space Jumpers guarding your room, anyway? They're supposed to be banished. If Queykay finds out, he'll surely notify the Council. He's a member, you know. They could cause a lot of trouble, Ketheria."

"Many things are changing, JT."

"Yeah, well, I'm not one of them."

I stormed out of Ketheria's room and past her Jumpers.

"See ya, popper," one of them joked.

I spun around. "What does that mean?" I yelled, and shoved him. The other Space Jumper slammed the butt of his rifle into my stomach. I heard them both laughing as my body and mind were torn through space and time yet again.

5

The stink and decay were familiar to me now, so I knew I had jumped to Murat. The nausea returned, too; I felt my stomach tighten and push toward my throat. I was once again in an alley. I leaned against an abandoned transport — one wheel was missing, and the engine had been ripped out. I figured it wasn't going anywhere, so I just lay back and closed my eyes. The cold metal felt soothing against my neck, and I took this private moment to catalog the recent events in order to establish some direction in my life.

It was obvious to me that the awakening was changing Ketheria on a deeper level than I had even imagined. She seemed so different to me now. I felt like the Rings of Orbis had taken my sister from me. It was one more reason to hate it here. It was almost as if she was on *their* side now, but I couldn't figure out when that line had been drawn. And where did that leave me? Ketheria had always been on *my* side. I felt more isolated than I had on the *Renaissance*.

My problems with Max were not making any of this easier. How could I keep my promise to her now? Could I really take care of Ketheria if I was no longer part of her inner circle? The fact that I was being shut out of Ketheria's life simply dumbfounded me. What if being the Tonat was the only way I could protect my sister? But if I became the Tonat, I was certain that I would lose Max, and I was not prepared to do that.

Sitting against the cold machine and feeling sorry for myself certainly wasn't going to help me. I knew that much. I needed a plan. What could I use to my advantage? Well, I could move freely about the ring, while Space Jumpers had to stay in the shadows. Maybe there was some way to control this spontaneous jumping. I also had my arm. Its robotics had come in handy more than once. And there was my alliance with Vairocina. That relationship was very important to me. But best of all, I could get inside their precious central computer whenever I pleased. *My side* was looking pretty good. It was time to learn what they knew.

"Vairocina?" I said.

"Yes, JT?"

"Can you determine my location?"

"Yes. You're in Murat. What are you doing there?"

"Long story. Do you know about the place where the Keepers do their charity work on Orbis 4?"

"I believe it's called the Center for Relief and Assistance. It's 3.7 kilometers from where you are now."

"Great. Which way?" I asked, getting up.

"Up ring. It will be on your right near the center of the city but, JT, I would like to talk about the information you asked me to find."

"Oh, sure, but can it wait, Vairocina? I need to talk with a Keeper right now. We'll chat when I'm done."

"Certainly."

I may not have decided to be the Tonat yet, but I was certain I could garner valuable information while they tried to convince me. Drapling's defenses were down. He wanted me to become the Tonat so bad, I could almost smell it on him. I was going to leverage his desire to get something from *me* to get what I wanted from *him*: information.

A large, scarred metallic orb drifted over me. Six bluish lights crawled along the orb's surface and scanned the area around me. *Security?* The searchlights converged on the ship's belly and focused on me for only a moment. The orb then rotated and drifted away. I figured Vairocina must have sent it, so I followed my makeshift escort.

Murat's buildings grew taller as I marched toward its center. Instead of building out, Murat had built upward. I began to notice a larger, more modern city beneath the refuse. Skyscrapers fashioned in the images of those you might find on Orbis 1 poked through the city's poorer framework. I followed a narrow canal of green silt, which seemed to flow in and out of the city, and stopped just inside the densest part of Murat. Next to me, a metal and glass pod cracked open and a gangly alien unfurled himself. I looked up and saw more pods mounted above that one, each attached to the same narrow beam that arched up and over my head. I could see more aliens lumbering inside the dull, well-worn pods. They were roughly the same size and shape as the nurture pods we had used on the *Renaissance*. In one capsule, I saw a female with two small children. I could not even imagine having to *live* inside one of those things.

I moved away from the pods and squinted through the mountains of oxidized metal framework that formed a forest of trading chambers and makeshift shelters. There was no sign of the Center for Relief and Assistance, so I kept moving.

"Vairocina? Can you tell if I'm close to the Center yet?"

There was a pause before she replied. "You need to walk about six hundred meters and you will find it on your left."

"Thank you."

As Vairocina predicted, the slanted glass structure appeared like a distress beacon amid the chaos of Murat. A steady stream of aliens flowed through the Center's pristine doors, and I stepped into the flow.

Inside I found more aliens, sitting at O-dats, while three Keepers emerged from light chutes located behind a large oval counter. I watched as each Keeper retrieved a new Citizen and then left with him or her through the same chute. I searched for an empty O-dat, but they were all occupied, with at least two or three aliens waiting their turn. How many aliens did the Keepers help? I decided to find out for myself.

"Excuse me," I said to the Saliman standing in front of me. I could always spot a Saliman because they had big hornlike ears that pointed backward. "Are you a Citizen?"

"Lot of good it does me," the alien grunted, waving one of

her thick pink forearms in the air for emphasis. "The First Families have the system so rigged, I was better off as a knudnik."

"What will the Keepers do for you?"

"Keepers? Don't confuse the Descendants of Light with the Keepers. They may look the same, but they are definitely two different breeds. Watch out for the DOL," she said in a gossipy tone, and then glanced at the Keeper standing a few meters to her right.

Another alien had been eavesdropping on our conversation. "Get your pass and get out of here," he said.

"Pass?" I said.

"Through the wormhole," replied the Saliman. "It's the one good thing about the DOL. They love to see you go."

"And I'm going to keep them happy," added the other one. I turned toward that alien. His face was almost as wide as his shoulders. It was a Roshilon. His eyes blinked at me as they struggled to peer around his big bony face. "There's no way I can afford to live on these rings, and there is absolutely no way I can afford the tax to travel through that wormhole. The DOL arranges your passage for free. It's the best assistance this place can offer."

"Is everyone here leaving?" I whispered.

"If they're smart, they will."

The Saliman squatted in front of the terminal and reached up with his short arms. I stood back, digesting what the aliens had told me, when I heard my name.

"Johnny Turnbull!" Drapling called out to me. "What a pleasure. Are you lost again?"

I saw the Saliman glance at me over his shoulder.

"No," I said. "I was hoping we could talk."

"Absolutely," Drapling cried. "Follow me."

"Get your pass!" hissed the Saliman.

I followed Drapling through the light chute, then emerged to find him waiting next to a tall green crystal anchored in the wall. It was one of many that lined the polished stone hallway.

"This way," he said, motioning.

I followed Drapling down the hallway and across the glossy floor. Below my feet, buried about ten centimeters under the clear floor, I could see rows and rows of loosely arranged hand-fashioned copper slabs. These plates were separated by globs of rust-colored grout, just the sort of sloppy brick-and-mortar job one might find in Murat.

"What are these?" I asked, pointing at the floor.

"Keepers who have served their purpose beyond all expectations," he replied.

"They're graves?"

"This is much more honorable," he replied.

"Walking on them is honorable?"

"They're still serving the greater good. I find that honorable, don't you?"

No! How is spending eternity as a paving stone honorable? I stepped away from the tombstones, tiptoed along the grout, and followed Drapling into a room near the end of the hallway. He sat in a sloped chair made from some sort of greenish, silky material. There was no place for me to sit.

"How is Ketheria?" he asked.

"She says she's fine," I replied, walking past amber lights embedded in the floor.

"I take it you do not agree."

"Tell me about the Tonat, Drapling. I may have been hasty in my decision."

Drapling stood up. There was that pause again. He was thinking about the proper response, but at least I had his attention.

"What would you like to know?" he asked carefully.

He was stalling. I could feel it.

"Have there ever been other Tonats?"

"Of course."

"Is the Tonat always a sibling of the Scion?"

Drapling got up and slid along a narrow table near the back of the room. I watched as he lifted a thin carafe and poured an opaque liquid into a fragile fluted glass. He placed the glass on the table before answering me. I knew this entire charade was just a way to give him time to think about his answer.

"That is hard to say," he finally responded.

"Well, is it a condition of their relationship?"

"We are all connected in more than one way, Johnny. Even you and I are connected within this universe. OIO tells us—"

"Just answer the question, please," I interrupted.

"I am confused as to the point of your question. I should inform you that I have not met any other Scions. Your sister is my first. A Scion is a rare and extraordinary individual, but unfortunately most do not live long. Your species has destroyed many."

"You mean humans?"

Drapling nodded but said no more. I think he was waiting for my response to his doomsday claim, but I didn't take the bait. "Not every Scion has found his or her Tonat in time. I believe Ketheria is unique in having a Tonat who is also her brother, although you seem indifferent to her safety."

"I care for my sister more than you know. Tell me more about this *connection*."

"You must be feeling it now. You became sick as the awakening started, did you not?"

"I did."

"See? And your movements through space and time, despite being so unorthodox, are, I am convinced, also connected to your relationship to the Scion. As her awakening continues and as you move closer to your destiny, I am convinced this little anomaly will disappear."

"How is that possible?"

"You are connected to her like no other creature in this universe. You feel her pain and sense her danger. This will grow stronger as the awakening continues. You cannot escape this. A Tonat is burdened with all the pain the Scion experiences. You are like a valve that releases this pressure so that she may live in the light and bring harmony to the universe. You, in turn, must use this pain to protect her. You must fashion this energy as a soldier fashions a weapon. It is your greatest strength. That is why you are feared. As the Scion grows and takes on the pain of all those suffering in the universe, so, too, does your power grow. The longer the Scion lives, the more feared you become.

This pain and suffering will strengthen you and allow you to do what others cannot. Feel her, sense her, think like her. There is not a Space Jumper in the universe that will protect your sister as you will. You and the Scion are connected like no other individuals in this universe."

"But *how* did this happen, Drapling? Who made this connection? I'm certain not every brother and sister has this kind of connection."

Drapling sat the glass down, but did not respond—again.

"Drapling, tell me how this happened. Please!"

"You may want to sit down," said a voice from the door. I spun around to find Theylor entering the room. He extended his arm toward the chair. "Please, sit," he said. "I believe the answer to your question might not please you."

6

I slept straight through the next two cycles. My head was so full, I couldn't hold it up, anyway. I spent the first diam of the third cycle simply staring at the ceiling. Ketheria came to visit me while I was awake, but I pretended to be asleep. I figured her telepathy would give me away, but she let me be, all the same. Even Queykay left me to myself, but there was nothing unusual about that.

I finally got up and washed. Moments later I heard a soft tapping at my door.

Go away, I thought

When I didn't answer, they did go away. I had already made my decision about what I was going to do, and I didn't need others trying to change my mind. Despite the odds, I was even more resolved to have it my way now. *How dare they do this to me? How* dare *they?*

When I felt ready, I ventured out into the building. The first person I wanted to find was Max. I found her in her room with Grace and that other kid, whatever his name was.

"Hi." I waved from the doorway.

"JT!" Max shrieked, and bolted to her feet. Grace got up, too, and kicked the other kid to do the same.

"We were just on our way out," Grace declared. "Good to see you up, JT. Max, we'll talk about it more later."

"Sure," she replied, looking anxious for them to leave.

I nodded at the other kid as he and Grace slipped out of the room.

"What's his name now?" I whispered to Max.

"Dante," she replied.

"What were you guys talking about?"

"Nothing. Sit. Are you all right? Theylor said you got sick in Murat. He told us not to disturb you."

"Was that you who knocked earlier?"

She smiled. "Yeah. I'm sorry. I just needed to apologize about the other cycle. Knowing you were here and I couldn't talk to you—well, it was driving me crazy. Ketheria is your sister and that *is* precious. I had no right to say what I did. It was horrible. Can you forgive me?"

"You don't need to be forgiven, Max. I was the one who was acting like a malf—to everyone. I know that now, but that's going to change—I promise. It's just like you said: one more rotation and then we can do whatever we want. We can even leave the rings if you want. I'll lead the way."

"Really?"

"Really," I assured her.

Max just stood there, smiling. "So, now what?"

"Let's have some fun."

A large furry knudnik with thick arms appeared at the door. It was a Garin, and they were only assigned to Trading Council members. "Queykay sent me to retrieve you. Your sister has requested you."

I looked at Max and then back to the messenger. "Tell Queykay I'm sure the Council can deal with the Scion. Tell Ketheria I'll come by later. Much later."

I grabbed Max's hand and pulled her out of the room as the Garin stepped aside. I really don't think he knew what to do, but I didn't care.

"You do not have permission to leave," he challenged me.

I turned and faced him, Max's hand firmly in mine. "This is not your fight. Are you going to stop me?" Max stepped next to me.

The Garin sucked the air through his teeth, and I adjusted the controls in my arm just in case.

"Well?" Max said.

He glared at us for another moment. "I must report this," he spat, and then stormed off.

"You should get sick more often," Max teased.

I could only smile. The fact was that my stomach had been doing backflips ever since I refused to go to Ketheria, and I was afraid to open my mouth in fear of what would come out.

Live with it, I told myself. *That's your new motto.*

• • •

Typical of Max, she had already found a secret route into Murat. I followed her through one shortcut that was nothing more than a crack in a concrete barrier. The maze of trading chambers and living quarters was like second nature to her.

"Where are we going?" I asked.

"It's a surprise."

I followed Max down a series of steps that ended in a small amphitheater carved into the foot of one of Murat's superstructures. The building's green glass bathed the entire courtyard in its reflection of a distant, dying sun. Max found a spot on the stone seats and settled into the eerie afterglow. I must admit, the effect did a pretty good job of masking the city's decay.

"What are we doing here?" I whispered as we sat among other aliens, some of whom seemed to be sleeping.

"This is a special cycle on the Rings of Orbis. Not one that everyone celebrates, but quite a few do. Look up in the sky."

Max pointed down ring and up about sixty degrees. I followed her finger to see what she was pointing at. "See it?" she said. "The rings. They spell OIO."

In the sky, Orbis 1 and Orbis 3 were positioned next to each other, and Orbis 4, the ring we were on, ran up between them. It did spell OIO—well, kind of, anyway.

"The golden thing is that OIO works in any language. It's really a symbol."

"I always thought the central computer translated it for us."

"Everyone gets the same translation. That's one of the things that makes it so special. The alignment happens once every rotation."

"What's going to happen now?" I asked.

"It's a celebration. Remember that place you took me to on Orbis 3? The place with the musician?"

"He was amazing."

"Then I think you might like this. Watch," she said, holding her fingers to her lips.

I looked at the stage near the bottom of the amphitheater. A few aliens were setting up musical instruments among the rubbish. Single notes washed over me as they tuned their stringed devices. I watched more musicians join the group, and the air soon resonated with a cacophony of notes and sounds as they set up their instruments. I fidgeted in my seat, anxious to hear them play. Max looked at me and smiled.

"Thanks," I whispered.

Then she leaned toward me and rested her head against my shoulder at the precise moment the musicians came together. A wall of sound fell upon us, and anyone who had been sleeping now sat up. It was amazing that amid all this atrophy, a sound so pure and so promising could lift me up and turn my dingy surroundings into the most exquisite concert hall in the universe. I sat with Max and listened without saying a word. We let the music fill in the spaces around us, and for that moment, I had everything I had ever dreamed about when I was on the *Renaissance*. It did not matter what they had planned for me. It didn't even matter what Theylor said they had done to me. I could resist it. I knew I could.

Then I threw up. The feeling came so fast, I barely had time to react. As my mouth filled with vomit, I tore away from Max, horrified that I might puke on her. I unloaded the contents of my stomach on the unfortunate alien to my right.

"JT! Are you all right? What's wrong? Are you still sick?" she cried.

I couldn't face Max. I was so embarrassed and I didn't want her asking why I was still sick because I don't think could have lied to her just then.

"I'm sorry," I said to the alien next to me, but he didn't seem to mind. Instead he picked through the remains on his shirt as if I had passed him the leftovers of my meal (which I kind of did, in a way).

I wiped my mouth and turned back to Max. "I guess I'm not a hundred percent yet," I said.

"Let's go back," she insisted.

"No, I said. I love this. I'm sorry."

"Don't be sorry. You're sick. What if it's something serious?"

It was serious, *very* serious. But I couldn't tell her I was going to be like this for the rest of my life and that it was only going to get worse. My head was splitting now, and my underarms were soaked as well. If Max knew the truth, if she knew what Theylor had told me, I was certain that she would never accept me and I would lose her.

Live with it! I reminded myself.

"Let's get some water," she said.

"Good idea."

Reluctantly, I left the amphitheater, following Max back up and into the street, mumbling to her the entire time that I was sorry.

After I assured Max that I was fine, I told her, "That's such a golden place. How did you ever find it?"

"That's the thing, JT. There is so much like that here in Murat, but the Trading Council won't fund any of it. In fact, they made it illegal for certain groups, like those musicians, to even perform concerts anymore."

"That's stupid."

"But it's happening. The city is jam-packed with these little pockets of creativity. It's really inspiring. I mean, despite the conditions these people are forced to live under, they are still able to connect to the Source."

"The Source?"

"Creativity is the best way to connect to the Universe," she replied matter-of-factly as she dashed into the surface street, pausing for a makeshift tram to pass.

"Do you really believe all that stuff, Max?"

"You mean OIO?"

"Yeah. I don't get it. It just smells like another system of rules."

Max stopped in front of a fountain where water bubbled out of a plastic pipe. "Here," she said. "Drink this."

"Is it clean?" I asked her.

"Crystal," she replied, and I drank. "OIO's not like that at all. It's really an investigation of truths and principles that guide our Universe. It helps a lot of people remain calm in the presence of all the trouble and chaos around them. You ever see a Nagool get upset?"

"None that I can think of. So that's it? It just makes you calm?"

Max turned to me and chuckled. "No! You really don't get this stuff, do you? I'm so surprised. Look. It's very simple. The Universe is energy. Our thoughts and actions contribute to this energy and have influence over every creature within it. Negative or deconstructive energy created by individuals, and even societies as a whole, contribute to behaviors that are self-destructive, like a hidden virus undetected in our psyche. That deconstructive energy feeds certain forces in our Universe and has the power to corrupt entire cultures—look at the Trading Council. Even when they know their actions are destructive, they continue because they are addicted to this energy. Remember Theodore and those tetrascopes?"

"What does this have to do with Ketheria?"

"Some say the Universe chooses a Scion. The balance of constructive and deconstructive energy flowing from the Source is very delicate. The universe can self-destruct under the sheer mass of unopposed deconstructive energy. When Ketheria has completely awoken these negative forces will no longer influence her. Her nodes will be in perfect sync with the brightest part of the Source. Nagools consider Scions to be the only enlightened individuals in the universe. A Scion's presence alone can raise the consciousness of another individual by absorbing all their deconstructive energy. To become conscious is the greatest gift a Scion can give you, but it scares the crap out of the Trading Council."

"Why?"

"There is a direct link between consciousness and a sense of self. When your nodes are clogged by deconstructive energy, you feel worthless and incapable of achieving anything, which makes you very easy to control. The Trading Council likes their knudniks that way. On the other hand, a higher consciousness can make you feel like you can do anything. Even run these rings."

"No wonder so many Scions have been killed," I said.

"It reminds me a lot of the way you acted around Switzer on the *Renaissance*. You really kept your head when most people wouldn't."

"I don't consider those the finer moments in my life. I'd rather forget them," I said.

Max smiled, moved toward me, and put her arms around me. "Did you like me back then?"

"Did you like me?" I asked, resting my nose against hers.

When I breathed, Max winced and pinched my lips together with her fingers. "You shouldn't talk. C'mon, let's get something to eat. Something that will settle your stomach."

"What? Does my breath stink? Great!"

"C'mon. I know another place," she yelled as she ran ahead.

I looked at Murat a little differently after what Max had told me. Instead of seeing trading chambers simply filled with junk, I began to notice exquisite little dolls fashioned from scraps of plastic and thread as well as detailed paintings on discarded scraps of metal or wood, all hung neatly in the chambers and ready for sale. Windows were no longer stacked with discarded electronics but rather parts used by skilled technicians repairing anything their customers could bring them. Despite the obstacles created by the First Families, these new Citizens had carved out an existence for themselves.

Just like you, I whispered to myself. I sure was going to try.

I saw Max stop under a huge splash of red light outside a tiny chamber. The doorway was so small, I was forced to turn sideways to enter, and once I was inside, the smell of cooking grease violated my senses. To my right, I saw three Bachaks stuffed behind a tall counter lined with mismatched metallic stools. I watched as these brawny-looking aliens with thick forearms jammed pouches of fried foods under tiny light chutes that delivered the food to smaller tables along the wall. Max and I sat at the farthest table from the counter. She was giggling as we sat.

"Golden place, huh?" she said.

"Small," I remarked.

"This is only part of it." Then Max knocked on the wall behind her bench. A few moments later, part of the wall slid back.

"Max!" cried the alien who opened the door. I stepped back. It was a Belaran. Her inky black skin and sharp features immediately brought back memories of Madame Lee, who had tried to kill me on Orbis 1.

"Hi, Tic. I brought my friend, the one I told you about. I hope you don't mind," Max said.

Tic looked me over and smiled. "Of course not. Come in!" Max squeezed past, and I followed. "Who would refuse the Tonat?" Tic whispered as I passed. I spun around to look at her, but the alien's back was to me while she locked the little door.

I turned back and followed Max down the narrow hallway and into a much larger, circular room. We stepped over cushions scattered on the floor, and I ducked under one of two metal pots that hung from the center of the ceiling. The pots leaked blue smoke that wove its way through the silks also hanging from the ceiling. Max plopped onto one of the cushions, and I did the same as Tic gathered some drinking glasses. The Belaran appeared much older than Madame Lee and walked with a slight stoop. To me, Tic seemed like a bland version of the warrior I once knew, but I was still nervous. Belarans had a fierce reputation.

"JT wasn't feeling well, and I didn't want to go home," Max said.

"You are always welcome here," Tic exclaimed. "I have just the thing that will help your friend as well."

When Tic left the room, I whispered to Max, "What's a Belaran doing here?"

"We are not all as fortunate as some of our race," Tic answered for herself, returning to the room with three glasses.

"I'm sorry," I said. "I didn't mean to be rude. I was just surprised to see someone from Zinovia in Murat."

"Zinovia is an amazing planet, but far too ruthless for my

tastes. I like the simplicity of Murat. Don't you?" she said as she passed me a glass and then another to Max. I noticed that mine was filled with a black liquid while Max's was yellow. "Drink it. It will help your stomach."

"How did you know it was my stomach?" I asked.

Tic did not reply. Instead, she took a sip from her own glass and glanced at Max. "I trust you're feeling fine," she said.

"Yes, but I do need to use your bathroom."

"Of course. You know where it is."

After Max left the room, I sat in awkward silence while Tic just stared at me. I tried to drink the liquid, but the smell only twisted my stomach more.

"Trust me: it will help you. I have more if you need it."

"Thanks, but this will pass."

"Will it?" she asked.

I glanced up at Tic. What did she know?

"The Belaran believed that they possessed the Scion at one point, as well you know," she whispered. "In fact, I believe you met her once."

"Who?"

"Madame Lee believed that she was the Scion, or at least she wanted to be. Such a taste for power, that one."

"Really?"

"She was livid after the Keepers had proven her unworthy. She even had a Tonat."

"Where is he?"

"Why do you assume it was a male?"

"I'm sorry. Where is *she*?"

"Dead. The genetic alterations killed her, as often happens when individuals try to force what should be a natural process."

"You know about that?"

"It's written all over you."

"Don't tell Max. Please!"

"Don't tell her what? That the boy she loves has been genetically altered by the Trust to protect his sibling? That her partner will forever feel the tug of the Scion even to the point of physical ailment?"

"Max loves me?"

"You miss the point. As the Tonat, your cell structure has been coded to respond to the needs of the Scion. Even if you do not want to be the Tonat, you cannot escape its effects."

"I know. The Keepers told me already. Theylor explained to me that even if I choose *not* to be the Tonat, my genetic structure will fight me every step of the way." I stood up. "I can't believe they did this to me."

"Understand that the Trust, those five patriarchic Space Jumpers, are wired to do one thing: create the Space Jumper that protects the Scion. That's all they care about. The Trust knows what they are doing. They've been getting ready for this just as long as the Nagools. Maybe longer. The Scion needs a Tonat."

"But this is supposed to be *my* life. How can I have my own life and choose what I want to do when a bunch of aliens have already rewired me to protect another?"

"Do you think it's fair not to tell Max? Do you think that's fair to either of you?"

"Nothing seems fair on the Rings of Orbis."

"Then you should feel welcome here."

"What are you guys talking about?" Max asked as she returned.

I looked at Tic. I wasn't ready to tell Max. *Please don't,* I thought.

"JT was telling me how my little concoction was making him feel much better."

"Golden!" Max exclaimed. "I knew it was a good idea to come here."

"You must take some home with you," Tic insisted. "In case you feel a relapse."

"Thanks," I replied.

We sat and talked with Tic for some time. She was so much different from Madame Lee, although I sometimes caught glimpses of a ferocious warrior hidden in her chiseled bone structure and jet-black skin. Tic told us she had lived on Orbis since before the Citizens' uprising on Orbis 3. That's when she moved to Murat and began living like a knudnik. I was interested, but my thoughts began to drift away from the conversation. I was thinking about what to do with Max. Would she find out on her own? She wouldn't let me live like this, even if I explained to her that it wasn't that bad. Theylor told me that the symptoms would get worse the farther I traveled from Ketheria, but I figured I could live with throwing up every once in a while. Besides, I could always get more of Tic's magic drink.

The truth was, all *I* wanted was to be with Max. The fact that my genetic structure had been altered to help protect Ketheria was not going to get in the way. Whoever did this to me had no right to do so. I would protect my sister, but I would have my own life as well. I had always protected her in the past, and I didn't see why I couldn't continue to do so. Ketheria had enough Space Jumpers around her, anyway. One more wasn't going to help. I would keep this a secret from Max and have my own life. At least that was my plan.

By the time Hach had returned from his business dealings, my plan seemed to be working. I had programmed the chow synth to create more of Tic's drink, and I drank it in private at the start of every cycle. I also tested Theylor's distance theory and began going out with the other kids to distribute taps around Murat. The only new symptom was a sharp headache stabbing at my temples as I ventured farther from home. It was still plenty of distance to lead my own life, despite what the Keepers had warned.

The guilt, however, was something I couldn't escape. Ketheria must have known that I had no intention of becoming the Tonat. She *was* a telepath. But if she was disappointed in me, she never let it show. In fact, it seemed to me that Ketheria did her best to accept my decision; she was always assuring me that she was well protected. I made her promise to inform me if anything seemed out of the ordinary or dangerous. The thing was, Ketheria seemed so loved by everyone around her that I didn't understand why there was so much worry about her safety, anyway. Still, to demonstrate my ability to protect her, I made alliances with the knudniks who served her, cleaned her room, and worked in the building. I asked them to report anything suspicious. They eagerly agreed to help, but only reported that Ketheria spent every cycle with the Nagools. When I questioned her, she said that she was learning about the Universe and preparing for the Cycle of Witnessing. She never left the building, and the Space Jumpers always guarded her door. It seemed like a boring existence to me, but Ketheria looked happy and she was safe. That's all that mattered.

"There are some in the universe who are appalled by your sister's very existence," Hach told me when I asked about her security a few cycles later. He was dining in his room and had asked me to join him. "Her existence is an affront to their own beliefs, and they refuse to see the truth."

"So you believe in it too?" I asked.

"There's nothing to believe. OIO does not ask you to have faith in anything or follow anyone; it simply is. They say OIO is a seamless part of your own existence."

"I still don't get it."

"You don't have to. Listen to me. It is believed that the Ancients *made* the first softwires."

"Made?"

Hach stuffed a piece of meat in his mouth and shook his head. "I don't know folklore. Don't drill me on it, but it's common knowledge that the Ancients gave them the technology for their belts, and we know the Ancients picked the first Trust—

that council of Jumpers who now govern and train all Space Jumpers. You see, the Ancients knew that there would be many individuals in this universe, even believers, who would see any Scion as a threat. They have been right in the past. I'm afraid you can't fight this."

"I've heard that," I mumbled. "So you're not upset with all these Space Jumpers hanging around here?"

"I'm not, but I do worry for the Keepers. They are running a huge risking by parading them in the open like this. I can't help but feel they are taunting the Trading Council. The Keepers cannot afford a war. We've made certain of that."

"Then why do you allow the Space Jumpers to remain here?"

"I suppose some things are worth the risk. At least the Keepers feel that way," he said, stabbing another piece of meat with his fork and winking at me. It was nice to have Hach back.

A knudnik entered the room. "Your guests have arrived," he announced.

Hach swallowed and said, "Good. Have them wait. I'm not finished with the Tonat just yet."

The thin alien nodded before leaving. Hach put down his fork and knife and said, "I know you're not happy with this arrangement, but as I'm sure you are well aware, you are in no position to deny me."

"I've been in Murat. I've passed out the taps. I've done everything that has been asked of me."

Hach nodded. "The Scion's first public appearance is a few cycles away. The Cycle of Witnessing. I certainly can't have a bunch of Space Jumpers lining the stage, now, can I? Your presence will be required."

"Why? These people worship her. No one is going to hurt her," I complained.

Hach leaned on his elbows. "On the planet of Sorlinda, maybe ninety million light-years from here, a very advanced society discovered that a Scion was among their ranks. They rejoiced. They celebrated. As far as they were concerned, *they* were the chosen ones, but as they waited for the Scion to fully awaken, others on the planet decided that they, too, were worthy of this title. If the Universe had chosen one Sorlindian, why shouldn't it choose them all?"

Hach grabbed another hunk of meat from the tray in front of him and plopped it onto his plate. He sliced it as he spoke. "Come the Cycle of Witnessing, a powerful arm of its government seized the Scion and ceremonially sliced her up, serving her flesh for consumption to anyone in attendance at the Witnessing. They passed around pieces of her on plates, just as you might do at a banquet." Hach shoved a piece of meat into his mouth for emphasis. My stomach rolled over once, but it had nothing to do with my illness.

"Where was the Tonat?" I asked.

"They had tricked the Tonat and drugged him. He was unconscious during the entire event. When he awoke, he was so enraged that he slaughtered every single person who had attended the Witnessing, and there were many. He piled the dead bodies in a pyramid on the exact spot where the Scion had died. Then he stole their precious metals and entombed the bodies in a silver shrine so no one would ever forget what they had done to the Scion. It was quite ghastly. In fact, the Tonat is now considered a monster in Sorlindian folklore."

"The Keepers never spoke of this," I said.

"I can see why. Even your own people have destroyed their share of Scions. One fable talks of a Scion who was nailed to a piece of wood while he was still alive; those who worshipped him stood around and watched him suffer. He died eventually, of course." Hach sipped from a goblet. "Shall I go on?"

I shook my head. "You're just trying to scare me," I said.

"I know you want to live your own life, but believe me when I tell you that your sister *needs* you. I do not trust the Council. Do it for your sister, Ketheria, not for the Scion."

That was a dirty trick. "Fine," I said. "But since I'm not trained as a Space Jumper, I don't know what I'll do if anything happens at the Witnessing."

"Presentation will be our best defense." Hach said, and stood up, pushing his chair back. "People fear the Tonat," he called out as he left the room. "Use that."

The Cycle of Witnessing was sort of like Ketheria's coming-out party. Anyone who had heard rumors about the Scion was now allowed to see her firsthand (if they paid the fee, of course). I stood back and watched as the corridors of Hach's newly created temple buzzed with gossip and the workers scrambled about under Queykay's precise, military-like instruction. He oversaw every detail, including the new robes he ordered us to wear. It was clear that the Trading Council wanted everyone to know that they were in charge of the Scion.

The new cream-colored robes were detailed with a broad, deep red collar marked with the OIO symbol. My outfit was different, though. Instead of a robe, I was given bloodred pants that matched the collars on everyone's robe. My pants flared behind my legs, leaving a short train of fabric as I walked. I wore a belt marked with the OIO symbol and a long, double-breasted jacket lined with gold buttons, each one sporting the Orbis emblem.

"I think you look . . . great!" Max exclaimed, tugging at the jacket as I got dressed in my room.

"I look ridiculous," I complained.

"No, you don't. In fact, you look impressive."

Max put her arms around me and kissed me.

"What's that for?" I asked.

"I don't know," she said, blushing. "Just because."

"Well, your robe looks very nice, too. You wear it . . . well," I said, searching for the proper word.

"You think?" Max said, rubbing her hands over the material. It was so hard for me to compliment her without sounding like a malf. Did I tell her how much I liked the way the material stretched over her legs as she walked? Or the way it clung to her waist? It sounded stupid in my head. I couldn't imagine saying it out loud. I was staring at her and she saw me. Max kissed me again. "Thanks," she whispered in my ear.

Theodore charged into my room. "Have you seen all the people out there?" he exclaimed. "The place is already full, and it doesn't start until the next spoke. No wonder the Trading Council wants to charge for this." He turned to Max. "Queykay also wants us to hand these out among the crowds."

Theodore held up four huge sacks filled with more taps. The bags were three times as big as anything we had ever handed out in Murat.

"Wow!" Max remarked. "Where is he, anyway?"

"Not a clue. These were left outside my door with a note."

"We better get going. It will take all the time we have to hand them out," Theodore said.

"Queykay left me a note with my clothes. He asked me to stay with Ketheria," I told them.

Max frowned. "Aw, come with us. Please. I was getting used to you in your new clothes."

"Yeah, that's way more golden than what we have to wear," Theodore added.

I looked at Max and Theodore, with those huge bags of taps. "What can it hurt?" I said. I'd get to the stage in time. No one was going to carve up Ketheria and feed her to the Citizens. I would much rather be with Max than stand around like some stupid trophy. My stomach reacted to my thoughts, turning over once before settling. "Let me grab something, and then we'll drop by Ketheria's room before I help you with the taps."

I made sure not to let Max see me chug Tic's drink from the chow synth. The liquid's effect on my stomach was instant, and I was thankful for my encounter with the Belaran even though her warning about Max crept back into my head. *I* will *resist their genetic tampering,* I said to myself. *I don't care what they're trying to do. I will live my own life, and right now I want to be with Max.*

Theodore handed off two of the sacks, one to Grace and one to Dante (I think that's what he was calling himself at the moment). Then we stepped outside with the remaining bags. I stopped when I saw the crowd outside waiting to see Ketheria. I think every alien from all four rings was standing in the open courtyard. I looked out and saw more aliens pouring over the concrete walls and stuffing themselves into the walkway leading to the building. Over the farthest points of the audience, huge O-dats floated in the sky as everyone was straining to see the platform extending from the roof and over the crowd.

"How many people do you think are here?" Max wondered aloud.

"More than I ever imagined," I mumbled.

I walked next to Theodore while he handed out the taps to aliens thrusting their hands toward him. No one pushed or grabbed at Theodore, but you could tell they were anxious to get any information they could. As I walked through the crowd, people whispered and moved out of my way. Max stayed at my side, scooping taps from her sack and handing them to anyone who wanted them. Theodore then fell in behind.

"We're going to need more than this," Theodore declared.

"Can't they share?" I asked.

"I don't think they want to. They keep these taps like souvenirs."

I tried to read the faces. Some immediately averted their eyes when I looked at them, and I even caught the odd daring sneer. What did they think I was going to do? Chop *them* all up and eat them? I imagined parents threatening their unruly offspring with horrible stories about the Tonat. Would I ever live up to those fears? *Impossible,* I thought. I mean, look at the outfit I was wearing. Who would be afraid of me?

A Choi stepped in front of me and grabbed my hand with her scaly paw. The familiar knobby stumps poking out from her shoulder blades reminded me of Weegin, our first Guarantor. The alien rubbed my hand along her face, mumbling something I couldn't understand, an odd display of affection by a Citizen over a knudnik. Did they realize I was still a knudnik? I stopped and looked at Max. *What do I do now?* my eyes pleaded, but Max only shrugged. With my other hand, I stroked the top of the Choi's bumpy head. Others, seeing my reaction, poured in around us as if by invitation. They pawed at my shoulders, my hair, and even my legs. A sea of hands engulfed Max and me, reaching out to touch any part they could reach. There was no way to move.

"Stop!" I shouted.

The aliens pulled back as if I had used some sort of invisible battering ram. The Choi in front of me started crying. Dirty yellow tears puddled at my feet, and I moved around her to get away. I had no idea what to do.

"This is creepy," Max whispered.

"Let's get out of here," I said.

"What about Theodore?"

"He'll understand." I turned to him and called out, "Theodore, we'll be back in a bit. We'll meet near the right side of the platform when Ketheria comes out."

"Hey!" Theodore tried to protest, but the aliens reaching for their taps closed in and smothered him. Max and I slipped into the crowd.

"I feel bad leaving him like that," Max said.

"He'll be fine," I assured her, straining to locate a private spot among the throng of aliens. I grabbed Max's hand and pulled her along as the crowd parted for us.

"Where are we going to go?" she asked.

"Anywhere," I replied.

Beneath one of the huge O-dats floating over the crowd, I found a tower holding speakers and smaller O-dats; it was draped in some sort of black material. I poked my head under the cloth. Nothing but the metal frame. *Perfect,* I thought. I lifted the cloth and motioned Max to get under. She laughed and looked over her shoulder. It felt good to be doing something I wanted to do.

Inside, the light barely penetrated the thick material. "I can hardly see you," I whispered, but Max only chuckled in response.

"Use your hands then," she said, and placed mine on her face. I ran my fingers around the edges of her face, across her cheeks, and along her lips. We were silent as I explored her face, but I swear I could have started a fire in the space between my fingers and her soft skin. Her warm breath seemed to quicken against the palm of my hand and then I cupped the back of her neck.

"Kiss me," she said, and I obliged.

We remained tangled in each other's arms, invisible to the pageantry that surrounded us. I felt happy, truly happy. This was all I wanted—to be alone with Max. We could have been hidden under those drapes for a parsec or an entire light-year. I had no idea. Time was not relevant at that moment; I just wanted more of it.

Without warning I felt like a Neewalker had dug his claws into me and ripped out my stomach. I pushed away from Max and doubled over in the dark.

"What's wrong?" Max cried.

"I don't know," I croaked. I could hardly breathe.

"JT! Are you sick again?"

Clawing at the fabric, I dug my way into fresh air. The light slammed into my eyes with a searing bolt of pain to my brain, and I screamed. Or maybe Max did—I couldn't tell. I stared into the crowd and a found a Neewalker, directly in front of me, setting up a long-range plasma rifle. I cried out, lunging toward the creature, but found myself with my hands wrapped around the throat of a terrified knudnik, scrambling to get away from me. I spun around, but the Neewalker was gone. *What's happening to me?*

"JT! What are you doing?" Max cried.

The pain seized my brain again and squeezed mercilessly. Another flash, as if someone pointed the sun directly into my eyes, but this time I saw Queykay running along the rooftop.

"Queykay!" I screamed, and pushed through the crowd, stumbling toward him.

Max was at my side. "JT, Queykay's not here. Talk to me. What's happening?"

I looked at the roof. She was right. Queykay was gone. Then another flash. More pain.

"JT! Talk to me. Please!"

I turned to Max and saw a wormhole pirate standing behind her. Max saw me staring and spun around. Then I saw another and another. The pirates revealed weapons cloaked at their hip.

"Max, something's wrong!" I yelled.

"I see that." She grabbed me by the shoulders. "Look at me, JT. Tell me what's happening to you."

"I'm seeing things. It has something to do with Ketheria— I'm certain of it."

And as I spoke her name, my sister stepped out onto the rooftop platform.

"I have to get to her, Max!"

I lunged forward as the crowd around me broke free like a solar flare. The sound was deafening. A wave of people pushed toward the platform, and Max was swallowed up in the rush.

"JT!"

But I couldn't respond. Another bolt of pain stabbed at my head, and this time I saw another alien remove a strange-looking device from under his emerald-colored cape. The device was electric of some sort, its long barrel crackling from some unknown power source. I blinked and he disappeared.

I spun toward the platform. I could see my sister waving to the crowd.

"Welcome," her voice echoed through the loudspeakers. "I know some of you have traveled far, and I thank you."

"Ketheria!" I screamed.

And then I heard it. I knew instantly.

A sting ripped over the crowd, like an electrical cable had been cut free. There was a short pause followed by a crack. I looked up and saw Queykay moving away from Ketheria, just as I had envisioned earlier. Then I saw Ketheria fall. The crowd gasped and fell silent. I heard nothing but the sound of Ketheria's body hitting the platform before the air was gobbled up with mayhem. As some screamed, others began to run. Instantly, more than a dozen Space Jumpers appeared on the platform.

That's when I felt it.

I didn't try to jump. It was as if someone was *making* me jump. My mind and my body struggled to gain control while some psychic tether yanked me through space and time.

For a nanosecond, the world about me appeared frozen before I was torn from my current moment in time and placed next to my sister on the platform without lapse. The chaos and pandemonium roared back in as the universe caught up with me. Four Nagool masters moved toward my sister, and I spotted Drapling running across the platform. I turned to see where Queykay had gone, but I could not find him. Then four Jumpers closed in around me. Each one grabbed onto Ketheria, and then they were gone, my sister with them. All of this happened within a single breath.

"Wait! Where are they taking her?" I screamed, staring at the spot where they had just been. I ran to the next Jumper, but he disappeared before I even got close. Each Jumper followed, one by one. "Where are you taking her?" I screamed at them.

With Ketheria gone, my head felt like it was going to crack open and its contents spill out on the platform. I was drowning in a wave of nausea as I tried to focus, to unlock some hidden link to the Space Jumpers or to Ketheria herself. Surely the Trust had wired me with something like that. I fixated on being with Ketheria, being off this platform, being next to her. Precious seconds slipped away. *Where are they?* Then my mind unhinged and I pushed myself forward, not from where I was standing but rather through space and time. Instead of darkness, my mind exploded with pure light, and I felt relief as I slipped away from the here and now. I let the Universe guide me and prepared myself for what was to come. I even welcomed the sickly scent of smelly feet.

8

I had an idea where I was. The pain in my head had subsided the moment I jumped, and even my stomach felt better.

Ketheria was close.

I recognized the steel beams and walls rooted in the black rock from the last time I had been held here a rotation ago. The Space Jumpers had taken Ketheria to the Trust — I was certain of it. Standing in a wide corridor, I saw blue light glowing along the ceiling's edge and sparkling on the textured floor, just as I remembered. The fact that I had left the Rings of Orbis and jumped to the Trust was not an easy concept to understand, but, as with my softwire abilities, I chose to simply accept it. Right now I only wanted to find Ketheria.

The Trust was powerful, and my last meeting with them had not been a favorable one. They could inflict pain without laying a finger on me, and they could track my movements whenever they pleased. Besides that, whenever the Keepers spoke of the Trust, I always sensed both fear and respect in their tone. When Theylor had informed me that I was genetically altered to be the Tonat, he told me that it was under their instruction. Theylor also told me that the Trust had been instrumental in arranging our trip from Earth. The Trust's main mission, he told me, was to search for a Scion and then, once he or she was found, to help the Scion awaken. But who gave them this role? I assumed it had been the Ancients.

I heard footsteps around the corner to my right. I bolted across the corridor and slipped down another hallway on my left. I had to move quickly, before I ended up in some hole waiting to find out what had happened to Ketheria. I knew she wasn't dead; I sensed it. *Is that from their programming?* I wondered. Or was it simply because Ketheria was my sister? I couldn't even imagine how my body would react if she died.

I slipped along the corridor, searching for some connection to the computer that ran the place. What would I say to Ketheria once I found her? Certainly this incident proved that the security around my sister was inadequate, despite their manpower. I knew Ketheria would say that none of this was my fault, but it was. It had been my decision to handle security in this manner, yet the first time Ketheria appeared in public, she was attacked. What was I thinking? I should have been next to her. It *was* my fault.

Max! I had simply left her in that mob of aliens. *Have I failed everyone? Would she even understand?* I hoped she would.

I stopped in front of a glass panel embedded in the wall. It was the best chance I had. I pushed into the device.

"Ouch!"

I pulled out immediately. My teeth were ringing from the shock, and I could taste a peculiar metal tinge on the roof of my mouth. I tried to shake it off, but it stuck to me like radiation gel. The Trust was using some sort of security device to keep people out of their computer. I moved on, looking for something else, but all I found were more and more corridors with more useless little panels.

Again the sound of footsteps resonated down the hall. There were lots of them this time, and they were marching. I searched for a place to hide and found a small impression in the bedrock. I pushed against the wall, trying to make myself as small as possible, when the wall opened up and I fell inside.

"It doesn't take a softwire to use one of those door panels," said a voice from somewhere within the room. Actually, it was more like the voice was everywhere in the room.

"Who said that?" I called out.

"I did," the deep voice replied.

The room wasn't much. In fact, all I saw were two sloped chairs similar to the ones in Drapling's rooms. There was also a small table. That was it.

"Please sit if you feel more comfortable," the voice offered.

"Thanks," I mumbled, with no intention of sitting.

The walls were the most active things in the place. Lights seemed to flash through the room as if circulating through the rock. Tubes and pipes filled in most of the blank spaces, and then I saw it. To my left, in one corner of the room, I saw a hand, as if it was stuck in the rock. A small control panel was placed within reach of the hand's fingers. I began to notice more body parts spread out through the rock and around the entire room.

"Who are you?" I asked.

"That's rather rude," the voice replied.

"I'm sorry. This is a little strange for me. I'm worried about my sister. She's hurt, and I want to get to her."

"Ketheria is fine. They are attending to her now."

"You know! Can I see her? Do they know who did it?"

"They know who wasn't protecting her."

"Oh."

I knew it. And so did they. I wasn't going to live this one down, that's for sure. I failed Ketheria on my initial test. The anger flushed through my skin. Anger at myself.

"I do not know why you resist it," the voice said. "It is your destiny,"

"Says who?"

"Says me."

"Who are you?"

"Every cell in your body has been programmed to protect that girl. It does not matter how hard you try to avoid your responsibility; you cannot escape it. That sickness you feel? Can you imagine what that would be like if she left this galaxy?"

"I can handle it. I handled it when she came here," I said.

"This asteroid is simply orbiting the rings, you fool."

Well, that explained all this rock.

"What you feel now is nothing compared to what you will

feel if you don't stay close to the Scion. You'll need more than those foolish little potions you drink."

The lights in the rock flared with the sound of the voice, as if agitated.

"How do you know this? Tell me who are you," I said.

"I'm surprised you haven't figured that out. You haven't read those files I gave you, have you?"

"Files? No one gave me any files," I complained.

"Were you not given a device by a Space Jumper and told to keep it with you at all times?"

I reached into my pocket and touched the cold metal disc given to me by one of the Space Jumpers.

"Yes," I muttered.

"Were you not curious to examine the device, to see what you were asked to carry around with you? Obviously not. This is why you need training. You must join us, son. Protecting the Scion is the one thing I cannot program into you."

Program into me? I removed the disc and pushed inside it. Nestled behind the intricate tracking device was a single nugget of data. I willed it open, and my parents' missing files flashed in front of me, all 321 of them.

"You're . . ."

"Quirin," the voice replied.

"My father?"

"By definition."

I didn't look for the chair; I simply sat on the floor and stared at the body parts spread around the room.

"How can it be?" I whispered. "What happened to you?"

"When the *Renaissance* was attacked, I attempted a jump that I knew was not possible. I tried to take everything with me and move backward through time. I failed, and now I will be like this forever."

"But my mother. You left her there."

"Your mother never left Earth."

"What?"

"You will find everything in those files. I'm afraid most of it will upset you, and I caution you against telling the others any of what you find, but that is your choice. I would rather use this time to help you accept your fate. The Scion needs you."

The weight of this revelation tightened around my chest. I tried sitting up to let some much-needed oxygen into my lungs, but could breathe in only a little. It seemed every time some inexplicable part of me was explained, I was left feeling emptier and even more hollow. A million new questions crept in to fill the void. Why had I not seen my father sooner? What did he mean that my mother never left Earth? Would he be a part of my life now? If he was my father, was I even human?

I rubbed the smooth disc across the palm of my hands, afraid to look inside it again. How could my life have strayed so far from my own desires? Where was the promise of happiness on the Rings of Orbis? I didn't want my father to be some freak pieced together inside some asteroid. I wanted the man in the photo — the human who had left Earth to create a better life for his family.

"I don't want any of this," I told him.

"You're willing to sacrifice the future of the universe for your own selfish desires. This obsession with free will is ridiculous. There are no options after this. That is why everything has been sacrificed to save the last possible Scion. There isn't a species left in the universe that can fill this role. We've tried.

"Only a Scion can raise the consciousness of the universe. Without a Scion, the universe will implode under the mass of deconstructive energy that its inhabitants will produce. But before that happens, the universe will be fed upon by beings I can only begin to describe. Ketheria is the last possible candidate. If we fail, the universe will fall."

"Why? Why her? Why me?"

"Only your ego, that sense of yourself, would ever ask such useless questions. There is no *you* or *her* in this equation. The fact that you are involved is nothing more than a random outcome. You were simply the embryo I reached for. You were nothing more than a group of cells that took the genetic information I gave it. The others did not survive. . . ."

"What do you mean, 'the others'?"

"It is far too risky to prepare only one Tonat. Once the Scion was stable, I needed to make absolutely certain to link a Tonat. We could not wait for it to happen naturally. Had the ship not been attacked, I would have tried several combinations. I must admit, though, your abilities have exceeded my expectations. I am grateful you survived. I believe the remaining candidate would have proven even more difficult."

"There's another Tonat?"

"You are the only Tonat."

"You are not making any sense. This is only confusing me more."

"Before the *Renaissance* was attacked, I had time to prepare two cell specimens to receive the required genetic coding. You and one other survivor. The one you call Switzer."

Now I really couldn't breathe. I swallowed hard, hoping that some oxygen would sneak in as well.

"I need to know more," I croaked.

"The wormhole pirate you helped capture had received similar genetic coding to yourself. He was prepared as a backup, if you will—a replacement should something have gone wrong with you. I fear his sociopathic behaviors and narcissistic tendencies are the direct results of my procedures. If I had had more time to give him the attention required, I would have adjusted those anomalies. I would have made him more like you."

"So there would be two Tonats running around the rings?"

"No, I would have destroyed one of you before the *Renaissance* ever arrived on the Rings of Orbis. In fact, I would have destroyed all the embryos except for you and the Scion. That was the plan."

"You would have killed everyone?"

"Yes. Why does this matter?"

"It matters."

A world without Max? Without Theodore? Without Switzer? I felt dizzy even though I was already sitting. I wanted to lie down.

"I don't feel good," I said.

"This is why you need more training. Your emotions are too strong. Your sense of self blinds you. Stay with me and become who you are destined to be. I offer you one of the greatest roles in the history of the universe. Your name will be emblazoned in the hearts of every creature in every galaxy. With Ketheria as the Scion, every human in the universe will be given a unique path to enlightenment. She will guide humans to fulfill their new role in this universe. The Ancients are gone, my son. When the Scion completes the fourteenth step of the awakening, then humans can succeed the Ancients and bring harmony to this universe. It is our last defense against the Knull. An entire universe will stand behind you. You are poised for greatness, John Turnbull. You only need to accept it."

I could only think about Max and Theodore and Grace and even the guy whose name I had trouble remembering, and Switzer. They existed only because the Trust tried to grow their own Scion and Tonat—Ketheria and me. Switzer is sitting in a cell, probably for the rest of his life, because of me. Now, more than ever, I wished I had waited until I was inside his spaceship on Orbis 3, so he could have escaped. At least he would have some sort of life right now.

"It still matters," I mumbled. "It matters a lot."

Every one of them had suffered life as a knudnik on the Rings of Orbis. Suffered because of me and Ketheria. Of course I didn't think Quirin should have actually followed through with his mission and destroyed everyone, but I wanted desperately to be back on the *Renaissance,* trying to help Switzer steal the ship.

I was staring at my hands. It would be Switzer standing here right now if a single one of my cells had mutated in some errant fashion. It would be Switzer poised for all this "glory," not me. I was feeling worse by the second. I really didn't want to be me right now.

I looked up at the wall. "Wait," I said. "Did you do this on purpose? Did you bring Ketheria here so I would hear this?"

"You had to come on your own."

"So does this mean that Switzer is my brother or something?"

"You both share my genetics."

Wow! Too much. I needed to get out of here.

"You, however, have proven to be a much better candidate. I abandoned him for you."

"I want to see my sister," I whispered.

"But we are not finished."

"I was finished a long time ago," I replied. "In fact, I want to go back to the rings. You said Ketheria is all right, didn't you? I want to go home." The word struck me as odd. I had never referred to the rings as my home before. "I need time to swallow all of this."

Quirin did not reply.

"Look, I'll come back so we can talk again," I lied, purely to let him believe that I was considering the situation."

"Certainly. If you remained, however, and if you studied, you could jump back to the rings yourself."

"I said we would talk some more. That is all I can offer you right now."

"There is no way you can fight this," he warned me.

"I can find a way."

"Then I suggest you act quickly. It is dangerous on the rings for your sister."

"Then keep her here."

"The awakening must be allowed to continue. She must do so among those whom she will enlighten."

"Or those who will kill her."

"We must not interfere."

"You are *way* beyond that," I reminded him.

The door to Quirin's room opened, and a Space Jumper stepped in, someone I had never seen before. This Jumper was not as militarized as the others and was dressed in a sleek grayish material. His belt, however, was still prominent.

"He will return you to the rings," Quirin said. "Your sister will be fine. She will follow you there shortly."

"Good-bye . . . Quirin," I said. There was no way I could call him Father, not now.

"Good-bye, son."

The Space Jumper returned me to Ketheria's room on Orbis 4. We did not speak even once, and that suited me fine. I was eager to get back to my own room, lock the door, and open my parents' files. For so long I had wanted to see what was on those restricted documents, but now I had almost forgotten about them. When Madame Lee destroyed the copy from the *Renaissance,* I had thought that was the end of it.

What would I find now? I was almost too afraid to look.

"JT!" Theodore stopped me as I stepped into the corridor outside Ketheria's chamber. "Where's Ketheria? Is she dead? Where did she go?"

"She's fine. The Trust has her."

"Is that where you went?"

I nodded.

"All those Space Jumpers!" he exclaimed. "Everyone is talking about war. So many people saw how easily they moved about the rings. The Citizens are really going crazy. Queykay arrived with the entire Trading Council. They put all these new laws into place. You can't even move from ring to ring now. They said it was to protect the Scion, but Hach was furious. They took him with them when they left."

"Where's Max?"

"She's with Grace and that guy—what's his name?"

I shook my head.

"Come on, I know Max will be glad to see you. They're having a meeting or something. Max has Grace getting everyone together."

Theodore tried to guide me in the direction he was going, but I pulled away.

"I can't," I told him.

"Why not?"

"There's something I've got to do first."

"Fine," he said, turning back in my direction. "We'll go after that."

"Alone," I said.

"Oh."

"I'm sorry."

"Don't be. I understand. We'll come by later. Max will want to see you when she finds out that you're back."

"I don't want you to tell her you saw me," I said.

Theodore just looked at me. "What's wrong, JT? Let me help you."

I shook my head. "Not this time. It's not like that."

"But—"

"I'm sorry. Really." I turned and headed toward my room. "Don't tell her, all right?" I yelled back.

But Theodore did not respond.

Inside my room, I sat at the edge of my sleeper and slipped the disc from my pocket. I ran my finger along the impression that circled the face of the disc. I pushed in and grabbed a random file.

NEXUS ACCESS 12B-532-AFG

TIME POINT: 12:45.2: 227

CONTACT: QUIRIN NE YARNOS

The genetic enhancements on specimen 1325b appear to manifest the desired traits far more rapidly than the original candidate (specimen 334). My fears that I may not be able to procure an alternate now seem unfounded.

Cleavage of the Scion zygote coupled with the experimental regermination may prove to have created an exceptional candidate for the Tonat.

If success continues, I will destroy specimen 334 prior to the standard schedule.

Transmission successful.

It's true!

I pulled out of the storage device. The residual burn of Quirin's entry still sparkled against the inside of my forehead. It would fade, I knew, but the knowledge would stay with me forever.

Was *I* specimen 1325b? I had to be. When Theylor admitted that I had been genetically altered, I never once thought it happened on the *Renaissance.* I assumed it was when they replaced my arm, or when I almost drowned in the cooling tank on Orbis 2.

If this was true, then Switzer must have been specimen 334. What did they do to him? Did Quirin start to turn Switzer into the Tonat and then stop? If Quirin had never touched Switzer, would he be like the other kids from the *Renaissance?* Out of the two hundred children born on that ship, Switzer was the only one we feared. He was a monster, and they had made him that way. It was not fair.

If success continues, I will destroy specimen 334 prior to the standard schedule.

They had planned to flush everyone on that seed-ship. The thought horrified me. Where were all of our parents? Were they already dead? This didn't make sense. Quirin said my mother was still on Earth.

"JT?" Vairocina's voice whispered inside my head.

"Yes," I replied, welcoming the distraction.

"I was hoping we could talk now."

"It's not a good time."

"But I think it is too important for you to wait any longer. I've located the information you requested."

"What information?" I stood up and paced the room.

Vairocina formed to my left. "You asked me to gain a better understanding of your transfer to the Citizen Hach," she replied.

"I did, didn't I? I'm sorry. I forgot. Did you find anything?"

"Yes. It seems that Charlie had made arrangements for his possessions to be distributed through an advocate."

"Is that normal?"

"Absolutely. Advocates are usually appointed by the Trading Council to ensure a fair and honest allocation of assets in the event there are no relatives."

"Like that would ever happen. No wonder I ended up with Hach."

"No," Vairocina interrupted. "The unusual aspect is that Charlie had *already* chosen an advocate well before he died. In fact, the same cycle he became a Citizen and only moments after an enormous sum of chits was transferred to his personal holdings."

"Who? Who did he assign?"

"Well, it wasn't a single person really. . . ."

"Who, Vairocina?"

"The Descendants of Light. Drapling signed the transfer. Drapling is also the one who then bequeathed you to Hach."

"What?"

"The Descendants of Light. The trans —"

"I heard you. I just can't believe it. It doesn't make sense. Charlie was no fan of the DOL, especially Drapling. I even heard them fighting once when I was half-conscious. I'm sure it was Charlie and Drapling. This just doesn't make sense."

I sat down on my sleeper and hoped the room would stop spinning.

"Is there anything else I can find for you, JT?"

"No," I said, "but there is something you can do."

"Certainly."

"Can you tell Drapling I need to meet him? It's an emergency."

"I'll do it now."

I pushed back into the storage device. This time I discovered a small interface along with the hidden data. *Only a softwire would find this interface,* I thought. The interface displayed a projection mode, which I initiated, then pulled out of the device and sat the metal disc on the lid of my sleeper. Using my softwire, I interacted with the display projected on the wall in the same manner I would with an ordinary O-dat. I opened another file at random.

NEXUS ACCESS 6F-448-MGH
TIME POINT: 14:40.9: 814
CONTACT: QUIRIN NE YARNOS

Long-range subspace tracers have detected a distress signal in the Dorvum system. Ion Signatures identify craft as a Zinovian class 4 cruiser: nonmilitary issue.

Threat: none.

Current systems are stable. Recommend jump interaction. Please advise.

Transmission successful.

Zinovian class? Was that Madame Lee? Did she trick him? I opened another file.

NEXUS ACCESS 11C-102-MKL
TIME POINT: 03:03.1: 019
CONTACT: QUIRIN NE YARNOS
AI programming was initiated as per instructions. Earth-like histories for all specimens now loaded. Scion and Tonat entered as siblings. The AI has been time-stamped to display death of parents, children, and crew upon arrival. Birth sequence initiated for Scion and Tonat and scheduled to arrive on the Rings of Orbis near their thirteenth Earth year.

Transmission successful.

Ketheria and I were supposed to arrive on the rings as the same age. I tried to think of Ketheria as seventeen, just like me. It was too weird. What would she look like? I retrieved the first file I had opened. What did the words *zygote* and *cleavage* mean? Were Ketheria and I twins? Impossible!

"JT?" Vairocina whispered inside my head.

"Did you find Drapling?"

"He will meet you at the Center for Relief and Assistance."

"When?"

"Whenever you are ready."

"I'm ready now."

9

"I want to see Switzer," I told Drapling. We were seated in the same room underneath the Center for Relief and Assistance.

Both of Drapling's heads converged on me. "I'm sorry, but that is impossible," he stated.

"I'm learning quickly that nothing is impossible. I want to see him, Drapling. He shouldn't be there. What happened to Switzer is not his fault. In fact, it is more the Rings of Orbis's fault than his."

"Your friend is a criminal, a wormhole pirate. He will never see the surface of the ring for as long as he lives. Your request is denied."

I stood up, marched over to Drapling, and leaned in close. Any other person would have shrunk back into their seat, but Drapling remained indifferent. "Listen carefully," I whispered. "This is not a request. I don't need your answers anymore. I *know*. Do you understand me? I met with Quirin. He gave me the missing files. As far as I can figure, you guys sent him to snatch a bunch of embryos from Earth and grew your own Scion. Except your plan didn't work out the way you wanted it to, and now you have all of *us*. Switzer isn't just a friend; he's my brother."

"Technically, I believe you would call him a half brother. You share only the genetic coding of Quirin. You and the Scion share a common human egg."

"Shut up! No matter how you spin it, the life Switzer now has is directly the result of *your* actions."

"This means nothing. You feel this way only because you have been adjusted to exhibit a greater care for your sibling. For Ketheria, *not* for Randall Switzer."

I pulled back and stepped around Drapling. It took eight strides across the shiny floor to reach the door. I *pushed* into the control panel and locked it. My old feelings for Switzer were gone. *Now* I wished that I had helped him steal the *Renaissance* when we first arrived. *Now* I wished I had let him escape on Orbis 3. I had to make it up to him before I did anything else. It was not right for him to be forgotten and left to rot away in some cell. I wanted to apologize to him. I wanted to apologize for everything.

I turned toward Drapling. He hadn't moved a muscle. "I know about the Descendants of Light," I told him. "I know that you helped Charlie become a Citizen. Yet I was wondering if Theylor and the other Keepers know everything. If I remember correctly, when Theylor came to greet us on the *Renaissance,* he was expecting to find a ship filled with adults. Or was that a ruse as well?"

Drapling did not respond. Instead he looked toward the glasses at the far side of the room.

"Is something wrong, Drapling? Was that information restricted? I don't know what it means yet, but I think I can use it."

"You cannot comprehend the magnitude of the situation," Drapling declared.

"Let me see him."

Drapling spun toward me.

"Why can't you just accept it? You *are* the Tonat. This is your destiny!"

"Let me see him!"

Drapling just stared at me from across the room. Then, without speaking, he stood up and strode toward the door.

"Please unlock the door," he said. "And follow me."

Drapling led me from the room, across the floor of tombs, and past the light chute we used to descend from the Center for Relief and Assistance. He stopped at the end of the corridor in front of another chute.

"Can this take us off the ring?" I asked. "Switzer's at the Center for Science and Research on Orbis 1, isn't he?"

"No," Drapling replied. "I am afraid you underestimate your adversary."

"*I* could never escape from the Center," I reminded him.

"You never tried."

Had Switzer tried to escape? I doubted he was the easiest prisoner for the Keepers to deal with.

"Please understand that if Quirin had failed with your enhancements, Switzer would have been the Tonat. All that remained for Quirin to do was to initiate the proper gene activation sequence and Switzer, too, would have been a softwire."

"I thought softwires were rare. If it's so easy to cook one up in a test tube, then why don't you just make an army of them?"

Drapling was about to punch the code into the panel next to the purplish light chute when his right head turned and said, "Believe me when I tell you that we have tried, but it is not as simple as you suggest. You must appreciate how fortunate Quirin was to have two workable specimens at his disposal. I only wonder if Quirin may have made the wrong choice, as Switzer certainly exhibits the ruthlessness required for the job."

"It sounds to me like you built a monster that you cannot control and now you're going to imprison him for the rest of his life to avoid dealing with your own mistake."

"What do you suggest? That we kill him?"

"No! Let him go. You made him this way."

"We also made you."

The edge in Drapling's voice and the sneer rubbed across his face reminded me of the Keeper I first encountered when I had arrived on the Rings of Orbis. Any niceties he had recently shown were gone. I watched him over my shoulder as I stepped into the chute.

When I exited the light chute, the first thing I felt was cold.

In fact, it was freezing. I moved away from the chute and into a gray, lifeless corridor. Drapling was behind me in the next instant.

"Where are we?" I asked. I could see my breath in front of me.

"Deep within Orbis 4," Drapling replied, stepping past me.

He walked beneath a single bluish light source embedded in the ceiling of the concrete corridor, and I followed, avoiding his purplish robe, which dragged behind him. I glanced at my surroundings and noticed frost gathering in places where the walls met the ceiling. I could only assume Switzer was somewhere behind one of these walls.

A green electrical field blocked us from continuing down the corridor. I watched as Drapling turned and placed his hand inside a device mounted on the right wall. The green force field appeared to drop away and run along Drapling's arm before scanning his entire body. He removed his hand and ordered me to follow him.

Once we passed through this entry point, I saw a series of thick chrome doors along the wall every three meters or so. Each door flashed an LED symbol embedded right at the Keeper's eye level.

"What is this place?" I asked Drapling.

"It does not have a name."

"What do *you* call it?"

"Terminus," he mumbled.

"Why is it so cold?"

"I hadn't noticed."

Drapling stopped in front of the second door. I waited as he reached inside his left sleeve and a small bench slid out from the wall on the opposite side of the hallway. He sat but motioned me toward the metal door.

"What am I supposed to do?"

Drapling reached under his sleeve again, and this time the door disappeared. A paler version of the electrical field I saw earlier remained in its a place.

On the other side, I saw Switzer lying on the floor.

"Switzer!" I cried.

His body only jerked in response. I turned to Drapling. "Open it!"

Drapling reached under his sleeve, and the field fell away. I raced in and knelt next to Switzer. He was balled up in a fetal position, clutching his stomach and moaning. Someone had removed the piece of screen over his eye but had left the wires sticking out of his face.

"Switzer!"

He cracked open his eyes and stared at me through the pus that had crusted around his lids.

"Switzer, it's me, JT!"

Switzer didn't respond. Instead, his body convulsed as if he was trying to throw up, but nothing came out. I looked around the room. By the looks of the mess near the toilet I didn't think he had much left to throw up, anyway. I turned to Drapling. He had replaced the barrier to the room.

"Does he have the same thing as me, the sickness when Ketheria is too far away?" Drapling nodded. "How could you leave him like this?" I screamed at him. "Do you have any idea what that feels like?"

"You appear to be doing fine," he reminded me.

"That's because—"

I thrust my hand into my pocket. I had the medicine that Tic had given me. I pulled it out and chewed off the lid as I propped Switzer's head up.

"Drink this. It will help. I know what you're going through. I would be just like you if it wasn't for this stuff."

I expected Switzer to resist, but he raised his chin a little and parted his lips. They were dried and cracked. Scabs had grown over the smallest crevices, but thick, bleeding sores were visible at the corners of his mouth. I poured the liquid over his lips. He pawed at my hand, forcing me to pour more liquid into his mouth.

He pulled his head away and fell back onto the floor, his arms flung out. Then he bellowed with laughter and cried, "Sweet golden universe! Where was that stuff when I needed it?"

I sat back, relieved to see the liquid working so quickly. "I'll bring you more. You won't have to feel that way again."

"You can't even imagine what I felt," he mumbled, and tried to sit up.

"Yes, I can," I replied.

Switzer looked at me and then looked out at Drapling. "What's he doing here?"

"Forget him. We need to talk."

"About what? You want to rub it in my face a little? You want to tell me how you were right all along?"

"No, Switzer. *You* were right. You were right about everything. They did this to you. They made you this way. They messed with your genetic code, trying to create a security force for Ketheria. I'm sorry."

"Sorry? For what?"

"For everything. I should have listened to you. I should have helped you get out of here." I leaned toward him. "I should have left with you. It's my fault you are in here."

Switzer pushed himself up to his sleeper and then struggled to stand. He walked over to the door and stared at Drapling. "Don't take the blame for everything, split-screen. These two-headed space monkeys aren't telling you the whole story. I'm sure of it."

"I don't need them now. I know all the answers now. I found the files from the *Renaissance*."

Switzer turned to me. "And?"

"On the *Renaissance*, they messed with your genetics to create a Space Jumper who would be the Tonat. Then they made me. You were supposed to be . . . well, let's say that when the ship was attacked, they didn't have time to finish with their experiments and you were born. They made you who you are and they should be responsible for you. You should be out there learning to be a Space Jumper. Enjoying your life. Preparing for great things."

"But somehow I'm stuck in here, regretting my every waking moment." Switzer turned and looked at me. "And don't think that an apology is enough, Dumbwire."

He was right. Words weren't going to change anything. I stood up and marched toward the door.

"Drapling. You have to let him out. Let Switzer study with the Space Jumpers. Let him go with the Trust.

"I will not let Switzer roam free," he insisted.

"The Trust will take him away from the Rings of Orbis. He won't stay here. He'll leave Orbis. I know he will." I turned to Switzer. "Won't you?"

"Forget it. He's not going to do it," Switzer mumbled.

"Drapling, Switzer's wanted to leave here ever since he knew about the Rings of Orbis. He has the same genetic enhancements I have, so let him fulfill his role as a Space Jumper. You owe that to him, Drapling. It's the right thing to do. He deserves at least *that*, not a life like this."

Drapling stood up and walked toward the force field.

"Fine," he said. "But with one condition."

"Anything," I replied.

"You go with him."

10

I returned to my room and found Max kneeling in front of my sleeper with half a dozen tools scattered about the room. She had the front panel of my sleeper on her lap and was picking through a fistful of knotted wires.

"I don't know why that makes me nervous," I said.

"Should you be?" she asked without looking up, and then placed the ball of wire between her teeth. With her hands free, she snapped the plastic panel back into place and snatched a laser drill off the floor to secure her handiwork. She looked satisfied and stood up, tossed the wires onto the sleeper, and turned to me.

"Don't I need those?" I asked.

"You could have let me know you were back," she said.

I walked toward her and took her hand.

"I'm sorry, Max. I really am."

"What happened?"

What was I going to say? I knew *too* much now. Should I tell Max that her entire existence was a mistake? Should I tell her that the Trust had messed up and she was never meant to be alive? The life that she and the others had suffered on Orbis was all because of Ketheria and me. What about the others, who I hadn't seen since we arrived? What were they suffering?

"I went to see Switzer," I told her.

"What?"

"He shouldn't be there, Max."

Max pulled away, but it felt like someone had chopped my hand off. "What caused this turn of events, JT? You've hated him ever since you were born. He tried to kill you. He was directly involved in Charlie's death and who knows what else? Trust me: he's supposed to be wherever he is."

"It's not his fault, Max."

"What do you mean? I can't believe you can even say that. It's certainly not *your* fault. I don't get this, JT. You went to see Switzer instead of coming to see me? Ketheria I could understand, but him?"

"Max, you *don't* understand."

"Apparently I don't. I had no idea what happened to you. First you start going crazy, then someone tries to assassinate Ketheria, and then, *bang,* you're gone, too! I was going crazy wondering what happened to you. If it wasn't for Theodore telling me you were all right, I don't know what I would have done."

"Theodore told you I was here?"

"Don't get mad at him. He was just being a good friend."

"Some friend," I mumbled.

"You could take a few lessons from him, Johnny Turnbull."

Max turned and walked out of my room. I didn't try to stop her. Maybe it was the best thing, anyway. I didn't have a clue how to tell her that I was leaving.

Ketheria returned the next cycle along with an army of Space Jumpers and a half dozen Nagool masters.

"This isn't good," Theodore said as we watched Ketheria's entourage pile into the antechamber of her room. I caught Queykay watching from down the corridor. He did not look happy.

"What do you mean?" I asked Theodore.

"All those Space Jumpers, JT. The Council is having a fit. They're saying that the Keepers have broken the treaty." Theodore glanced toward Queykay. "Look at him. I would stay out of his way if I were you."

"But I thought most of the people on the rings loved this OIO stuff. Isn't Ketheria their leader now or something?"

"Not really. The OIO philosophy is basically a set of tools to aid in enlightenment. The Scion acts as a seed. Her purpose is to awaken the Universe and help it protect itself against the Knull. I can understand why the Council is nervous. Who's going to listen to them now?"

I turned toward Theodore. "Where did you learn this stuff?" I asked him.

Theodore grabbed me by the arm and pulled me away

from the crowd. He stopped when it appeared no one could hear him. "From Grace and Diablo."

"Diablo?"

"That's what he's calling himself now."

"And you know this because?"

"I have joined their group. Max started it, actually."

"What group?"

"Shhh!" Theodore pulled me farther down the corridor, but I didn't think anyone could hear us anyway.

"We call ourselves Knudnik Nation. We're convinced that if the Citizens go to war against the Keepers again and we, the knudniks, work behind the scenes to undermine the Citizens' efforts, then we can sway the outcome of the war. Do you know how much business on these rings is dependent upon knudniks? Just by collectively refusing to work, we could bring the Citizens' cycle-to-cycle activity to a halt. We have so much power! We simply need to unite. Our biggest hurdle is to get the word out. The taps have helped. Max has hacked into them and we've begun leaving little messages after the original propaganda. They're only viewed once and then the tap is destroyed. There's no way it can come back to us."

I didn't know what to say. It was as if someone had shone a light on Theodore. He had been in the room all along, but no one had ever noticed him. Theodore was empowered by this mission in a manner I had never seen.

"Well, what do you think? Join us. We could use your soft-wire abilities. You could use it to spread the message and connect to the other rings inside the central computer. Even Vairocina could help."

I shook my head. "I don't think I can," I told him.

"Why not? Max is there. She's practically our leader. I think Ketheria would actually promote it. She knows how evil the Citizens are; that's why the Council is so afraid of her."

"It's not that."

"Then what is it?"

How was I going to explain to Theodore that I was leaving to become a Space Jumper in order to free the one person we had both despised? Our hate for Switzer was a common bond that Theodore and I had shared our entire lives. If I told him now, I knew I would be hurting our friendship, maybe permanently.

"It's nothing," I said. "Of course I'll join. Are you crazy? When do they meet? Is it soon? I'll come with you."

"That's golden, JT. I knew I could count on you. This is going to strengthen our effort like you can't believe. We meet in Murat next cycle. I don't have the location yet, but I'll let you know the moment I do."

"Sure," I said, and motioned back toward Ketheria. "I want to check on my sister. I still haven't seen her yet."

"Oh, of course. Go. Do you want me to say anything to Max for you? We're going to deliver some more taps."

"You and Max?"

"And a bunch of us," he said.

"No," I replied. "I have to deal with Max myself. It's only fair."

"I'll tell her you're with Ketheria; she'll understand," he said as he turned away.

"No!" I yelled after him. "Don't say anything else. Please. Let me deal with Max."

"All right, but remember: say nothing. To anyone."

I nodded as I watched Theodore trot down the corridor in the opposite direction of Queykay. I was jealous. *I* wanted to be going to see Max. I wanted to make plans with them, but all I was going to do was disappoint Max and Theodore. I couldn't tell them. Not yet. I needed a better reason, one that everyone would understand and one that would not expose the fact the each and every kid from the *Renaissance* was never meant to be alive.

Inside the first chamber of Ketheria's room, I found two Nagools discussing something quietly. They both looked up when I entered and smiled. I returned the gesture.

"We welcome your participation," the one Nagool said, his voice like still water.

"And thank you for your decision," the other added.

"You're welcome," I muttered. Truth was, Nagools made me nervous. I didn't understand them, and I didn't want to. In fact, I didn't really know what they did. I made a mental note to ask Ketheria.

Inside Ketheria's main room, I found my sister sitting up in her bed. Seated on the far side were Theylor and another Keeper I had never seen before. This Keeper had only one head. I had never seen that before, either.

"Hello, Johnny Turnbull," Theylor said when I entered.

"Hi, Theylor. I didn't know you were here."

"I wanted to make sure your sister was comfortable. She has been through a great deal."

"Hi, Ketheria," I whispered.

She smiled weakly, her eyelids looking heavy upon her eyes. I saw a yellow bandage wrapped around her left shoulder and arm. Tiny sensors protruded from the bandage, and one of those blue med-lights glowed in a semicircle over the headboard of her sleeper. Seeing my sister wounded by some unknown attacker only reinforced my decision to become a Space Jumper. Suddenly, my own desires seemed selfish and childish to me. Was I feeling this way because of their genetic tampering? *No*, I thought. Ketheria needed me. No one had to alter any part of me to understand that.

"Does anyone know what happened?" I asked Theylor. I moved closer to my sister and let my fingertips caress her hand. She felt warm.

"She was attacked by a long-range plasma rifle," he informed me. "The most disturbing aspect is that our security sensors never picked it up."

"What does that mean?"

"Someone had to program the sensors around her platform to ignore the signature of that weapon."

"Who?"

"Our first suspicion was that someone close to her had done it. Someone with access to the platform, but we have questioned everyone. I am afraid that we have found nothing." The Keeper stood up and walked toward me. "Your acceptance will go a long way to eliminate these holes in their security. I am confident you will rise to be the greatest Tonat ever. An achievement only possible as Ketheria's brother."

"So you know about my plans?" I said.

"This is a great cycle for everyone. I am proud of you."

"Let's hope I can live up to the hype," I said.

"You will," he said, and then Theylor and the single-headed alien slipped away, leaving me with Ketheria.

"Thanks," she whispered.

"Don't thank me yet. I haven't told you about the details."

Ketheria closed her eyes and attempted to smile.

"You know?"

She nodded.

"Aren't you upset?"

"I'm proud of you as well. To put your hatred aside and seek a path to help undo the misfortune set upon another — a person with whom you have such a tattered history. I couldn't be more happy, JT."

"I'm afraid," I told her.

"I know that as well."

"Not just for me, but about what Max will think."

Ketheria winced as the light around her bed pulsed red.

"Don't talk anymore," I whispered, and helped her to lie on her pillow. "Get your rest." But I don't think she heard me. Whoever was monitoring Ketheria had put her to sleep as soon as the pain registered. I stood over the bed and watched my sister rest. *Such a little girl with such an enormous responsibility,* I thought. How could I *not* protect her? Whatever the

Universe had planned for Ketheria, I knew in my heart that she needed me. I had made the right decision. Now I had three cycles to convince Max of my decision before I left the Rings of Orbis.

It simply wasn't enough time.

When I left Ketheria's room, I found the two Nagools still waiting outside. One of them drifted my way when Ketheria's door closed behind me.

"She's sleeping," I whispered.

The Nagool simply reached into his robe and removed something with the OIO symbol marked on one side. He handed it to me.

"What's this?" I asked, turning the card over in my hand.

"It's an OIO key," he replied.

"What do you do with it?"

"It's simply a reflection of the energy that is moving through you right now. Use this gift as you see fit."

"Um, thanks, I guess."

When he turned back to the other Nagool, I slipped past them and returned to my room. I flopped on my sleeper and looked at the OIO key. I turned it over and brushed my fingers over the raised letters. I tried to push into the thing, thinking it was some sort of computer device, but there was nothing. It was simply a piece of plastic. It read:

> *Many entities in this universe feed on fear. They seek out fear, and when they find it, they encourage it. Their efforts are often*

subtle but effective, and you are completely unaware of their presence.

Understand that your fears are learned and compounded by others around you. Simply let this energy pass through your nodes and do not give it attention, as this fear is not yours.

Fear Nothing.

I read the words again. There was something in their meaning that struck a chord deep within me, like the music I enjoyed so much. It felt like the OIO key was speaking directly to me, as if the author had followed me my entire life, experienced everything I had, and eavesdropped on that inner voice that only I heard. Is this what OIO was all about?

I read the card one more time. The words empowered me. They allowed me to release the ownership of my fears and look at my needs with intense clarity.

It was time to talk to Max.

Before I even placed my feet on the floor, there was a knock at my door.

"Come in," I said, hoping it was Max. The door disappeared, and Hach entered my room.

"I've been informed about your decision," he said. "I am pleased by this, especially after the incident with your sister."

"It was a little more than an incident," I pointed out. "Someone tried to kill her. Someone who might even be involved with this place."

Hach checked the door. He seemed nervous. "So you know?

This is the reason for my visit. The Trading Council believes that one of you—one of the humans—is responsible for the attempt on your sister's life."

"One of us!" I jumped off my sleeper. "Are you crazy?"

"May I remind you that I am still your Guarantor? And please keep your voice down. I understand the mood of many of the knudniks and the new Citizens on Orbis 4. I hear the whispers of war. Many feel cheated and rightly so, but it is no reason to upset the balance that we have worked so hard to maintain on these rings."

"At the expense of others," I reminded him.

Hach could only nod.

"Has anyone looked at the Council?" I asked.

"Don't be ridiculous. The Council needs the Scion."

"So what are you getting at?"

Hach checked the door again. "At first I, too, thought it might be the Council that staged the attempt on the Scion. It certainly helps their position. But Queykay informed me that someone has been tampering with the taps. A concerned Citizen returned one to us, but the additional information had been wiped. I have authorities attempting to retrieve the missing data and trace the source of the tampering, but I must assume that one of the renegade groups of Citizens on 4 has something to do with this. My concern is that a few of *you* my have been persuaded to join their ranks."

"Why are you telling me this?"

"If this is true, I can only warn you that such an action is a threat to their lives."

What had Theodore gotten himself into? Then I remembered: it wasn't just him. Max was involved, too, and so were Grace and that other kid.

"You look as is if you have just remembered something," Hach said.

I stared at Hach and tried to put on my best liar's face. "I don't know anything. Look, I'll be gone in a few cycles. My new training should help me track this person. It's not one of us, I assure you. I'll find whoever it is—I promise."

"That's good, because that *is* your job now. You are the Tonat. Even if you discover that your friends are the culprits, Queykay will make you punish them. He may not own you, but he will use you." Hach turned to leave. "Get some rest," he said. "You look tired."

"Thanks," I muttered as the door closed. I fell back onto my sleeper. *What had I done?* I couldn't leave my friends with Queykay. I needed to know what he knew. I jumped off my sleeper and peeked out the door to make sure Hach was gone. I slipped into the corridor but realized I had no idea where Queykay stayed when he was here, if he even was here.

"Vairocina?" I whispered.

"Yes, JT."

"Do you know where Queykay rests when he visits us?"

"Not exactly, but I do know there is a section of your building accessible only by council members."

"Can you help me locate it?"

"It's only for council members," she reminded me.

"That's never stopped us before."

Using my staining, Vairocina located where I was in the building and directed me to the far side of the complex. I figured a good conversation with Queykay might reveal a few of his suspects, or at least get him thinking in another direction.

"I believe these are his quarters," Vairocina stated, and I stopped in front of a set of double brass doors stamped with the Orbis emblem.

I knocked. No one answered.

"Is he here?" I asked.

"It is impossible for me to know," she replied.

Looking for an access point into the central computer, I spotted the entry pad to the left of the doors. When I pushed inside, I found Vairocina waiting for me.

"He is a Trading Council member," she reminded me. "I don't want to see you get in any trouble."

"Something's not right about this guy. If I'm going to go away, I need to be certain he won't hurt my friends. I just want to talk to him."

"What if this is not his room? What if he is not even here?"

"Then it won't hurt to look around a little."

Vairocina paused before she stepped aside. "Thanks," I whispered, and then I unlocked the door and slipped out of the central computer and into Queykay's room.

I was glad that he was gone. It would be easier to snoop around to find some answers than actually trying to get it out of him myself. I crept down the entry to his quarters, staying close to the cold walls. The only light seemed to emanate from plants spilling out of tall vases that were set back in the walls. It reminded me of an underwater cave.

At the end of the main hall, I spotted an open door. Warm light spilled into the hallway and mixed with the cool green light from the hall plants. I stopped just outside the door and peeked around the corner.

What I saw caught my breath. Queykay was naked, lying on a stone slab, his robe on the floor beside him. His porcelain skin was covered with hundreds of little wriggling wormlike creatures that seemed to swell in unison as they nurtured themselves off Queykay's body. I stared in horror when one of the parasites, no more than six centimeters long, pulled away from Queykay. The moist sucking sound made me choke as the creature turned in my direction. Its beady red eyes lit on fire when they caught mine. Then it opened its bloody mouth and screamed.

I ran.

I did not leave my room the next cycle. I had no intention of bumping into Queykay and his brood. I had wanted to see Max, but everything I needed to say was now bottlenecked by the enormous amount of information that had been dumped on me. The missing files I had read before falling asleep only thickened the logjam with more of Quirin's reports.

The history of our parents, whom we thought had died on the *Renaissance,* had been manufactured and placed within Mother purely for Ketheria's and my benefit. The depth of their elaborate ruse was actually inspiring, as Quirin and the Trust had created backup contingencies for every possible scenario. What they never anticipated, however, was two hundred of us arriving on the Rings of Orbis. Their intentions had been to destroy all the embryos and blame it, along with the death of the adults, on the failed cryogenics. Madame Lee's attack now looked like a convenient coincidence, but her actions must have been the catalyst for Quirin to abort his mission.

Coming to grips with the fact that there never were any human adults aboard the *Renaissance* was like cutting the tether that secured me to the ship. I grew up thinking my parents had chosen to come to the Rings of Orbis to begin a new life. I had openly adopted that dream for Ketheria and myself, but now . . . all of that was a mirage. The dreams, the hopes, and even the girl I loved weren't ever meant to be. She wasn't meant to exist, according to the plan set forth by the DOL and the Trust. But why? So they could rig the outcome of their fate with the Knull? That's what it seemed like to me. And what was the Knull, anyway?

The craziest part of all was that I was going to accept this new reality and become a Space Jumper, the Tonat, or whatever they wanted me to be, so I could protect my sister. I was also forcing them to release my lifelong enemy—who apparently was my half brother. Argh! How in the universe could I explain any of this to Max? It didn't even make sense to me.

I let another cycle slip past. I stopped in on Ketheria while they were changing the sensor bandages. Whoever had attacked her had done a nasty job on her shoulder. The medical AI was attempting to fabricate new bone tissue before tackling her muscles. I couldn't stomach anymore. I left Nugget with Ketheria and returned to my room to find Theodore waiting.

"You're coming next cycle, right?" he asked.

"Sure," I told him. "When?"

"Third spoke. I don't know the location yet. It's kept secret until the very last moment."

"Are you sure this is safe, Theodore?"

He looked at me and chuckled. "Since when did you get concerned about *safe*?"

"How does this group feel about Ketheria? You know, about OIO and all of the stuff that's going on."

"There are a lot of believers. Most agree that Ketheria's awakening is a sign—a sign that it's time to act. I think most of them would follow Ketheria to the corners of the universe."

"And you?"

"What do you mean? I know Ketheria's your sister, but she's every bit a sister to me as well. We are a family."

"In more ways than one," I muttered.

"What?"

"Nothing," I said. "Do you ever wonder why Ketheria and I are the only siblings from the *Renaissance*?

"What are you getting at, JT?"

"Think about it—all those kids and only one pair of siblings. Seems odd to me, don't you think?"

"More odd than you being a softwire and Ketheria being the Scion?"

"Good point."

"What's wrong, JT?"

I wanted to tell Theodore everything I had found out. I wanted to share it with someone. I needed to. I couldn't keep all of this inside me. But how could I tell Theodore he was a mistake? Just one of a thousand embryos brought along for the ride — just in case?"

"My dad is alive," I told him.

"What?" Theodore jumped off my sleeper.

"I met him after Ketheria was attacked. He's the reason why Ketheria and I are the way we are. He's not human. Well, not completely. He was a Space Jumper, just like they said. He messed around with our genetics. The Keepers wanted us this way."

"That explains a lot."

"Does it?" I asked him.

"Well, first off, it explains your softwire abilities and Ketheria's awakening. No one else on the ship has the powers you guys have. *That* I always found strange. It was only natural you were siblings. If your evolution had been affected somehow by space travel, why wouldn't it have happened to some others?"

"You sound envious."

"Why wouldn't I be? I would kill to have some of what you have. Why was it that only you two got to race down the evolutionary highway at the speed of light?"

"We aren't the only ones."

"What do you mean? Who else? There's another softwire?"

"Switzer."

"No!"

"And we share the same genetic code from Quirin, my father."

"You and Switzer are brothers?"

"Kind of, but not really. We both received genetic anomalies from Quirin, so in some sense we *are* connected genetically. Ketheria and I are actually from the same human female egg."

"So you and Ketheria are twins?" Theodore slumped onto my sleeper, the weight of the information visible in his posture.

"Just imagine how I feel," I said. Theodore's blank stare told me he was trying to digest everything.

"And now Switzer is locked up."

"Because of this, the way I see it."

"Doesn't seem fair, does it?" he remarked.

"I feel the same way," I whispered.

"What are you going to do?"

"I've already done it. I've agreed to become a Space Jumper if they let me take Switzer. He doesn't deserve to be where he is. It's not his fault."

"JT!"

"I know."

"Max is not going to like this."

"You can't tell her. I want to tell her."

"When? You've been avoiding her like a case of space scratch. Everyone sees it. She's crazy about you, you know."

"Does she say that?"

"Everyone knows."

"I'll tell her at your meeting tomorrow. It's right before I leave. I think it will be easier that way."

"For who?"

I glared at Theodore, but he was right. It wouldn't be easier for Max. I'd been sitting with it for cycles, and now I was just going to dump it on her at the last minute. Now I felt twice as bad.

"You're not helping any," I said.

"She deserves to know," he said as he headed for the door.

"I can't."

"But you should."

When Theodore opened the door, a messenger-bot entered with a screen scroll.

"I didn't think knudniks could get those," Theodore said.

"I think my cycles as a knudnik are numbered," I mumbled.

"Fortunately, mine are, too," he said, and left me alone.

I pushed into the screen scroll thinking it was from Theylor. The scroll read:

Human: Turnbull, J.

An escort will arrive on the next cycle during the third spoke to retrieve you. Your training will begin the moment your escort arrives. You are prohibited from bringing any possessions.

THE TRUST

The third spoke! It figured. Well, they would have to find me, because I was going to that meeting with Theodore.

• • •

At the start of the next spoke, I went to say good-bye to Ketheria. I didn't know how long I would be gone, but I assumed it would be a short trip. How else was I supposed to protect her? I figured the Trust would make me uplink a few codecs, give me a belt, and then ship me back here before anyone knew I was gone.

The two Space Jumpers standing outside Ketheria's room only glanced at me as I slipped past them. I found my sister sitting up. She was alone and sipping from a small ceramic bowl.

"You look better," I told her.

"I don't feel it yet," she groaned. "Who would want to do this to me?"

"I'm afraid more people than you realize."

Ketheria gestured for me to sit on her sleeper, and I did.

"We need to talk before you go," she said.

"About?"

"The Nagools have a ritual they call awakening a self. It is a fourteen-step spiritual journey that allows the individual to discover some part of him or herself, usually an important part on their path to enlightenment. Even I'm experiencing these steps on my path to truly becoming the Scion."

"Theylor told me about that, but why fourteen?"

"Fourteen nodes in and around your body . . . fourteen levels to the labyrinth . . . fourteen keys to enlightenment. Fourteen is an important number. But that's not why I bring it up. Sometimes it can take an entire lifetime to awaken a single self. Sometimes it never happens. Space Jumpers use the same technique to awaken the selves that exist within them. Above all else, they believe in courage, self-discipline, and integrity."

"So? Those are good traits, aren't they?"

"Yes, but they don't let you wait a lifetime to awaken that self. This is one aspect of their training I do not agree with. They use force to awaken those parts within you whether you're ready or not."

"How do they do that?"

"I don't know exactly. I can't get anyone to tell me, but I wanted to warn you. I know you can be a little . . . stubborn sometimes, but that won't work with the Trust. You need to open your mind and allow them to do their work. Otherwise, I'm worried that the training will be a horrible experience for you."

My sister's eyes ballooned with tears ready to pop. I loved her for that. "I can take care of myself," I whispered. "They're just going to zap me with a couple of codecs and then I'll be back. Don't worry. Everything will be all right."

"I know," she said, and tried to smile, "but this is different. Please listen to me and try to understand. Don't fight them. Let it happen. It will be good for you, for me, for us."

I held Ketheria's hand in mine. "I promise," I told her. "I know it seemed I was resisting before, but I will make this work. Besides, the training will help me to protect you so that nothing like this will ever happen to you again."

"Good. Now, I also want you to think of something else to say to Max. What you're going to say won't work with her. In fact, it will probably make matters worse. Try something different. Tell her how much you feel for her, and blame this on me. She can't stay mad at me."

"Out of my head, little sister!"

Ketheria laughed and swiped at a wayward tear that trickled onto her cheek. "All right. But really, think of something else to say to Max. I'll be fine. They'll let you come back and see me, I'm sure. You're not in prison."

I got up and walked to the door. Before I left, I turned to Ketheria and asked, "Hey, with all your power to read minds and whatever other miraculous things you can do now, did you see who tried to kill you?"

Ketheria shook her head. "I was too busy soaking up all the love coming toward me. That's why I need a Space Jumper, big brother. Finding the bad guys is your job."

Ketheria's eyes were welling up again. She looked past me, as if trying to fight back the tears. She stood up, and I moved toward her. "Ketheria . . ."

She shook her head and pointed toward the door. I turned to find Nugget standing there.

"You're so handsome!" Ketheria gushed.

Nugget stood at attention while holding his chin up like some dignitary. His big clumsy feet poked out from an absurd-looking military uniform with mismatched epaulettes and a crude set of medals pinned to his chest. I leaned in and noticed that the medals were made from pieces of plastic and crystal rocks stitched or pinned to his jacket.

I tried not to laugh. "What's going on?"

"Nugget is on a mission," Ketheria said, and moved next to

him. Nugget stood a little taller. "I have made him a mediator on his home planet. It's one of his fourteen keys." Ketheria rubbed his chin, and I remembered the first time she did that back on Orbis 1, when she was the only one who could control him. "Nugget is going to return to Krig and help reunite the Choi and the Choival. Nugget will do so with the blessing of the Scion. He will be an extremely important person on his planet. They will write songs about Nugget some cycle."

Ketheria couldn't stop the tears now. Nugget practically fell on her and threw his arms around her waist.

"It's all right," she cooed. "I will miss you so much, you can't even imagine."

What was she doing? I wanted to step in. I wanted to say something. The race wars on Krig were legendary. Nugget didn't stand a chance. This was a death sentence for him.

"No, it's not," Ketheria said, reading my mind. "Nugget is going to do great things. If he has any trouble, he knows that I will be in his heart. All he has to do is reach out to the Source, and I will be there for him."

"I don't know about this, Ketheria," I said.

"Of course, it will be difficult, but I know Nugget can do it."

"I am not afraid," he declared.

"But—"

"Walk us out, will you, JT?"

Nugget spun on his heels and marched through the door.

"Why him, Ketheria?"

"Why not him? You're judging him on his size."

"I'm judging him on more than that. You've seen what the Choival did to the Choi. Look at Weegin's wings."

"Trust me, JT. I have a knack for these things now. Nugget will perform magnificently in his new role, and he will bring peace to his planet like they have never experienced."

"You can see the future now?" I asked, almost mocking her.

"No, but I can see into Nugget's Source, and he is the only one capable of performing this task, just as you are the only one capable of being the Tonat. It's your judgment of his ability that clogs his nodes and weakens him. So many creatures in this universe are repressed by the thoughts and discriminations of others. You need to stop that, JT. You must stop that now."

Ketheria reached for my hand and then smiled, taking the edge off her demand. I obliged, and we followed Nugget past the Space Jumpers and out into the open hall. Ketheria stopped short and glanced down the hall to her right. I could hear some sort of commotion coming toward us, as if someone was being dragged down the corridor. The sound was quickly succeeded by the spectacle of four faceless guards dragging the kid whose name I could never remember over the stone floor. Queykay marched behind them as Max and Grace hurried to keep next to him.

"Max!" I cried, and rushed toward her.

The four guards stepped between us and took an aggressive position between me and the kid. Their long chrome chest plates extended and then locked together to form a barrier.

"What are you doing?" I yelled.

"Leave it alone, JT," Max called out.

"He is my prisoner," Queykay responded as he stopped in front of the wall of guards.

"What did he do?" I asked

"Darja didn't do anything!" Grace said, and kicked one of the guards with her boot. The guard only glanced over his shoulder at her.

Queykay threw back his crimson robe and reached behind the guards as if digging into a shipping crate. He surfaced with his rigid white fingers ensnared in Max's hair and dragged her to the front.

"Maybe I should arrest everyone to prove my point," he said with a snarl.

"Don't you touch her!" I yelled.

"I can do whatever I want. I am a Trading Council member. *You* are nothing."

Queykay's brood scrambled down his arm and reached for Max's hair as well. They were getting bigger now, more than ten centimeters long. Queykay barked something at them, and they scurried back into his robe. Max's toes clicked on the floor as he lifted her higher off the ground.

"Stop it!" Ketheria yelled at him. "Put her down."

"If you hurt her, Queykay, I swear, I'll—"

"You'll do nothing unless I tell you to do it," he hissed. I watched in vain as Max clawed at the alien's hand.

"We'll see about that," I said, and moved toward the guards.

"Don't!" Max screamed, but I would not stop.

As I moved, I adjusted the strength and torque settings in my right arm and used it as a battering ram on the four guards. I hit the middle one, hoping to buckle its armor and send them scattering. As my arm made impact, I heard the metal crunch and then snap apart as the guards scattered. I spun around, ready to attack Queykay, but the guards re-formed and surrounded me, their plates locking together again without a scratch.

"How pathetic," Queykay sneered. "You? As the Tonat?"

"Let them go!" I yelled from within my makeshift cell.

"He is my prisoner. He is charged with treason. I have proof that he has been tampering with the taps and spreading lies around the rings. His punishment is death."

"No!" Grace cried.

Nugget ran toward Queykay, his big snout open. He clamped onto Queykay's leg as the guards broke rank and turned on him. As Nugget bit down, Queykay screamed and released Max from his grip. She fell to the floor and rolled away from Queykay. I moved toward her.

"I'm fine," she said.

I looked up and saw Queykay remove a long, silvery talon from under his cloak.

"Don't!" Ketheria screamed.

He raised it over Nugget's head. The four guards that circled me broke rank and lashed at Nugget with black metal prods. In an instant, they had each secured one of Nugget's limbs with a lasso of sorts that was attached to the end the prod. They pulled, lifting Nugget off the ground as I leaped toward them.

"You're hurting him!" Max yelled.

Just as Queykay was about to bring the talon down upon Nugget, the hallway went silent. Queykay slid into a state of motionlessness, his eyes locked on Ketheria. The air around us was so still, I could hear my heartbeat. I could even hear Max breathing behind me.

I looked down the corridor and then back the other way. It seemed as if everything was a little less colorful, a little less in focus. Frozen in their attack, Queykay and his goons did nothing as Ketheria moved toward Nugget and untangled him from the metal prods.

"Are you doing this, Ketheria?" I asked.

But she didn't say anything. She worked quickly to get Nugget loose, and I moved in to help, snapping the prods in half with my robotic arm.

"What sort of powers *do* you have?" I whispered.

Once Nugget was free, she looked at me and said in a hushed voice, "I don't really know. I find new ones every cycle."

With everyone still locked in some sort of alternate reality, Ketheria turned to me and said, "I suggest you leave."

"Wait!" I protested. "He's not safe." I pointed at Darja. "Queykay will take revenge on him—I guarantee you that."

"Queykay will not remember a thing. Nor will the guards. At least I don't think so," she replied, and turned to Darja. "Where were you when this all started?"

"I was in my room," he said.

"Go back there. I will meet you there shortly. Queykay will attempt to arrest you as he did before, but I will be there with a Keeper and a Nagool. They will not let Queykay take you. Max, Grace, take him there now, please."

Then Ketheria put her arm around Nugget's shoulder and started to lead him away.

"But wait. I don't know when I will see you again," I said.

"You will. That's all that matters."

Ketheria disappeared down the corridor and I turned to Max, but she had already disappeared with Grace and Darja.

"Max?"

I looked up at Queykay, who was still staring at the spot where Nugget once was. I stepped toward him and reached up with my hand, waving it in front of his icy face.

"I wish you could stay like this forever," I whispered.

With my forefinger and thumb, I picked at the edge of Queykay's sleeve and lifted it up, hoping for a glimpse of the tiny creatures nurturing themselves off Queykay's body. Before my eyes were able to crack the darkness of his sleeve, two bloodred eyes launched themselves at me. A zipper's worth of pointed white teeth sparkled as they broke from the shadows, and I fell back, horrified. The little worm landed on my leg screeching as it tore at my pants, trying to burrow itself into my leg. With a quick sharp blow, I struck the abomination with my right hand and watched it skitter across the stone. I was on my feet and down the corridor before it even turned around.

I sat up in my sleeper. *Theodore will be here soon,* I thought. I had tried to sleep, but instead I'd lain awake berating myself the entire spoke. I was ashamed at how useless I had been against Queykay and his goons. What good was I going to be to Ketheria? What could the Trust teach me that wasn't better than these powers she kept developing? I hoped I had made the right decision.

Since I couldn't sleep, I decided to stop at the chow synth before I went to the meeting with Theodore. I needed to get that food dispenser to manufacture Tic's lifesaving potion into some sort of solid form, like the food tablets we ate at Weegin's World. There was no one at the chow synth when I entered, and I was glad for that. I poked into the synth's chip, and despite the infinite array of choices, I could not figure out how to change a liquid to a solid. The synth would let me freeze and dehydrate, which I thought might work, but it would not let me make a tablet. I pulled out and called Vairocina for help.

"I was wondering when you were going to call," she said.

"Can you help?"

"Let me link through the chow synth," she replied as she materialized before me.

"I guess you know I'm leaving."

"I do," she said.

"I should have called you to say good-bye."

"Good-bye? I assumed I was coming with you."

"Oh." I hadn't thought about bringing Vairocina.

"I was told I could not bring anything—I mean anyone!" I said, correcting myself and trying to sound as if I had already thought about this. "Besides, I would feel much better if I knew you were still here keeping an eye on everyone for me. I have no idea what my training is going to be like or even how long I will be gone. I really need you here. I'm sure if anything goes wrong, you can get a message to me through Theylor or Drapling."

"So, this is good-bye then?"

"It's more like see you in a while."

Vairocina dropped her head as if she were looking at the ground.

"It's getting boring in here," she whispered. "It's so much more exciting when I'm inside your arm, going places with you."

"I'll be back, and it will be like I never left. I need you here, V," I said, hoping Theodore's nickname would help.

She smiled. It was a small smile, but it was better than nothing. "I'll try to find the link the Keepers use with the Trust, and maybe I can communicate with you through that," she said.

"That would be perfect," I told her. "Now, any chance you

can help make this thing spit out some magic tablets for me? I'm going to need a lot." I was also thinking about taking some for Switzer.

"My pleasure," she replied.

By the time I returned to my room, Theodore was waiting for me to go to the secret meeting. I had half expected to find a couple of Space Jumpers waiting for me instead.

"I thought Max was going to be with you," I said.

"She went with Grace."

"Does she know I'm coming?"

"Yes, she does, but Darja doesn't think this is a good idea."

"Darja?"

"You know, that kid. He changed his name again."

I shook my head. "How long do these meetings take?" I asked him.

"Usually most of the spoke," he replied.

With the tablets spread between two pockets in the legs of my pants, I slipped Quirin's disc into my back pocket. I had become used to traveling light, and I saw nothing else worth taking. I tossed my skin onto my sleeper.

"You're not coming back, are you?" Theodore asked. There was a little worry in his voice.

"Not for a while, I'm beginning to think."

Theodore checked and rechecked each corridor leading to the far end of our building and away from Queykay's quarters, counting his steps as we moved. When he was sure no one was watching, he overrode the security panel at the back exit of the building using a crude-looking uplink attached to his neural port. A small blinking box dangled in the middle of the hard-wire. When it turned blue, the door opened.

"How did you learn to do that?" I whispered.

"Max showed me."

As we sprinted across the open compound and into Murat, Hach's suspicions that one of us was involved in the attack on Ketheria trickled into my thoughts. *That's just ridiculous,* I told myself.

The city was rotating into shadow, and the building lights blinked on in sequence as the city was slowly swallowed up by the encroaching darkness. I stayed close to Theodore as he picked up the pace and raced toward the darkness. This was my favorite time on the rings. Sparkling reflections of red and gold replaced the dirt and grime, which seemed to wash away with the receding light. Things that once looked decrepit and uninviting now shimmered in the golden dusk.

This was also the same time of cycle that Max had taken me to the concert in Murat and the time we'd held hands while watching the musician play those strange glass bowls on Orbis 3. This was also the time Max and I would leave the Laby-rinth and head home after a Quest-Nest match last rotation. It was in this same dusky glow that Max and I would walk in the garden behind Charlie's, and it was the same time of the cycle that Max and I often strolled through Murat. I loved this time of cycle.

Theodore and I stopped in front of the podlike living quar-ters that stacked up and over the street. Using a control pad, he punched in a long access code, one I would never have been able to remember.

"We can't possibly be meeting in one of these things, can we?" I said.

"Keep it down," he whispered. "We're not."

One pod broke rank, rotated silently to the street level, and then cracked open. Theodore reached inside and pulled out a tap that he attached to his neural port.

"What's it say?" I asked.

He pulled the tap out and dropped it on the ground. Then he crushed it under the heel of his boot. "I got it," he announced, and turned up the street. All I could do was stare at the shards of plastic on the ground. What had happened to the Theodore I knew? The one who avoided trouble like a Trefaldoor avoided a lie?

"Wait up!" I called after him.

"It's not far," he said, pointing up ahead.

"Does everyone find out about the meeting this way?"

"Pretty much. It changes, though, when we think someone might be watching us."

I turned and looked behind me to see if that was the case, but I saw no one. "Who sets this up? I mean who's going to these great lengths to keep this hidden?"

"We are," he replied.

"I know that, but who's the leader, who's the head guy?"

"Oh, we've never met them. We're just one cell. There are hundreds, just like us, waiting all over the ring."

"Waiting for what?"

"For orders."

"Orders for *what*?"

"Well, obviously we're waiting for the big order, the one that tells us we're going to fight for our freedom. When the Keepers and the Trading Council go at it, we'll be ready to spring into action. But mostly it's little things. Like that tap back there. I'm sure someone in some cell was given an order to place that there. They had no idea why; they just did it."

"Have you ever had one of these orders?"

"Lots."

"Wait," I said, stopping in the street. "What's going on here, Theodore?"

"What do you mean?"

"Everyone running around following these orders, with no connections to the big picture. Think about it. How easy would it be to set up an assassin to take out Ketheria? No one would really know what had happened. All these little things could be put in place without anyone ever knowing they were helping to kill the Scion. Think about that."

Theodore stopped and cocked his head, his eyes wide. "We wouldn't kill Ketheria. The Scion is one of us. The Scion is a knudnik, JT. She came here just like we did, to work for the Citizens, to labor in their system, to dream *their* dream. We have more in common with the Scion than we do with anyone here."

Was this where I told my friend that he had nothing in common with the knudniks on the Rings of Orbis? Did I tell him that he never had parents who chose to come to Orbis to work—that his life was an accident? Did I tell him that if Madame Lee had never attacked the *Renaissance,* he would have been flushed with the rest of the embryos on the seed-ship?

Of course I didn't.

"I'm sorry," I mumbled. "I didn't mean to imply anything. It's just that Hach told me that someone on the inside was involved."

"And you thought it was *me*? You thought I would try to kill Ketheria? Are you crazy? I can't believe you would think that." Theodore glanced over his shoulder toward the building to my right.

"What's wrong?" I asked.

"I don't know if you should come, JT. People in there aren't going to take that kind of thinking lightly. We are the last people who would try to kill the Scion."

"Theodore, I'm sorry. I won't say anything. Please, I need to talk to Max. I'll be *gone* by next cycle."

"I don't even know if she'll talk to you. Now is not the right time. You should have done this earlier, JT."

"But I didn't. This is my only chance. Please. I won't say a word. I'm sorry for even thinking it."

Theodore waited. It was a long pause. He was actually considering not bringing me. The thought freaked me out a little.

"Not a word, then?" he whispered.

"I promise."

As we slipped off the main street and down an unlit alley, I was reminded that this was the second time I had followed Theodore to some unfamiliar place under his direction. The first one was the Shed, where he'd sneaked off to use a tetrascope. I only hoped this was a better place than that. When Theodore stopped, there was no light chute this time, no industrial cavern, just an unmarked metal door. He opened the door without knocking, and I followed him down a narrow hallway lit with golden glass balls that were embedded in the mottled walls.

"Whose place is this?" I whispered.

"I don't really know. No one ever tells me," he replied.

"Has the meeting started?"

"I don't think so."

We passed several unmarked doors before stopping in front of a double metal door at the end of the hall on the right-hand side. I waited as Theodore ran his hand over some sort of scanner before reaching down to grab a cable that hoisted the door up. I don't know why the scanner bothered me. Maybe because it meant that there was some record of the people who were allowed entry into whatever club was now meeting on the other side. I had always thought anonymity was the best defense when doing something you weren't supposed to.

There were several people on the other side of the door. They looked up at Theodore and me when we entered. I saw Grace and that kid immediately.

"What's he doing here?" the kid said. I didn't like his accusatory tone. If any knudniks were involved in the attack on Ketheria, I would check him out first. Maybe Queykay had something when he picked this kid up.

"What's wrong with JT coming?" Theodore confronted him in my defense.

"He's a softwire. He's not on our side."

There was that side issue again. This little group was quickly getting on *my* bad side.

"He's still a knudnik," Theodore argued.

"Hardly," the kid spat.

"What is your name now, anyway?" I interrupted.

"Why do you want to know, so you can run and tell them?"

"Tell who? Queykay? It seems he knows you're up to something already. Need I remind you that you're stained, just like me? They don't need your name to find you."

Grace jumped in. "His name is Ganook now. He won't be changing it again," she said, smiling and placing her hand on his shoulder. Grace's smiled seemed to put the kid at ease. *Ganook?* His choice, not mine.

"Besides, I think you should be thanking me for rescuing you last cycle."

"You? Rescue *me*? The Scion did everything. In fact, as I recall, you were rather useless."

I stepped toward the kid. Even Theodore moved next to me.

"That is enough," a voice said behind me.

I turned and saw a slender alien approaching me. Large green eyes eclipsed his narrow forehead, and two small bones protruded from his slanted shoulders. The bones supported a deep burgundy cloth that wrapped around him, almost like a loose cocoon.

"Remember: we are against no one," he said, his voice deep and soothing. Instantly, I felt relaxed. "We are for freedom and the sanctity of the moons, just as the Ancients were so long ago. We only wish to awaken from the dream, the dream of the Trading Council."

"You must agree with the Keepers then. They want the same thing," I said.

"Some, maybe. But greed has corrupted many of them as well."

"Then what *do* you guys want?" I asked him.

"Freedom from the way of life that has destroyed the hearts and minds of so many here on the rings. Freedom from the tyranny of the Citizens and freedom from the deconstructive energy that plagues these rings and anyone who walks among us. It was not always like this, you know. The Rings of Orbis were once the glowing epicenter of true Source energy.

"So I've heard," I said.

"Please join us. My name is Horgan."

Horgan extended his arm and motioned toward a large green and gold curtain suspended from the ceiling. I could see more light through the sheer material and more people. The room was larger than I had realized.

Horgan walked next to me as the group moved toward the curtain.

"We could benefit from the abilities of a softwire. I'm sure you appreciate this. Your powers could single-handedly disrupt the lives of the Citizens."

"I'm afraid I've heard that one before as well."

"You are far more powerful than you realize, and so many of your friends are already with us."

On the other side of the curtain, I saw Max sitting at a huge round table in the center of the room. Her shadow, created by open fires placed around the table like gigantic candles, flickered on the wall. Everything was afire in an orange glow.

"I can see that," I replied, "but I'm afraid I can't stay long."

"Maybe after you sit with us, you will decide to stay longer."

"Maybe," I said.

When Max saw me, she looked at Theodore and then back at me. Max turned away and struck up a conversation with Grace, who had slipped in next to her.

My ears were burning. I almost used the sweat from my palms to cool them off. Max was going to freak when I told her I was leaving to train as a Space Jumper. I knew it. I hesitated to sit next to her, but I knew there was no more time to waste. In fact, my escort could show up at any second to take me away. I was moving toward the empty seat next her when a small Honine, her forehead spotted with small spikes, sat down before I could.

"Excuse me. Do you mind if I sit here? I would like to talk to my friend," I said. I made sure Max could hear the last part so at least she would be aware of my intention.

The Honine smiled and moved away without incident. I sat next to Max, but she continued to talk with Grace. I hadn't been this close to Max in a while. Just her scent made my eyes close, and I secretly breathed her in. When I opened my eyes, she was looking at me.

"What are you doing?" she hissed.

"I was just—I mean, I . . ." It was hard to talk over the lump that was now formed in my throat. Why was this so difficult?

"I mean, what are you doing here?" Max said.

"I need to talk to you about something."

"We've had plenty of time to talk since your return. I don't think this is the appropriate place for you to be apologizing to me."

"Who said I was—? I mean, I *am* sorry."

Max kind of grunted. "Do you even know what you're sorry for?"

"I know what I'm going to be sorry for," I mumbled.

"What?" she asked, but then Horgan stood up and raised his arms to quiet everyone down.

"Welcome, all. There are some new faces around the table. It makes me happy to see our ranks swelling."

Max's arm was about ten centimeters away from mine—so close. I wanted to touch it. I wanted to tell her what I was about to do while I was holding her, not like this. Theodore was right. It was the wrong place and the wrong time. I was such a malf.

"Max, there's something I need to tell you."

"Shhh," she shushed me as Horgan continued.

"As we discussed last time, signs of war are increasing. It was just this cycle that the Trading Council suspended all new petitions for work rule from inquiring races."

"What?" I said out loud.

Horgan paused and nodded. "Oh, yes," he said. "The Council has even suspended education for knudniks and Citizens nationalized in the last five rotations. And there is talk to suspend all work-rule expirations until the Council feels it appropriate to continue normal contracts. They want to make sure they have control of everyone and everything if they choose to go to war against the Keepers."

"But why would they want war?" I asked.

"The Keepers have broken the treaty set in place almost two thousand rotations ago. The Council is using the Keepers as scapegoats and rallying the Citizens into a unified frenzy over the need to eliminate all Space Jumpers, and the Keepers with them. The Keepers' arrogance has given the Trading Council the perfect enemy to go to war against."

The crowd seated at the table fidgeted in their seats each time Horgan spoke. Some nodded anxiously while others called out in agreement.

"But why would they want war? They will only hurt themselves," I yelled over the others. They went quiet when I spoke.

"War will give them more power. War will give them more control over the crystal moons with less interference from the Keepers and the Trust. The Citizens could rule the rings the way they want to, without restriction, and *that* would be devastating for the likes of you and me on the Rings of Orbis."

Horgan began speaking to the entire crowd now. "Can you imagine what it would be like on the Rings of Orbis if the Trading Council controlled the laws? Can you imagine how many races would suffer under the hand of slavery? Enticed by wealth and greed, many more people would flock to the rings unaware of the consequences that await them.

"The Trading Council also wants to set their own prices for the crystals harvested from Ki and Ta. Many civilizations that rely on these energy sources would be shackled under the exorbitant prices set by the Council. With no intervention from the Keepers, economies would grind to a halt, societies would crumble, and, all the while, the Council would grow fatter from their obscene profits."

"And how do you plan to stop them?" I asked.

"Do we have to explain ourselves every time someone new comes along?" Ganook complained. "This is a waste of time."

I stared at the kid I had grown up with on the *Renaissance*. "What's your problem?" I asked him. "What do you have against me?"

"He has nothing against you," Grace interrupted, putting her hand on the kid's shoulder.

"Let *him* answer," I said.

Ganook stood up, shaking off Grace. He kicked his chair back and walked away from the table. Then he turned toward me. "Don't you see it? You are their instrument," he growled. "Just your presence gives the Trading Council another excuse to act."

"But if you want the Keepers to stay in power, aren't you going to need the Space Jumpers on your side? When I become a Space Jumper, I—"

I stopped mid-sentence and looked at Max. She spun around, her mouth agape.

"I'm sorry. I can explain," I whispered.

Max's eyes filled with tears. She shoved her chair back and ran from the room. Grace got up to go after her, but I stopped her. "Let me, please," I said.

I chased Max through the curtains and found her against the wall, her face in her hands. Her shoulders shook in unison with her sobs. I placed my hand on her back.

"Don't!" she cried, and pulled away.

"Max, please, it's not what you think. I don't have a choice."

"We always have a choice!"

Without warning, an explosion ripped through the building. Chunks of concrete tore through the curtain, and I threw myself over Max as the debris rained down upon us. I heard screams and felt my skin turn warm as the open fires leaped from the their containers and crawled over anything that would burn.

"Theodore!" Max cried from underneath me. She pushed me off, and we both jumped up. Max sprinted through the dust and smoke that now choked the room.

"Theodore!" I yelled, but I heard only moans and crying as the last pieces of rubble trickled to the ground. "Be careful, Max!"

I bumped into Grace, clawing her way through the smoke and debris. She was bleeding from her forehead, and her hands were covered in blood.

"Ganook!" she screamed, looking around. "Ganook!"

I grabbed her by the shoulders. Tears and blood raked

through the dust on her face. "Grace! Grace, we'll find him," I yelled, shaking her back to reality.

"He turned blue!"

"Blue? Who turned blue? What do you mean?"

"Ganook. He turned blue just before the explosion! His whole body."

"Blue? Grace, you're hurt. Sit down."

"No! He was a target. They wanted him. They knew!"

It was Queykay. I was certain of it. If Ketheria's little stunt had not completely erased his memory, then a trace on Ganook could have exposed his whereabouts. Could they simply kill us from an O-dat whenever they wanted? I certainly hoped not.

"JT, find Theodore," Max cried.

"I'm here. I'm all right," he shouted from somewhere in the smoke. "You have to find Grace. Make her stay where she is. Don't bring her over here."

"Why!" Grace screamed. "GANOOK!" She ran into the dust before I could grab her.

I was wading through the debris, looking for Max, when I saw streams of light materialize in the dust. They rippled before merging into a single point. A moment later, I was staring at two Space Jumpers standing in front of me.

"Not now!" I cried, but the Space Jumpers looked at the destruction around me and worked quickly. One armed his plasma rifle, while the other moved toward me and gripped my forearm.

"What happened here?" he said.

"I don't know. Let me find out. Give me a minute. Please! Max!"

Max stepped through the dust and saw me standing between the two Space Jumpers. "Please, Max, not like this," I pleaded. "Try to understand. I never wanted to hurt you."

Max didn't say anything. She just stood there amid the debris. Tears streaked the soot that had settled on her face. She lifted her right hand as if to wave good-bye. I didn't know for sure because I was ripped away before I could respond.

12

My arrival at the Trust was as uneventful as a solar flare on the surface of the sun. The two Space Jumpers dumped me into my room and left without even a welcome. The stone floor and metal fixtures were an exact copy of the room they had put me in before, the first time I was taken to their comet. I looked up and realized, however, that something was different. This time I had a roommate.

"Of all the rocks in the universe, they have to put me with you?" Switzer grumbled.

I sat on the floor, Max's image still emblazoned on my mind. "Give me a minute and I'll call someone to see if they have anything else available, something more suiting a wormhole pirate."

"At least your sarcasm has gotten better," Switzer said, and leaned back on his sleeper. He hoisted his huge boots over the edge and let them clunk on the metal as he clamped his thick hands behind his even thicker neck. It was difficult for me to get used to the older Switzer. I had to look carefully, past the scars and muscles, to see the kid I had grown up with. If it wasn't for his cocky attitude, I don't know if I would have recognized him at all. "But really," he went on in his deeper, Switzer-the-man voice. "Thanks. I thought I was going to rot in that awful cell. I owe you one."

His grateful remark caught me off guard. So much had happened between the two us, and none of it was pleasant. Yet I couldn't help but glance at him and blame myself for his very existence. "It was the least I could do," I said without sarcasm.

"Yeah, I've been thinking about that. Why *did* you do it, anyway? From what I've seen, you had a pretty good thing going on down there. What possessed you to drag me out of prison?"

"I told you already. It's not fair what they did to us. They made you the way you are. They are responsible for you. They can't just lock you away. Your actions are just as much their fault as yours."

"Not sure I see it your way, split-screen. I've done a lot of bad things that had nothing to do with them, but thanks all the same."

"Please stop calling me that."

"What?"

"Split-screen, Dumbwire, or whatever witty little tag you can come up with. Call me JT or don't call me anything."

Switzer paused before muttering, "Sure. Whatever you want. Hey, how did your girlfriend take it?"

I stood up and moved in front of his sleeper. "Do not talk

about Max," I told him. "Ever! Understand that I do not want to be here. I did it to get you out. My goal is to get through this stupid training and then get back to the Rings of Orbis. I need to protect Ketheria. You're not the only one I feel responsible for. When you're done with your training, I want you to accept some post in another galaxy, all right? But after you become a Space Jumper, I never want to see you again. Understood?"

"Wow, one minute you're feeling sorry for me and the next minute you never want to see me again. What's with that?"

"Nothing that I'm going to tell you," I said as I turned away.

"Suit yourself," he replied, and leaned back only to sit right back up again. "Hey, do you have any more of that stuff you gave me back on the rings? I could really use some right now. Just a little. I don't want to get used to it."

I reached into my pocket and pulled out the bag of tablets I had made for Switzer. I took a couple from the bag and popped them into my mouth. My head had been killing me ever since I'd arrived. "Here," I said, and tossed the bag to him. "They'll do the trick."

Switzer caught the bag and held it up, admiring it. Then he looked at me and said, "You'll make a good wife some cycle, split-screen."

Switzer's teasing was the least of my concerns. I went to sleep worrying about how they'd gotten to Ganook and woke up wondering what Max was doing. How long was I going to be here? *It couldn't be that long,* I told myself. Then I remembered slow-time. The Keepers had used it in the Center for Science and Research, and the Trust even mentioned it the first time I was here. Surely they must be using it now. If they wanted me to protect Ketheria, how could I do it from here? All I had to do was finish their little course and I would be done. *Keep an open mind.* That's what Ketheria had said. How hard could that be?

Switzer's sleeper was closed, but I could still hear him snoring. I pushed back the lid of my own sleeper and stared at the metal door. A soft blue light lined the perimeter. I figured some sort of computer chip controlled all the doors on this ship, or rock, or whatever it was that they called this thing. I glanced over at Switzer. He was out cold. Since no one said we had started training yet, I figured now was a good a time as any to do a little exploring.

I slid off my sleeper, stuffed my feet into my boots, and went to the door. I pushed into the blue light and was surprised to find a rudimentary locking device, which I merely nudged open. The last time I was on this thing, the Trust had kept me locked up using a far more elaborate security system. *It's not like I could leave here, anyway,* I thought as the door disappeared. Outside, I dragged my fingers along the stony wall and slipped down the corridor.

I had no idea where I was going, so I followed the polished support girders that reflected the frigid glow from caged lights mounted above my head every meter or so. It was cold, and I could smell a slight medicinal scent lingering in the air.

I turned right down another corridor. *The place is bigger than I thought.* I found a short set of stairs at the end and climbed them into a small atrium. I stepped toward a large door at the far end, and it disappeared. Once inside, I found myself looking out at the stars through an enormous glass dome. It was some sort of observation deck, like the one we had on the *Renaissance*. I loved that place. I spent so many cycles staring out at the stars, wondering what my new home would be like.

I went up to the glass to look out over the ship, but what I saw really wasn't a ship at all. It was just a big rock—a huge comet falling through space. Behind me, a brilliant white tail of dust and ice lit up the empty blackness, and it was *empty*. There were no planets on the horizon, no nearby stars to light up the ship. But worse than that, the most glaring absence of all was that of the Rings of Orbis. I searched everywhere, running from side to side of the observation deck, but I could find no sign of it. *Where was I?* Everything I knew was gone. The home I had struggled to accept was nowhere to be found. *What had I done?* The enormity of my decision settled on my shoulders and forced me to the ground. I had felt alone in my life before, but never like this. Sitting there, on top of the comet, with nothing in sight, I felt *more* than alone. I felt dead.

"Do I really snore that bad?" Switzer asked.

I opened my eyes. I was still in the observation deck. I must have fallen asleep on the floor. "What time is it?" I mumbled, looking up at Switzer. There was a strange device hovering near his head, a golden light suspended over a metal spike like a torch.

"Um . . . you got something here," Switzer whispered, pointing at the corner of his mouth. I reached up and wiped away the drool that must have escaped while I was sleeping.

"Thanks. Who's that?"

"Him?" Switzer said, thumbing at the thing floating in the air. "That cheery little fellow is our escort. I think we're going to meet the rest of our playgroup."

"What are you doing here?"

"I didn't want to start my first cycle of school without my new buddy."

"Enough with the sarcasm. Do you have any of those tablets? My head is killing me."

Switzer tossed me a couple tablets and said, "Try to suck it up a little and use those only when it hurts. I don't know how long we're going to be on this icicle."

"So you know where we are?"

"I do now," he replied, walking over to the edge of the observation deck.

"Orientation is now assembling. Your presence is required. Please follow me," the floating thingy announced as its light flashed red.

"Ah, the universal color of danger. How long do we plan on letting them wait?" Switzer said, turning to me.

"I don't," I told him, and sprang to my feet. "Time to be a Space Jumper."

We followed our escort down several corridors before the light led us to a small lift suspended over a huge open area. The place was so big that I think I could have flown a ring shuttle through it. Directly across from our lift were a couple of enormous cylinders like two giant spacescopes standing next to each other, balanced on their lenses. I squinted to see what they were made of, but the black metal was punctured with an assortment of bright yellow, green, and white lights that made it hard to tell. I could see that each pillar was constructed from odd-size sections stacked one upon the other and that the sections were simply too numerous to count. *Theodore would have tried to count them, though,* I thought.

Then I heard some unseen motor clunk into action, and the two massive pillars began to rotate as we descended to the floor. I watched the enormous structures peel back and the room we were in flood with a brilliant blue light that hung at the center of the next room.

"This is what I call an entrance," Switzer remarked as we both stepped off the lift. There was another alien already on the floor, watching the pillars part. I elbowed Switzer and he glanced at our new companion.

"We aren't the only new kids at school," he said.

We followed the red light into the next room. It was circular, lined with balconies. It was difficult to see all the way to the top because the light source was blinding near the room's apex. I shielded my eyes and discovered rows and rows of Space Jumpers awash in the harsh light and staring down at us.

Switzer was gawking as well. "Guess being a softwire ain't as special as you thought," he whispered.

I guess it wasn't. I knew that all Space Jumpers were softwires and from what I'd understood, it was an especially rare ability. But when I walked past the cylinders and looked up, I almost felt common.

Switzer, the new guy, and I walked under a huge egg-like structure suspended by a thick metal cable at the center of everything. The thing must have been the size of a small spaceship. In fact, I actually wondered if it *was* a spaceship of some sort.

"Well, I'm impressed," Switzer said.

"Me too," I replied.

The other guy, an alien with thin tentacles that sprouted from his head, his arms, and even his back, did not respond. Instead, his many tentacles cautiously flicked about as if they were licking the air.

"What are we supposed to do?" I whispered to Switzer.

"Nothing. At least that's what I normally do when the odds are like this. Let them make the first move," he replied.

The egg thing started to descend, and Switzer and I moved back. Circling the center of the egg was a metal support mounted with half a dozen spotlights. Three of them fired up and focused on us. The two giant cylinders slowly swung closed as the egg began to speak.

"The Source has bestowed its most important gift upon you," a voice boomed from the egg. I recognized that voice. It was one of the Trust. "Do you accept this gift?"

"Yes!" cried the alien next to us.

"Absolutely," Switzer exclaimed.

I looked at Switzer. I guess this was it. I was going to do it. I was doing it for Ketheria, but I was also doing this for me in some weird way. I was finally able to make that "choice" I was always grumbling about.

"Yes," I added, with much less enthusiasm than the others.

"Your softwire ability is a prerequisite, but your Source is the admission into our family," the Trust continued. "Do you accept these terms?"

"Yes!" cried the other alien.

"You bet," Switzer added.

"What does that mean?" I whispered to Switzer. "Source? What source? I don't get it. What terms?"

"Just say yes, split-screen. There is no pamphlet to read, and I don't think they pay for the ride home if you want out now."

"Yes," I replied, looking up at the egg. I couldn't believe I was taking advice from Switzer.

"A Space Jumper is nothing without his family. His family understands his gift, and his family shares his unquestionable belief in the trinity," the egg said.

"Courage! Integrity! Self-discipline!" These three words stormed down upon us from the hoards of Jumpers who filled the balconies all around us.

"Your new family will guide you in your acceptance of these tenets. Only when these selves are awakened within you can you claim to be a Space Jumper."

The Space Jumpers responded by cheering and thumping on whatever was close to them, even if that included each other.

"Piece of cake," Switzer boasted.

"Please step forward as your name is called," the Trust ordered. "Gora Bloom!"

The alien with the tentacles practically jumped.

"Your connector will be Sul em Pah; your monitor will be Kebin Tam."

The crowd applauded, and Gora looked like he or she (I couldn't tell) had won some sort of award.

"Randall Switzer!"

"Here goes nothing. Wish me luck," he whispered as he stepped toward the egg.

"Your connector will be Che Tort; your monitor will be Temasos."

The crowd cheered again, and Switzer held out his arms. This made them cheer a little louder. Switzer always loved attention.

"Johnny Turnbull!"

Dutifully, I stepped toward the egg as Switzer returned to his original spot. The crowd had stopped cheering, and they were all staring at me. *Did they know about me?* I hated feeling this way, like I already knew things weren't going to be fair for me. I knew it was just in my head, but that's the way I always felt.

"Your connector will be Brine Amar." The Space Jumpers cheered just like they had for Switzer and Gora. *See?* I told myself. *It's all in your head.* "Your monitor will be Quirin Ne Yarnos."

That shut them up. The cheering had stopped immediately at the mention of Quirin's name, and I shook my head. I knew it. It was always like this. I moved back toward Switzer.

"You always have to be different, don't ya?" Switzer muttered.

Gora turned and spoke to us for the first time. His lipless mouth seemed to cut his face in half. "No one gets a member of the Trust for a monitor, especially Quirin," he said.

"Is that good or bad?" I asked.

Gora grunted. "I suppose that depends on you. I envy you, but I would not change places with you for a million yornaling crystals."

"There's a lot I would do for a million yornaling crystals," Switzer interrupted.

"Not this," Gora spat, and all his tentacles lay down at once.

I looked up and saw the Space Jumpers start to shuffle away as the huge egg rose silently toward the blinding light above my head. "Doesn't anyone explain things properly?" I grumbled.

"Why?" Switzer replied. "Why do you always have to *know*? You live in an alien world. Maybe they don't explain it because it's natural to them. Maybe it's like breathing for them. I don't see you going around explaining breathing to everyone you meet."

"It's not the same thing," I argued.

"Isn't it? Why do you feel so entitled to get an answer for everything? It looks like things have been going along just dandy here before you showed up. You think they're going to change how things are done just to suit you? Maybe it's you who needs to do a little changing. Keep your mouth shut and your eyes and ears open. Something tells me that this is a place you need to figure out on your own."

"Strong advice," Gora added.

Switzer made it sound so easy, but I still couldn't let it go. "Then what do we do now?" I asked, but it felt like more of a complaint.

"You follow me," said a voice walking toward us. The light was strong across the open floor, and three figures emerged out of the glare. They were Nagools.

"See?" Switzer whispered. "Let it come to you."

"I am Brine Amar," the Nagool greeted us. "This is Sul em and Che. Please follow me."

Brine Amar appeared a little more colorful than most of the Nagools I had encountered. While his face was still ashen, he sported colors of shimmering sapphire around his eyes and brow. His forehead formed a ridge just above this blue marking that crested up and over his head. As the Nagools turned back in the direction they had come from, I could see that this bone ran all the way to the back of his skull. Thin brown hair grew on the sides of his head—maybe to even it out, I thought, but it still left him with a long, oval-shaped head.

We followed slowly, as each of the Nagools shuffled their feet so delicately that it looked as if they were floating. I was careful not to catch their robes as I walked, staring at their high collars. Brine Amar's was decorated with a thick bouquet of colored animal feathers, while the others were a plain golden material.

As we were leaving, I glanced up at the balconies. They were all empty.

"Where did they go?" I said.

"Oh, would you shut up!" Switzer cried.

I glared at Switzer as we slipped through a tall, crowned doorway and into a coolly lit corridor. Wherever the Nagools had taken us, it was much different from the rock and metal section of the comet we were staying on. The corridor was molded from some sort of plastic, and a soft bluish light reflected off threads in the Nagool's robes. I noticed that crystal markers identified the different hallways and doors that we passed.

"I guess these guys live a little better than we do," I whispered, and then asked, "Why are you called connectors?"

Switzer jabbed me in the ribs.

"Ow. Can't I ask?"

"Certainly you may," Brine Amar said, turning to look at us. "That is part of our role: to help you understand the magnitude of your responsibility. Sometimes the answer to a seemingly insignificant question can mean the difference between life and death in your travels. As your connector, I am here to help your nodes establish a permanent link with the Universe. A Space Jumper's greatest accomplice is his connection with the Source, but understand that this is not a simple task. In order to make this link, you must be willing to abandon the dream that you are currently in. Through self-discipline and trust in yourself, you will be able to manifest a new dream, a dream in which you are in perfect harmony with the energy that flows through our universe. The Source is abundant. It can provide everything you need. It can connect you with the infinitesimal components of the atom and put you in harmony with the orbit of the largest planets. The Source is your point of singularity. The enlightened state is a Oneness in which there is no division of parts. The Source will present everything you need to reach your true potential as a Space Jumper. You simply need to accept it."

I only understood about a quarter of what Brine Amar said, but I liked the fact that he was answering questions. "All those Space Jumpers I just saw, have they all reached this enlightened state?"

"Again with all the questions," Switzer scoffed.

"Oh, no," replied Brine Amar.

"It is a difficult task," Sul em Pah remarked.

"Some spend a lifetime reaching and never move from the spot you occupy right now," Che Tort added.

"Most of the universe is unable to resist the negative distractions," Brine Amar said.

"Do I need this connection to be a Space Jumper?" Switzer asked.

"Be careful—that sounds like a question," I said.

"The path is just as important as the destination," Brine Amar replied.

"I'll take that as a no," Switzer said.

"But it will make your task much easier," Sul em Pah added.

The corridor opened into a small glass atrium similar to the Spaceway stations on Orbis, only much smaller.

"This is where we depart," Brine Amar announced.

"How do we get back?" I asked.

"I'm sorry. I meant, this is where we will separate and begin your individual orientation. The goal of a connector is to gain a deeper understanding of the candidate so that we may lay out the best path for your awakening. One-on-one encounters are a necessary part of this process. We will meet four times every cycle, between your training sessions. I thought we might begin with a relaxing tour of your environment. It may be our last chance before you begin."

The glass doors opened up and allowed us to access three small fliers, each large enough to hold three or four people. I followed Brine Amar into the middle one. I sat next to him in the back. Some sort of bot piloted each flier — it was hard to tell, as the pilot was encased in a dark green shield near the nose of the craft, but I was able make out someone moving inside. *Only a robot could see through that cockpit,* I thought.

The Nagools did not say good-bye to each other, but I nodded at Switzer and he did the same. We pushed away before he did, and as the flier wobbled over the expanse that opened up below me, I really got a sense of how big this place was.

"Are we on a ship or a comet?" I asked.

"Both," Brine Amar replied. "The Trust built a base within the comet and then eventually harnessed the mass to move at their will. The comet provides perfect cover when their work requires proximity to a young or primitive civilization. Are you aware of the nickname the other Space Jumpers have for the comet?"

"No," I said.

"They refer to it as the Hollow."

"Why the Hollow?"

"They've called it that for so long now that I don't believe anyone really remembers, but it certainly makes this place seem more friendly. Don't you agree?"

Brine Amar did not seem like a typical Nagool to me. My history had afforded me many encounters with Nagools, and they always seemed extremely isolated. In fact, I had hardly ever heard them speak.

"Friendlier? Maybe," I replied. "Brine Amar, will I be able to go back to the Rings of Orbis and visit my friends and my sister? I was hoping I could see them soon."

"I'm afraid that is not possible. You belong to the Trust now. It is up to them to decide when you are fit to leave."

"Well, how long will my training take?"

"That is up to you."

"That's not an answer."

"What would you like the answer to be, then?"

"I would like you to say *soon*. I would like you to tell me that I can see my friends very soon."

"If that is what you want, then you must believe that you will see them as soon as you want. As I said, it is up to you."

"That doesn't make any sense at all."

"It will. That is why you are here. You will understand in time."

Time was the one thing I didn't feel like wasting on this rock.

I glanced out the window as our flier cleared the bay where

we had boarded. Below us, I saw half a dozen spacecraft parked in some sort of landing bay that was carved into the side of the comet. I guess Space Jumpers need spacecraft on occasion as well. I didn't bother to ask. Near the top and on the far side of the bay, we entered an oval shaft that looked like some sort of connector tube to another part of the comet. When we emerged from the other end, Brine Amar gestured below us and said, "I'm sure you are familiar with this."

I was. Below me I could see a Quest-Nest arena, more like the one on the *Renaissance* than the one on Orbis 3.

"You will be spending a lot of time here. I understand you are quite accomplished."

"Switzer's better," I remarked, watching the Space Jumpers watching the labyrinth. They were running some sort of drill, and the different participants were waiting for their turn.

"Are they training as well?" I asked.

"I believe they are refreshing their skills."

"I don't mean to be rude. . . ."

"It is impossible for you to offend me," he asserted.

"That's good to know, but I was just wondering about *your* involvement, you know, as a Nagool, I mean. I thought Nagools were against violence and this sort of thing," I said, pointing at the Quest-Nest arena. "I remember witnessing a group of Nagools protesting outside the Labyrinth before the Chancellor's Challenge."

"The Citizens on the Rings of Orbis use the Space Jumpers' training field in a perverse manner. It is true that we oppose all violence, but Space Jumpers are not here to initiate violence;

they are merely here to protect and facilitate this universe's path to enlightenment. You will never find a Space Jumper who strikes first or one who uses his powers for personal gain. A Space Jumper serves the Ancients, prepares for enlightenment at the hands of the Scion, and eventually, if needed, will stand against the Knull."

"I've heard the Knull mentioned before, but I don't know anything about it," I said.

"You will know everything in time."

Brine Amar and I moved through more tubes and even smaller sections of the Hollow. My escort pointed out one of the eating commons, a relaxation area, a holographic recreation area, which looked interesting, a medical center, and even a commerce area with little Trading Chambers.

"This is like a city," I exclaimed.

"Much bigger, really. I've only shown you the highlights."

"Is that some sort of robot?" I asked, pointing to an individual attending one of the Trading Chambers. "That person there. The one with that metal thing around the back of his neck. He doesn't look like a Space Jumper."

"That is a Honock. You'll find many here at the Hollow."

"Honock? I'm sorry, but that didn't seem to translate. Is that a race?"

"No, they are workers for the Trust."

"Knudniks?"

"No, not at all. How do I explain? The Space Jumpers . . . make them."

"They make them?"

"Yes, in a way. During their travels, Space Jumpers come across individuals who have been killed, often wrongly so. When possible, the Space Jumpers can save certain parts of the unfortunate individual. It can be some tissue or some memories, and if they're lucky, a little bit of their Source energy, and then they instill that essence into these Honocks. They really are machines by most definitions, but depending on how much of the individual is salvaged, they are every bit as functioning an individual as you or I."

I thought about Vairocina. I wondered if she would be able to use a Honock for a new body. She had been searching for so long. I felt a tinge of regret for not bringing her.

"Do they ever leave the Hollow?"

"Oh, no, I don't believe they could survive outside this environment."

Honocks certainly sounded like knudniks to me. I couldn't help but wonder if a Honock ever wished that Space Jumpers hadn't saved them. I'm sure Max would spend a few cycles trying to find one or two who agreed.

Our flier returned to our original docking station while I was thinking about Max. I saw only one other flier parked next to us, but I couldn't remember if it was Switzer's craft or Gora's. I followed Brine Amar out of the small station and down the posh corridor.

"Your room is down here, two decks below. It will not take you long to learn the layout. It's one big circle, with most facilities located in or near the center. There is a schematic for you to upload if you like," he informed me.

Brine Amar paused in front of his door.

"When do I see you again?" I asked him.

"I will find you," he replied.

"All right. What do I do now?"

"Return to your room. There is someone waiting there for you."

"For me?" Who was it? Someone I knew? Suddenly I was anxious to find out. I spun around to go, but Brine Amar stopped me.

"JT, excuse me, but could I ask you a favor?"

I turned back around. "Yeah, sure. What do you need?"

"It seems the security access code on my door is not working. Do you think you could use your softwire to allow me entrance?"

"Me?"

"You are a softwire, are you not? I think that task would be quite easy for you."

"You're right, it's just that when most people ask me to help them with my softwire, it's usually for something illegal."

"I assure you my intentions are to merely gain access to my room so I may rest until we meet again."

"Of course. I didn't mean to imply—"

"You didn't."

I approached the door and pushed into the control pad. Once inside the chip, I expected to find something blocking the access sequence, but there was nothing. I simply switched the "access granted" algorithm to *true* and the door disappeared.

"There you go," I said.

"Your ability must come in handy," Brine Amar remarked.

"It just gets me in trouble mostly."

"Well, you helped me, and I thank you."

"It's just a door," I said.

"To you, maybe."

Nagools certainly were strange creatures. I turned and hurried down the hall, anxious to greet my guests.

"JT!" Brine Amar called out.

What did he want now?

"Yes?" I said, stopping and turning.

"Max is not waiting for you in your room, nor is Theodore, or your sister."

"How do you know about them?" I asked.

"There is a Space Jumper waiting to begin your training."

"Oh," I moaned.

"You're a Space Jumper now," he said solemnly as I turned and walked away.

Not yet, I thought, and took my time going back to my room. Who was I fooling, thinking that my friends where waiting for me in my room? *Split-screen.* The thought of Max and Theodore made me wonder what they were doing. I hoped they were all right. I hoped Max was avoiding Queykay. If only I had some way to know. It might make living on this comet a little easier.

Just as Brine Amar had promised, there was a Space Jumper waiting when I returned.

"Take your time, why don't ya!" Switzer cried when I walked in. "You kept our new friend waiting. Benas, isn't it?" Switzer asked as he slapped the Space Jumper on the shoulder. The jumper nodded in reply.

"He's not much of a talker," Switzer remarked.

Benas then stepped away from Switzer. I think he must have found Switzer's familiarity uncomfortable or at least odd. I took a moment to marvel at what Benas was wearing. It was a suit fashioned from a shimmering gray material with the texture of rough concrete. I couldn't tell if the pieces of metal and leather layered over the suit were decoration or padding. His Space Jumper's belt hung casually around his waist, but I could see no weapons attached to his body. I liked the leanness of his suit. I wondered if it was his choice.

"You are requested to dine with the others," Benas announced.

"Food?" Switzer said. "But I thought we would jump right into training. I'm interested to find out what kind of firepower this place holds."

Benas looked at him. It wasn't the kind of look friends shared, at least not my friends. "You are many phases away from weaponry training," Benas scolded him. "If you even make it that far. Pseudos usually don't last long at the Hollow."

I wouldn't say Benas pushed passed me to get to the door, but I honestly believe that if I hadn't moved, he would have walked right through me.

Switzer stared after him and then said, "Now, what's that all about?"

"Welcome to my world," I replied, and followed Benas.

The eating area was the same one Brine Amar had showed

me during the orientation. I wasn't really hungry. Those pills I took to combat the effect of being away from Ketheria always curbed my appetite. They also made it hard to sleep. I figured I should eat something, though. I didn't know how hard they worked new recruits, so I felt it best to assume I would need my energy.

The food commons was a large open area with individual tables that rose out of the floor, similar to the ones Odran used in his private quarters on Orbis 2. These seating stations, however, were able to move and connect into larger groups. I could see that several of them were now joined and about four dozen Jumpers were seated around the room in various-size groups.

Along one wall, behind the tables, I spotted rows and rows of little latch doors that protected a zillion little compartments of food. The food wall had an eerie similarity to the chow synth on the *Renaissance*. It was another similarity with my past that proved that my whole life had been orchestrated by the Trust.

Switzer had seemed unusually quiet ever since the comments made by Benas. I caught him checking out the other Space Jumpers in the room, and they were checking us out as well. Benas had slipped away the moment we arrived and had linked up with another group. It felt like he didn't want to be seen with us.

As I walked up to the food wall, a Space Jumper to my left whispered, "Hey, popper."

"What did you say?" Switzer retorted, but the Space Jumper ignored him and went on talking with his friends.

"This isn't good," Switzer grumbled behind me.

"Better get used it," I said. "This was my life on the *Renaissance*—my *whole* life, for that matter."

"What I don't understand is why you put up with it."

Another Space Jumper whispered, "Pseudos," as we walked past. Switzer spun around and scanned the crowd for the culprit, but everyone appeared to be minding their own business.

"What was I supposed to do?" I asked him.

"I'll show you what you were supposed to do."

Switzer turned and headed toward the largest group of Space Jumpers.

"Switzer, where are you going?"

"Just watch and learn," he called out.

I followed him but kept my distance. He strolled over to the table and stopped in front of the largest Space Jumper. This was one of those militarized Jumpers, the ones who used every spare inch of his suit to hold some sort of weapon. There were more weapons on the table than there were items to eat. I watched in horror as Switzer reached forward and shoved his fingers into the guy's food. Then he scooped out a handful of something I would never attempt to eat and shoved it into his mouth.

"Mmmm, that's good," he cried with his mouth full. It was loud enough that everyone turned to watch. "Where'd you get that? Mind if I have some more?"

The Space Jumper stared at Switzer as if he had just popped a circuit. When Switzer reached for another scoop, the Space Jumper clamped onto Switzer's forearm. The guy's paw was almost as big as Switzer's arm, and that's saying something, because Switzer is a big guy.

"Switzer!" I cried, but he didn't listen. After the Space Jumper clamped onto him, Switzer swung around, his fist clenched, and caught the Jumper right under the chin. The whole room heard the crack. The big Space Jumper fell backward, unconscious. Switzer moved around the table and pushed the guy's legs away. Then he took his seat. The other Jumpers at the table all stood up, but Switzer ignored them. I think it was the complete lack of fear on Switzer's face that scared the other Jumpers and thwarted any retaliation on behalf of their friend. They remained motionless, leaning toward Switzer and staring at him.

"What?" Switzer snapped. "He told me he was done. Didn't you hear him?"

Switzer dove into the guy's food.

"What's your name?" one of the Space Jumpers asked.

"Switzer," he replied. "Do you need me to write that down? Because you should remember it."

The Jumper did not respond, but he did sit down. Switzer scooped the last little bit of the slop from the plastic bowl and licked his fingers. Then he stood up and said, "Oh, that was good. I have to get some more. You guys want anything while I'm up?"

The rest of the Space Jumpers at the table either shook their heads or grunted, concentrating on their food again. Switzer strolled over to where I was standing and used his fingers to push my chin up, closing my mouth. His fingers were still wet from the guy's food.

"I think that's been taken care of," he whispered.

I followed Switzer to the food wall and asked, "Why that guy? Is it because he was the biggest?"

"No. Have you seen these guys fight? He was the only one I saw whose belt was on the table. I didn't want him slipping out and popping back up behind me. That's not a fair fight." Switzer looked over his shoulder and saw the Space Jumper getting up and returning to his seat. Switzer nodded at the guy, and he returned the nod. "The fact that he was the biggest is just a bonus," Switzer added.

I grabbed some food behind Switzer — a few things I could recognize — and we sat at a table with some of the other Jumpers. Switzer was already making alliances and starting friendships. As I ate and watched him, I realized that I would never be like him. If we were somehow picked from the same gene pool, then why were we so different? How come he could adapt so quickly to this new world when all I did was resist?

As a couple of Space Jumpers got up to leave, I overheard Switzer making plans with them to meet at Quest-Nest. I just shook my head.

"So I was just supposed to walk up to you on the *Renaissance* and knock your stars out?" I asked. "When we were eight years old?"

"Better than trying it now," he replied.

After we ate, I was informed by tap that we were to meet with our advisors. I uplinked directions to Quirin's quarters and then mumbled good-byes to Switzer. For the first time in my life, I found myself craving Switzer's company. His altercation at mealtime garnered us immediate respect with the other Jumpers, but I knew that the respect afforded me was due to my association with him, not from my own actions. Walking alone left me feeling exposed and I knew there was no way I was going to knock someone out, no matter how effective Switzer made it look.

Fortunately, I made it to Quirin's without the need to knock someone's head off and slipped inside his quarters.

"I was pleased to hear of your decision to participate, although I was concerned about your request to include the other human," he said. His voice seemed to come from every corner of the room.

"That other human is partly my brother, according to you. It was not fair what you did to us. It was the least I could do for him."

"I had hoped these sentiments would have been erased with your gene therapy."

"What do you mean?"

"You were not programmed to be so empathetic toward other life-forms. It was a human trait I clearly underestimated. Yet this Randall Switzer, from what I have heard, does not seem to share your feelings for your own kind."

"What do you mean by *programmed*? You make it sound like I'm some sort machine."

"In a way you are. Aren't we all?"

"No."

"Shall I say *designed*, then? As the Tonat, you will be placed in many situations where your only concern should, and will, be the survival of the Scion. You cannot fight that even if you try. All other life-forms will be of no consequence to you. They simply cannot be. That is why you have difficulty understanding the OIO philosophy. It was part of your design. As much as I believe in the value system, I could not have the questions it raises clouding your decisions."

"Well, I think there may be some flaws in your design," I told him.

"Then that is where we will start," he replied.

The light in the room focused on a point near the center of the floor. A sort of workstation with a seat and a panel of O-dats placed in a semicircle around the metal stool emerged.

"Sit," Quirin ordered.

As I obeyed, several wires snaked out from points in the wall, or rather from Quirin, that is, and connected with my workstation.

"We must upload traditional Space Jumper protocols into your cortex before physical training can begin. These rules, procedures, and themes are at the core of your studies. I will be uploading large chunks of data, so be prepared. The sooner this is done, the sooner your physical training can begin."

The O-dats lit up, and I began to feel a little nauseous. Hoping Quirin would not notice, I reached into my pocket and took a tablet, pretending to rub my nose as I slipped it into my mouth.

But Quirin saw it just the same. "You must learn to control that discomfort," he said. "It is a tool that allows you to physically estimate your distance from the Scion. Masking its effect is not the proper way to master the tool's important function."

"Some tool," I muttered.

"I am placing the files I need you to upload on the terminal in front of you. Please access the computer and install each one in sequence."

"Wait," I said. "How is Switzer doing this? He's not a softwire. I thought you had to be a softwire to be a Space Jumper. Are they doing it with his hardware?"

"The genetic structure for this gift was always within Switzer. The sequence was never initiated, as I found you a much better candidate. Once the genetic coding is manipulated, Switzer will share the same abilities as any other softwire. That is why he survived the jump from Orbis 2. The belt recognized the dormant genes and made a connection with him. Otherwise he would have died."

"He'll be just like me," I said.

"In some ways; in others not. Your ability to jump without a belt is a unique skill that no other Space Jumper has, although you are unable to control it. The mishaps you experienced early on, jumping without warning, will disappear. I'm convinced they were the result of Ketheria's awakening.

"Your softwire is merely used to connect with the belt. A Space Jumper's belt does most of the work under normal situations. It stores entry points throughout the universe and allows a Space Jumper to return to wherever he has been. You, on the other hand, simply need to remember a place in order to jump there. Unfortunately you cannot jump to a place you have never been without the use of a belt."

"But I've jumped to places I'd never been before. I've showed up in back alleys in Murat and other places on the rings," I told him.

"But you did not control those jumps. They were simply sparked by your emotions and sent you adrift through the Source. You are lucky you did not jump to the center of a black hole."

"Oh," I replied.

"May I continue?"

"Sorry."

"Your unique ability to jump without a belt parallels your ability to *push* into a computer, as you call it. Softwires merely connect to a computer without hardware and interface with the data. You can actually enter a computer with your mind, manipulating its contents in ways we are unable to do. Although I did manipulate your genetic structures, I believe you were the only candidate capable of evolving in this manner. But I don't know why. You are unique. You are the future of our kind."

"And you did all this for me?"

"Yes."

"Thanks," I said. "I guess."

The O-dats lit up, and I began downloading file after file. Most of it I didn't even acknowledge outside of the title. I knew that the information would come to me when I needed it, as long as I accessed it often enough to store it inside my long-term memory. That was the purpose of my physical training, Quirin said, to ingrain the information into my unconscious.

By the time we were finished, I figured I was going to have to do a lot of training to use all of this information. I uploaded data files big enough to knock out a whole class back at the Center for Wisdom, Culture, and Comprehension. I was exhausted and had to drag myself back to my room.

The moment I was settled in my sleeper, Switzer burst into the room.

"You've been hiding this your whole life!" he cried.

"What?"

"This!" he yelled, tapping his head. "I can't believe you've been ashamed of this."

"What are you talking about?" I asked him.

Switzer was prancing around the room as if he had just discovered a new planet.

"Your softwire," he cried. "They just turned mine on, or whatever it is they do. It's incredible!"

"Oh, that," I scoffed. "If I recall, you gave me a lot of crap over it when they discovered mine."

Switzer walked over to me and placed his hand on my shoulder. "Look, I'm sorry about that, all right? How was I supposed to know? I was just a kid, remember? And besides, how could someone else fathom this power?" Switzer took up prancing around the room again.

"It's done more harm than good," I reminded him.

"That's where you're wrong. Do you even realize the power

you have inside your head? I think half the training here is going to be about not abusing this."

"Abusing it? What are you talking about?" Suddenly, I felt extremely nervous about the fact that I had brought Switzer here. "Look," I said, standing up. "Don't do anything stupid, all right? I convinced them to bring you here because of what they did to us. It wasn't fair. Your situation is the exact result of their actions. Don't go proving me wrong, please."

"Don't get your uplink in a tangle. I'm not going to do anything. But that's why we haven't gotten the warmest reception around here. All these other Space Jumpers evolved this ability. It made them exceptional on whatever planet they came from. You and I, on the other hand, were tinkered with. They needed the process speeded up so baby-malf could be the Scion. Humans were their last hope."

"Don't call her that."

"Sorry. Old habits."

"So that's what they meant by calling us psuedos?"

"Yep."

"What about this popper thing I keep hearing?"

"Even *I* can figure that one out. It's because you were popping in out of space and time when you were getting angry. And you were doing it without a belt. No one else can do that, by the way."

"I've heard."

"I think it makes them a little jealous. We can't jump without a belt."

"We?" I said.

"Us *softwires*. I'm one of you now, my friend!"

Switzer punched me in the shoulder and laughed out loud. I couldn't believe how much he was enjoying this. I had spent my entire life hiding my softwire ability, and he was wearing it like some sort of medal. I couldn't even imagine acting like that. I wondered if the other Space Jumpers were stuffed with this much pride about their condition.

Switzer flopped onto his sleeper, still smiling.

"What are you thinking about?" I asked.

"The future," he replied.

"What about it?"

"How great it's going to be!"

As I lay in my sleeper, waiting to sleep, I tried to see Switzer's point of view, but it was impossible. Being a softwire was not something I looked at with such optimism. As a kid, my abilities had only garnered me ridicule and shame, but when I thought about it, Max was excited when my abilities were first discovered. It was just the Space Jumper part she didn't like. And I had promised her I wouldn't become one. *So much for keeping my promise.*

Insomnia. A side effect from the tablets that I kept popping despite Quirin's instructions. While Switzer snored in his sleeper, I lay in mine, staring at the darkened lid. It was no use. I wasn't going to fall asleep. I pushed the lid back and sat up. I was really missing Max. I wanted to know what she was doing, and the same with Theodore and Ketheria. I pulled on my clothes and headed for the observation deck.

Someone else was sitting there when I arrived. It was a Honock. He turned and looked at me when I entered.

"You bad!" he hissed.

I remembered that voice.

"Hey, I know you." It was the same voice I heard the first time I was taken to the Hollow, when I had popped during the Chancellor's Challenge on Orbis 3. This Honock was the one outside my room. "What's your name?"

The Honock stood up and moved away from me. "You bad," he repeated.

"No, I'm not. My name is JT. What's yours?"

He didn't reply. His back was against the glass, and he was sidling along it back toward the entrance. I didn't push him. I kept my distance.

"I'm not bad. Why do you keep saying that?"

He pointed at my waist. "You bad."

"What?" I said, patting my waist. "I'm bad because I don't have a Space Jumper's belt? Why would that make me bad?"

"You bad!" he yelled, and bolted for the door.

"Wait! Tell me why!" But the Honock was gone. At first I thought about following him. It made me wonder if Honocks even slept. How much of them were machine, anyway? Instead of following him, I sat near the glass and looked out at the stars. "Where are you, Max?" I whispered. "I miss you."

13

The next cycle, I was forced to endure Switzer's whistling as he strutted around the room, getting ready for the cycle's training. I allowed myself to take pride in the fact that he wouldn't be feeling this way if I had not gotten him out of that hole and brought him to the Hollow. Despite the rotations of abuse I'd taken from Switzer when we were kids, and even later when he was a wormhole pirate, I could see that he was a completely different person now. Secretly, I took a little credit for his change.

I started my cycle with a visit to Brine Amar, who asked me if I could help him fix his O-dat. I had to use my softwire ability again, and I started to wonder if the Nagool only thought of me as his own little handyman. Where was the connection to the Source? Where was the guidance? At least he was extremely thankful, and I liked using my softwire to *help* people, for a change.

Once at Quirin's, I uploaded more files — simulated experience memories, or SEMs, as he called them. This cycle, I learned how to pilot a shuttle that I had never even been on. Now, that was definitely something I would like to try. I could only imagine how much fun Switzer was having.

During mealtime, I caught myself thinking about Max again, as well as Ketheria. Switzer was knee-deep in friends now, and even I began to feel a little camaraderie with everyone sitting at our table. But enjoying myself made me feel guilty for not knowing what was happening down on the rings. I wished there was some way to contact my friends, but when I had mentioned this to Quirin, he'd quickly shut me down, saying it was out of the question.

During the sleep spokes, I often found myself back in the observation deck. This routine continued for many cycles, but the Honock never showed again. I did spot him once, working behind the food wall, but he acted as if he didn't know me. I don't know why the Honocks interested me so much. Maybe I saw them as knudniks and felt some sort of connection to them.

"You look like crap," Switzer said to me one cycle as he was headed out our door.

"Thanks," I replied.

"No, I mean it. When was the last time you slept?"

"I don't remember."

"Are you still popping those pills?"

"Yeah, aren't you?"

"No. I'm fighting it," he replied, but I found that hard to believe. The headaches, the nausea, it was too much to endure this far away from Ketheria.

"How?" I asked.

"I just *am*. It's not as hard as you think. You have to put the pain to the back of your mind and focus on something else."

Switzer would have made a better Tonat, I told myself. "I can't," I said. "I've tried."

"Well, try harder. You think you're going to be able find a lifetime supply of those things when we're done? What if you get stationed in another galaxy?"

"What do you mean *stationed* in another galaxy? Who told you this? I'm going back to the Rings of Orbis. I'm supposed to be protecting Ketheria. I'm not going anywhere."

Switzer had stopped at the door, but now he walked back to my sleeper. "Give it up," he growled. "*This* is your life now. You are an instrument of the Trust, a protector for the Ancients. You have a far greater purpose than all the split-screens on Orbis combined." Then he left.

Switzer *definitely* would have made a better Tonat.

The next cycle was the first phase of our physical training. Using the Quest-Nest arena at the most physically demanding settings I had ever seen, a team of seasoned Space Jumpers ran us through coordination, endurance, flexibility, and strength drills. And then we did it again. The playing field had been replaced with what was mostly an obstacle course, which re-formed on me when I was too slow. With each run at the course, the computer would slip in new elements that required the use of another SEM, usually one that I had uplinked in a previous session with Quirin. The Space Jumpers had us take single turns, as well as switching out partners, using Gora, Switzer, and one of the trainers. We were often in pairs.

"Do Space Jumpers always work as pairs when they are on missions?" I asked the instructor, a big militarized Space Jumper.

"Concentrate on the now, popper. You're in no condition to be thinking about a mission," he barked.

So much for camaraderie, I thought.

Whenever Switzer was asked to "run the Nest," as he began to call it, he didn't just walk up to it; he attacked it. Each obstacle was something else for him to conquer. I had to admire how good he was at it. He even completed one run ahead of the trainer. Not something he let slip by, either.

"You should have used that immobility cube on those spheres near the end. I find it acts as an adhesive on inanimate objects," he boasted.

The trainer did not snap at him. In fact, he seemed to be absorbing what Switzer was telling him. I often saw them discussing a move Switzer had tried or an unorthodox manner in which he employed his weapon.

"You were made for this," I said to him once at mealtime.

"Technically, I was," he said, his mouth full of something green. "But my experiences as Captain Ceesar taught me to be resourceful. I have to think it's going to get a lot harder than this if we are to live up to the Space Jumpers' reputation."

"What do you mean?" I asked. Switzer stuffed something with a tentacle into his mouth. I guess being a wormhole pirate had also broadened his appetite.

"Out there, in the real universe, these guys are gods," Switzer whispered. "On some planets, the mere mention of a Space Jumper can send an enemy scurrying for cover. I just thought it would be a little tougher."

"Or maybe you're just that good," I told him.

"Hey, don't worry—you're going to get better."

"I don't need your pity, thanks."

"I didn't mean it that way. Look, what are you now, seventeen? I have ten, maybe fifteen years' experience on you. That's all. How can anyone expect to be good at this right off the launch? That's what the training's for. I'm sure you're much better than me when you're using that thing in your head and jumping around computers and stuff. I'm still grasping working the interfaces on O-dats."

"You really like this life, don't you?"

"It's better than what I used to do."

We finished our meal in silence. We were both exhausted and sore. It even hurt to stand up. As I limped back to our room, I hoped I might get some sleep, but it did not come. I lay in my sleeper, thinking about what Switzer had said, about the reputation of Space Jumpers elsewhere in the universe. I thought about how they were feared. Max had heard those stories as well. I'm sure a lot of people on the rings shared the same sentiment. I wondered if Max would ever take me back now.

Over the next few cycles, I watched Switzer begin to dominate the trainers during the Quest-Nest drills. I then decided that instead of sitting there and grumbling about it, I would watch him and learn. Switzer was good, often combining two movements at once. But when I tried to repeat the task, it was simply impossible for me.

"Don't give up!" he encouraged me.

And I didn't. Whenever I trained with him, I stayed close, trying to reenact his movements even if it resulted in a painful drop to the floor or being blindsided by a moving obstacle.

Despite my exhaustion, I still wasn't sleeping.

One spoke, I caught another Honock in the observation deck. This one did not resort to calling me bad, but he was still afraid of me. I wondered if they had always been afraid. Had this individual almost been killed by a Space Jumper, only to be reincarnated as a machine and forced to live among us? How horrible would that be? No wonder he thought I was bad.

"Do the Honocks ever ask to go home?" I asked Brine Amar during one session.

"No. Why do you ask?"

"I've seen them in the observation deck, looking out at the stars, almost as if they were reminiscing about something. I thought they might be thinking about their former lives."

"Honocks are not designed that way. Yes, some of their personality is maintained, but you really must think of them as machines, just as you would a cart-bot or an android."

Before I left, though, he made the oddest request.

"Could you do me a favor?" he asked. "Would you play in a match of Quest-Nest with Randall Switzer? I would enjoy that very much."

"Me? I guess. Sure, why not? Whom will we play against?"

"No, I want you to play against Randall Switzer. You will use one of your instructors as your partner."

"*Against* him?"

"Yes. Do you mind?"

"Um, no. I guess not."

"When?"

"Now."

Instead of training this spoke, it appeared I was going to enter the labyrinth and play against Switzer. When I arrived, Switzer was already waiting, as were most of the other Space Jumpers I had seen in the Hollow.

"Just like old times," he said.

"You know?"

"Yeah, my guy asked me to play you."

"Mine, too. Don't you think that's weird? I mean everyone in the Hollow is here."

"Why should I? I'm looking forward to watching you lose."

Switzer yanked the helmet over his head and launched into the labyrinth. One of my trainers walked up and asked, "You want to be the bait or the tracker?"

"Tracker," I said under my breath, and pulled a helmet off the wall.

The labyrinth on the Hollow was different from the one I had been using on the Rings of Orbis, in that it did not have a sort. I was glad that I did not have to think of a sort strategy to use against Switzer. I was comforted by the fact that I would not be floating in a vacuum while trying to navigate multidimensional mazes after the door opened. No, this match would be familiar to me. This would be just like on the *Renaissance*.

Waiting for the computer to set, I felt the sudden urge to run. What if I was wrong? What if it was different here as well? *But you've already been practicing here,* I reminded myself. *Concentrate!* When the door peeled away, it was like stepping back onto the *Renaissance*. It was exactly the same! I sprinted along the curved purple walls and jumped over the blue lights embedded in channels on the floor. I knew the first obstacle of metal crates was just ahead to my right and the immobility cube would be waiting on the other side.

I dragged the metal crate next to the other two and used it to hop up and over a half wall. I grabbed the immobility cube and then used the ladder I knew would be there to sidestep two more obstacles, just as I had done so many times before on the *Renaissance. This is almost too easy,* I thought. It was obvious to me now that Quirin had designed our Quest-Nest on the *Renaissance.* Didn't they know I had played this version many, many times before? Was this some sort of trick? It certainly must have been boring for Brine Amar to watch.

I was ready for the four frontier pilots hiding in the deep trenches past the next doorway. An additional immobility cube and a plasma rifle took them down before they even started to scream. I ran across the darkened room, past a sparking electrical circuit that provided the only light. I was about to run through the doorway when I stopped.

The door was on the wrong side of the room. It should have been on the left, but it was on the right, on the other side of a snaking electrical wire that was torn loose from the wall. I wouldn't even have even thought about it if everything hadn't been so exact up until this point, right down to the color of the lights and scars on the walls. It was a complete reenactment of the *Renaissance*.

Except for this door.

I approached the door and saw that it was slightly open, as if someone had tried to open it but it had jammed. Had Switzer already been here and messed with the door to slow me down? I searched for some sort of control panel near the door, but there was none. I peered through the crack and saw a pink light flickering on the other side, so I figured this was the way to go. I even tried to pry it open with the butt of my fedaado blade, but the door was stuck.

I flexed my arm, used my softwire to adjust the torque and pain levels and then clobbered at the door with my right arm. The metal buckled, but I knew I was going to have to destroy the door to get through. I had to admire Switzer for jamming it like this. The delay was definitely going to set me back.

I pounded on the door several times; each effort widened the crack a little more. When I peered through again, it was mostly black beyond except for the beams of pink light that crisscrossed the darkness. I figured it was coming from some light source on the wall. With one final lunge, I hammered at the door, and whatever had jammed it came loose. The door jerked to the right with such a jolt that I lost my footing and fell forward, through the opening.

It was a hole.

I was falling through the beams of pink lights that flicked on as I passed them. *This is going to hurt,* I thought, but I didn't scream. Who would hear me, anyway?

And then I hit water. Water isn't as hard as concrete, but it still hurts. I felt my right leg jam up into my hip socket and the water crash in on my face.

It was over. I had lost.

I looked up through the tiny beams of pink light, waiting for the labyrinth to turn off. The water would drain away, and I would be left with my sore leg and my loser self. I had wanted to beat Switzer. I knew I didn't have a chance, but I wanted to beat him.

"Hey!" I called out when no one turned the maze off. "I'm down here. You win!"

But the water was not draining. In fact, I noticed that the water level was creeping upward, swallowing the little beams of pink light as it rose. Soon there were just as many pink lights in the water as there were above me.

Is this part of the match?

When I floated up to the door that I had fallen through, some sort of force field swallowed the opening before the water could spill out. The well, or tunnel or whatever I had fallen into, was filling up.

As I passed the broken door, I searched frantically for some sort of computer device. I knew I wasn't supposed to use my softwire to aid myself in the game, but that was on Orbis. Everyone here was a softwire. Everyone was on equal ground. I searched the walls for something to push into, but I found nothing. *What put up that force field?* I wondered. Where was the computer that ran this thing, for that matter? *Surely there must be something around here to manipulate,* I thought.

I could see the top of the tunnel, only a few meters above my head. There wasn't enough time to figure out why, nor was there anyone around who could answer my questions. There had to be a way out of here. If they weren't turning the labyrinth off, then that meant the match wasn't over. There must be a way out.

I swam to the edge and groped the walls for some sort of plate or panel, anything really, but the walls were smooth like glass. I couldn't even find a seam, nothing except for the little holes where the pink beams of light shone. Was that it?

My hand was now against the ceiling. There was nothing else to try. I held my breath and dove under, close to one of the lights. There was nothing to interface with, so I tried to push in, but I found nothing. I moved to another light, hoping it might be different, but again, nothing. I surfaced, gasping for air. There were only about fifteen centimeters left for me to breathe in. Surely they wouldn't let me die in here. This wasn't the Chancellor's Challenge. *Do I simply give up?* I wondered. *What if Ketheria was with me? Would I give up then?*

I dove back into the water, searching for any light that

was different in any way. Near the bottom, I spotted one that appeared slightly brighter than the others. I dove deeper, knowing that this was my last chance, since the water would surely be at the ceiling by now. In front of the light, I groped for a computer device but still found nothing! This time, I pushed in and discovered a single computer chip attached to a sensory timer. It was the smallest thing I had ever pushed into before, but at least it was something. I knew it had to connect to something larger. I forced myself inside the circuit and pushed against the resistance. It felt as if something was scratching at my skin, pawing for something to latch on to, something to hold me back with. The narrow corridor I found inside the chip then opened into a larger chamber of data cells stacked one on top of the other. I noticed that the one at the center was highlighted with a bright yellow glow as if it were a beacon to let me know I had arrived.

A simple manipulation of the data sequence, clearly marked for anyone who found it, set the tank on drain, and I felt the rush of water pull me down to the floor. The water drained through a grate that ran the circumference of the tank. I waited as the floor extended downward, enlarging the grate until I could simply walk out. My bait was waiting for me.

"Well done!" he cried. "You're the first."

"First what?"

"The first one to ever escape that trap. Nice job!"

The trek back was simple. The water obstacle was gone, and I exited the maze in front of the bait. Those watching erupted in cheers as we stepped out. A few Space Jumpers who had made friends with Switzer were coming up to me and clapping me on the back, hanging close to me and discussing the match with whoever walked up. I listened as some, in the excitement, even answered questions that were directed to me. It felt good.

Switzer was nowhere to be found.

Brine Amar walked up to me and said, "I must say, I am impressed. I'm sure your name will be carved into a rock around here somewhere. You should be proud of your accomplishment."

And I was. A little voice tried to creep up and remind me how scared I'd been, how I thought about quitting. *But I didn't,* I argued. I had figured it out and now I was here. The winner. If I had given up, I would have been the loser. If I had given up in real life, I would have been dead.

Switzer finally came out, shaking his head. "Nice job!" he cried. There were no jabs at my abilities, no taunts about next time. Switzer seemed genuinely proud of what I had done. "I couldn't get out of that tank. I tried everything. The softwire thing didn't help me at all."

"Ah, you just need a little practice. I'll show you," I called out to him as he walked over to the group of Space Jumpers standing around me. I expected the other Space Jumpers to turn to Switzer and leave me to myself, but they didn't. He joined us as if it was the most natural thing in the universe.

"Go on, smile," he whispered. "You deserve it. You won."

Things were different after our Quest-Nest match. I don't just mean with Switzer and me, but with everyone at the Hollow.

I enjoyed my friendships with Max and Theodore, and even my sister—in fact, I cherished them—but this was different. We were all joined by an ability we shared, a talent that had at one time made me an outsider, but not now, not here. Here you wore that ability like a badge. Your softwire was your admission to the Hollow, and it didn't matter anymore if some alien had tampered with your genetic structure or you had come to it through your own natural evolutionary process.

Despite our past, I felt that a bond had now formed between Switzer and me. We were in this together. I had finally accepted that. The fact that we *had* actually been in this together from the beginning did not escape me, either, but I was glad we had found a way to overcome all that. I looked forward to his company, and he had even begun asking me for help with his softwire ability. Switzer and I had become friends.

Then I found Charlie.

14

I tried to stop using the tablets like Switzer had suggested. It wasn't that I couldn't handle the nausea or the headaches—I really did want to live without the pills. The real problem was that whenever I began to feel sick, I thought about home. I thought about Ketheria and Max and Theodore. I ached to know what they were doing and to be near Max again. The Hollow provided an excellent distraction, but the sickness was a strong reminder of the people I had left behind.

As I did on most sleepless spokes, I snuck off to the observation deck instead of staring at the lid of my sleeper. I found that the stars relaxed me, and if I was lucky, I might even drift off for a diam or two. When I entered the deck this time, however, I wasn't alone. A Honock was there, staring at the stars. At first, I thought it was the one that was afraid of me, but when I got near and it didn't run off, I assumed it had to be a different one.

Leaving him to himself, I sprawled out in front of the glass, a good five meters away just to be polite. As I sat down, I glanced over to see if my presence had disturbed him.

But there was something about him that looked familiar to me.

I looked over my shoulder, trying not to stare. He was definitely a Honock — I could tell from the way his facial skin was pulled over his metal skull — so there was no way I could have known him. The skin stopped right at the jawline exposing a multitude of wires and metal bones. But despite the hardware, his profile was undeniable. It was Charlie Norton.

"Charlie?" I whispered.

The Honock turned and looked at me. It was Charlie, all right. The thick nose. The rugged chin. "Hello," he replied.

I jumped up. "Charlie, it's me. JT!"

I scrambled over to my old Guarantor, my friend — the person they told me was dead.

He scooted back a little when I rushed forward. His movements were precise and machinelike — very "un-Charlie," but there was no denying the resemblance.

"Don't you remember me, Charlie?"

I sat still and let him examine me. I waited as his eyes searched my face, and I stared back at his waxen skin. I had never been this close to a Honock before, but I could see why Brine Amar treated them like machines. The facial skin was an excellent plasticlike imitation, right down to the fake pores. I heard a humming sound coming from him, sort of like the whir of many tiny motors. Each gesture he made had a slight pause and the exacting execution of a machine.

What had they him done to my friend?

"Ketheria?" Charlie said.

"No, JT. But do you remember Ketheria? She was my sister. She loved you."

"Peanut Butter."

"Yes! Yes! Ketheria loves peanut butter."

"I don't eat peanut butter."

"You did," I told him.

Charlie turned and looked back out at the stars, casually sitting next to me as if the two of us had done so a dozen times before. It hurt to think that he didn't remember me, but what did I expect? I didn't even know what Charlie *was* anymore. I looked at his profile again, following the metal and wires down in to the collar of his green jumpsuit.

"What have they done to you, Charlie?" I whispered softly. I didn't think he heard me, but he turned and smiled anyway.

It hit me that I was not as surprised by his presence as one might think. They had brought Switzer back from the dead, didn't they? Why not Charlie?

"What are you looking for?" I asked him.

Charlie turned to me and said, "Chicago."

"I'm afraid we are a long way from home, Charlie. A very long way."

I wanted to blame the Rings of Orbis for what had happened to Charlie, but Orbis had nothing to do with it. Charlie was they way he was because of one person. Randall Switzer. It was Switzer's malf of a plan to steal the Ancients' Treasure that had gotten Charlie killed. Charlie's presence was a glaring reminder of every selfish act Switzer had ever committed in his life — from his tyranny on the *Renaissance* to his utter lack of concern when he entered us in the Chancellor's Challenge. Switzer was an animal, pure and simple. He was not my friend. Who was I kidding? I hated Switzer at that moment.

"Charlie, do you know who I am?"

"You're JT."

"I am, but do you remember me? Do you remember being my Guarantor on the Rings of Orbis? Do you remember Max or Theodore?"

"Your friends."

"Yes!"

"My friends."

"Yes!"

"They're sleeping."

"Who's sleeping?"

"Our friends."

Was Charlie talking about the other Space Jumpers at the Hollow? I'm sure he had seen me training with them. "No, Charlie. I don't know what our friends are doing right now. They're far away. Too far, I'm afraid."

"I watch them. I watch you. I watch your friends now."

I looked through the glass and out into the stars. Could he see the Rings of Orbis? "Don't you mean my friends here,

Charlie? On the Hollow? Do you watch me and the other Space Jumpers?"

"I watch them."

"I thought so," I mumbled.

"But I watch Theodore and Max and Ketheria and you."

"What?" I cried.

"Shh!" Charlie whispered. "I am not allowed. I watch when they aren't watching me."

"Charlie, you can see Max? Where? Show me."

"It is forbidden. I am not allowed."

"You have to show me, Charlie. Where is it? Is it here on the ship? I have to see them, Charlie. Show me, please!"

Charlie covered my mouth with his hand. To my surprise, it was warm. Charlie looked over his shoulder toward the door and then stood up. I followed him, something I had done so often that the back of his head had been emblazoned into my memory, but this was different; everything was different. The confidence in his walk was gone; there was a Honock-like stiffness to his movements, and the hardware around the base of his brain looked unnatural. Plus, he was bald.

Outside the observation deck, Charlie moved quickly, even with his awkward gait. I followed him down four decks and through the Honocks' living quarters. He never once paused to see if I was keeping pace. When he did stop, the only exit I could see in the dimly lit corridor was a ventilation grate that covered most of the wall.

"What is this place, Charlie?" I asked him.

"Shh!" he replied, and glanced back down the corridor. He lifted the thick metal grate out of the wall and set it down with a clank. The thing must have weighed sixty kilos, yet he moved it as if it was a scrap of plastic.

"Go," he whispered, and nodded for me to enter the tunnel.

I heard the grate grind back into place as Charlie followed, covering our tracks. A greenish electrical glow at the end of the tunnel was my only guide as I slid my foot forward to make sure I was walking on solid ground. When I reached the light, I discovered a patchwork of O-dat terminals, wires, and computer parts, all linked to a control panel that looked as if it had been hacked open.

"Charlie, did you make all of this?" I asked, staring at his makeshift control center. I think the hideaway was fashioned from some sort of a utility shaft off the main ventilation system.

I moved aside so Charlie could sit at a small stool he must have taken from the meal room. Then he pulled a scrap of polymer out of his pocket and attached the crude device to a hardwire that he coaxed from his arm. The makeshift O-dat sparkled to life, and Charlie began copying numbers into the larger O-dats in front him. After a few moments, I saw the screens light up with unrecognizable coordinates, each with small blinking dots near the right of the screen. I could see that one of the dots was moving slightly.

I looked at Charlie as he rested his head on his hands and stared longingly at the screens. What was he looking at? The markings made no sense to me whatsoever. They looked like some sort of radar coordinates, or maybe he had hooked into a deep-space probe. I couldn't break it to him that he was just staring at nothing, especially if he thought these were Max and Ketheria. Or *should* I tell him? I didn't know how much a Honock understood. What sort of feelings he had, if any at all. The creature in front of me looked like Charlie, but he *wasn't* Charlie. My friend never had a nest of computer circuitry mounted to the base of his skull. Suddenly, I felt sad. What had I done to him? What had Switzer done?

"That's nice, Charlie. They look good," I croaked, pushing down the lump trying to free itself from my throat.

Then, as if as an afterthought, Charlie flipped a yellowed toggle switch mounted to the frame of his contraption. The screens exploded with images of Max, Theodore, and Ketheria. They were all asleep except Max.

I pushed myself in front of Charlie, practically jumping into his lap.

"How are you doing this?" I grabbed the piece of polymer. It was filled with numbers and symbols. "What are these? Where did you get them?"

Charlie typed in some more numbers, and an image of my room on Orbis 4 came up on one of the previously blank O-dats.

"Charlie, how do you know how to do this? Who gave you these? Did someone put surveillance equipment in our rooms? Charlie, tell me!"

"I don't remember," was all he said, and then he went back to staring at the screens.

Max was not in her sleeper. She was sitting at her chair, her back to the camera. There was something in her hands, something she was looking at, but I couldn't make it out. How long had it been since I'd seen her? She looked just as she did in the image that was burned into my memory. Maybe her hair was a little longer, but that was it. The sight of her flooded my senses with her smell, her touch, the smoothness of her skin, the sound of her voice—all of it was inside me right now, igniting an ache I had been trying to bury. I wanted to be back on the Rings of Orbis. I wanted to be back on the rings *right now*.

I watched as Max placed whatever she'd been holding on her table and then walked toward her sleeper. She slipped out of her robe and climbed in. As the lid closed, she looked up—toward whatever was looking at her, I thought. For a nanosecond I was looking straight into her eyes again. It felt as if I had been impaled with a rod of hot metal. After the lid closed, I stood there staring at her sleeper, and then I slumped onto the floor. Charlie flipped the toggle switch, and the green dots came back up. He just sat there and watched them.

When I returned to my room, I found Switzer already up.

"Up early or just getting in?" he asked.

I couldn't talk to Switzer. Not right now. I crawled into my sleeper and closed the lid. I didn't even look at him. Knowing what he did to Charlie made me sick to my stomach.

"I'll take that as just getting in. You got to lay off those tablets, JT."

"Shut up," I muttered, and closed my eyes. How could we ever be friends? How could I ever forget what he did?

Switzer thumped his big hand on the lid of my sleeper.

"C'mon. Big cycle. We start looking like Space Jumpers. New uniforms. I want something mean-looking. What do you want to get?"

I didn't reply. I couldn't. Not a single word. I wanted to throw back the lid and rip Switzer's throat out. I wanted to hit him, punch him once for every one of the millions of stupid things he had done in his life. I wanted to hit him until he was dead.

"Suit yourself," he grumbled, and then I heard the door disappear.

Finally, I breathed. Then, for the first time in a long time, I slept. I didn't dream; my body simply wanted to check out for a while, to turn my brain off. When I woke, Switzer was back in his sleeper. I had spent the entire cycle asleep. No one had bothered me. No one had come looking for me when I missed my scheduled appointments with my connector or my meeting with Quirin. I found that odd, but I was relieved to find some freedom left in my life.

I got up and searched for Charlie. He was not in the observation deck, so I traced my steps back to the ventilation shaft. The huge grate was in its proper place, and when I went to remove it, I was forced to adjust the settings to my arm. How strong was Charlie now? I wondered. The clunk of the grate hitting the floor resonated down the hallway, but I didn't wait to see if I had alarmed anyone. With the grate back in place I headed toward the green glow.

Charlie was not at his screens, and all the O-dats were turned off. I searched the counter under the screens for the polymer, but that was nowhere to be found. *Where are you, Charlie?* I sat waiting for him to return, but he did not come. Instead, I stared at the blank O-dats. I wanted so badly to turn them on. I could simply push in and take a little peek into his handiwork. He wouldn't mind, I convinced myself, and so I sat at his stool and fired up the portal that was my only link to my old life.

Charlie's computer creation seemed designed for only one purpose: to spy on us. Once inside his array, I found hundreds and hundred of unlabeled files containing digis of Max, Theodore, Grace, Ketheria, me, and most of the other kids who had lived with Charlie on Orbis 3. Somehow Charlie had managed to locate each of us on Orbis 4. It was easy to figure out how he had done it — the staining. Everyone had been stained on Orbis 2 with a genetic mark that allowed Citizens to track us. After Switzer had jumped (and taken my arm with him), the Trading Council demanded that we get stained or be put to death. I remember Charlie railing against the staining at the time. I wondered if they gave him the tools to find us after he became our Guarantor. It all seemed plausible, but who had installed the surveillance equipment in our rooms and why? And how did a Honock find out about it?

Instead of watching the files inside Charlie's computer, I pulled out and displayed them on the O-dats. File after file, each of us sleeping or sitting in our rooms. Sometimes there was nothing but long passages of our empty rooms. I could find no pattern to what Charlie had saved. Every clip had a time stamp, the earliest dated right after we arrived on Orbis 4. Charlie, and whoever else, had been watching us since the moment we had arrived.

I pulled up a recent clip of Ketheria and began to watch. She was sitting with two Nagools, nodding as they spoke. What were they saying? All this equipment and no sound? It didn't make sense. I watched as one of the Nagools got up and left. Ketheria began to fidget, pulling at her robe and looking past the remaining Nagool. Then the first Nagool returned with another alien. He had his arm around the alien's waist, supporting him as he stumbled toward my sister. I think the creature was another Nagool. He had the same ashen complexion and OIO symbol marked on his face as the others, but he wasn't wearing the traditional Nagool garb.

I stared at the O-dat in fascination as the Nagool helped the alien kneel in front of Ketheria, and then the alien dropped his head onto her lap. The two other Nagools moved back and out of the frame. She looked up as the others left and then seemed to focus on the alien in her lap. Ketheria's shoulders slumped, and then her whole body flexed. The room became brighter, and I realized that Ketheria was glowing. The light seemed to radiate from her skin, getting brighter and brighter as she stroked the Nagool's forehead with her right hand, all the while clutching his left hand in hers.

The light continued to build around her, and she began to tremble. She was shaking now, and then she threw her head back as if to scream. The O-dat flashed white as the glow around Ketheria exploded, making it too bright for the surveillance equipment to register an image. When the flash subsided, so had the glow around Ketheria. She was no longer trembling, but her hair was soaked with sweat. The two other Nagools rushed back in, and one caught Ketheria as she collapsed onto the makeshift sleeper. The third Nagool, the one that had needed to be helped in, stood up without the aid of the others. His skin looked tighter, and he stood straight, smiling at the other Nagools.

Did Ketheria do that to him? What had I just watched? Was Ketheria healing people now?

I opened another file that had been recorded after my arrival at the Hollow. An image of Max jumped to the screen, making my stomach lurch. She was seated on the floor in her room, and I could tell she was crying. Theodore was seated next to her. When he put his arm around her, I immediately felt angry. *I* should be there comforting her, not Theodore. What was he doing, anyway? I pulled up another file of Max. This time Queykay was in her room, leaning over her. It looked as if he was yelling at her. About what, though? Max was holding her ground, at least she was trying to, but Queykay seemed very angry, very threatening. He waved his arms about, forcing himself into her personal space. At one point, I thought he might even hit her, but then he stormed out. Grace entered. She kept glancing over her shoulder as she spoke closely with Max. What was going on? I wondered. I flipped over to a file with the same time stamp. A file for Theodore, but he was not in his room.

I couldn't help but feel that something was wrong. I searched Charlie's computer to find some sort of live feed like the one he had shown me before.

"What are you doing?" Charlie said from behind me.

I spun around on the stool to find Charlie looming over me, a plastic pipe in his hand. He swung and struck me in the head before I had time to react.

I awoke to a pounding headache and a nice lump near the top of my head. Someone had put me back in my room. I pushed the lid aside and sat up. The blood rushed from my head, leaving nothing but the pain, which exploded and filled my entire skull. I pried open my eyelids to see if Switzer was sleeping. He wasn't there; I was glad about that. Had Charlie brought me back here? Had Switzer seen him? I couldn't tell what spoke it was, but despite the rocket that kept launching inside my head, I was hungry.

I found Switzer eating with our usual group of Space Jumpers, but he didn't see me enter the food commons. Switzer was holding up something attached to his uniform and showing it to the others while they ate. It looked like some sort of fabricated metal pocket. Our new uniforms! I had forgotten. *Who cares?* I muttered to myself while I searched the food wall for something to eat.

"Where have you been?" Switzer asked, coming up behind.

"Nowhere," I replied, and kept pulling food out and stuffing it into my mouth before even putting it on my plate.

"How can you be nowhere? You weren't in training. You

weren't around to get your uniform, and you certainly weren't in the room."

"What are you now, my Guarantor? I was doing stuff." I slammed the last door and pushed past him.

"Stop taking that crap. Those tablets are making you unbearable," he called after me.

"Yeah? What's your excuse?" I said, and left the food area.

Why had Charlie hit me? Had he not remembered me? I wanted to go back and find out. I also wanted to get something to protect myself with, or at least be ready to use my arm if Charlie attacked me again. He was strong, though. I needed to be prepared. Maybe there was something in my room to use, I thought.

When I returned to my room, Brine Amar was waiting for me.

"You've missed our scheduled appointments," he said.

"Sorry, I haven't been feeling well," I told him. It wasn't really a lie. My head was killing me.

"Did you go to the infirmary?"

"No."

"What is ailing you?"

"Um . . . my head. I'm having bad headaches."

"They can fix that immediately. Come. I'll show you the way if you don't know," he said, standing up.

"Now?"

"Yes, now, unless there is somewhere else you are off to, though I don't know where that could be since you're supposed to be with me right now."

Despite the fact that he had told me that I could not offend him, I detected a tinge of anger in Brine Amar's voice. Should I tell him about Charlie? What if that led to Charlie's little surveillance room? I couldn't risk that. I wanted to see Max again. I wanted to know how Ketheria was healing people.

"You know, I just had something to eat and I'm starting to feel a little better. Why don't we just have our session? I apologize if I messed up our schedule."

"That is fine as well. We have much to do."

I tried to concentrate on what Brine Amar asked of me, but I could not stop thinking about Charlie. How long had he been here? Why couldn't he remember anything? How much of him was really Charlie? My connector was instructing me to upload file after file of Space Jumper history, most of it dry and boring, while I thought of Charlie. The process reminded me of my first rotation at the Center for Wisdom, Culture, and Comprehension.

"What do I need this for?" I complained.

"Do you not wish to understand the rich heritage created by the many Space Jumpers that have come before you?"

Not really, I said to myself, but I had to admit, Brine Amar was right. There were a lot of Space Jumpers who had done some amazing things in the universe. Softwires didn't seem so rare when you looked at their entire history. I did notice, however, that there was little mention of the Tonat. Instead, I found stories that involved other categories of Space Jumpers. I read about units of militarized Space Jumpers, as well solitary Jumpers called Cenots, who worked undercover within unknowing civilizations. I read of one Cenot who lived among a warring race known as Forlians for more than forty rotations. He single-handedly created a new form of government that, once adopted by its people, allowed the Forlians to reach the stars and assist the Ancients in constructing the Rings of Orbis. I wondered why I had never heard of the Forlians before and why I had never encountered any on the rings. Orbis certainly held a lot of mysteries. Did anyone truly know everything?

I went slowly with the Cenot files. I found myself admiring these aliens and their dedication to the Ancients, but I could not understand why they sacrificed their entire lives yet had lapsed into obscurity. It just seemed strange.

"These Cenots," I said to Brine Amar. "Are there any here? You know, at the Hollow?"

"I don't believe so. It takes a special kind of Space Jumper to spend his or her life in isolation."

"Her? I wondered about that. So there are female Space Jumpers as well?"

"Certainly. Some of the best."

"I don't know how those Cenots do it," I said, shaking my head.

"Acceptance," Brine Amar replied. "Something you have much trouble with, I'm afraid. I hoped we would be much further along than this before you commenced the next stage of training."

"Next stage!" I cried. "I thought we were done. I thought we were getting our uniforms and that was it. Switzer has his now. I thought I could go back to the rings."

"But you don't even have your Burak yet."

"Burak?"

"Your Space Jumper's belt. Your most important possession."

"But I don't need a belt."

"You will if you ever need to jump *with* someone. *You* may be able to jump without your burak, but you would surely kill anyone you ever tried to jump with."

"Cenots don't jump with anyone," I reminded him.

"I'm referring to a rescue attempt. What if you were forced to jump and take the Scion with you? Without a belt, you would be unable to make the proper temporal allowance for your passenger. I shudder to think of the result."

I remembered the numerous times I had fantasized about jumping off the ring and taking Max with me. What if I had killed her? What else didn't I know? There was so much to learn, but I didn't want to stay here any longer. I wanted to be with my friends.

"When does the new training start?" I asked.

"When you are ready," he replied.

"I'm ready."

"Are you?"

Brine Amar's tone frightened me. "You don't sound very confident about my progress. What about Switzer? How is he doing? Perfect, I'm sure."

"Why don't we start with your uniform? It is a big step in accepting who you are."

"I know who I am," I told him.

Brine Amar didn't say anything, but he didn't need to; his silence said enough. He raised his hand toward the door, and I shrugged. I could use some new clothes, anyway.

Brine Amar took me to the small cluster of trading chambers located near the recreation area, just past the food commons. I had yet to visit this area. I had heard Switzer talking about going there with a few other Jumpers, but I had not been invited.

"Who works here?" I asked. "Do they live on the Hollow?"

"Most are Honocks. I believe there are also a few people who failed to complete the program but chose to stay."

"Or maybe the Trust didn't want them to leave and reveal the Hollow's whereabouts."

Brine Amar looked at me. "This is not an evil place, JT," he said. "You really must open your mind before it's too late."

"Too late for what? You don't have to be so cryptic. Just tell me."

"Here we are," Brine Amar said, stopping in front of an open trading chamber. It was nothing more than a few tables arranged under a concrete shelter.

"But where are the uniforms?" I said, staring at the bolts of material and piles of rubber, metal, and plastic.

"You don't think they stock uniforms for every species, do you? Your uniform is made specifically for you. It is unique, as unique as your softwire."

"That ability seems pretty common around here," I told him.

"You look only at what you see."

A Honock entered from a door in the back wall. I could tell

he was a Honock by the hunk of hardware around the back of his neck.

"Welcome," he said, beaming. "One last straggler for a fitting?"

This Honock seemed a little more "awake" than Charlie or the Honock that was afraid of me. This one acted like a normal person, despite the fact he was mostly metal, wires, and circuits.

"Just me. It must not be that busy around here," I said, pushing the Honock for information.

"Oh, you would be surprised. I also do repairs and tailoring. The Trust keeps me very busy, but it's always an honor to create a suit for a new Space Jumper. I've made every Space Jumper suit for . . ." The Honock looked up as if trying to remember. Then he gave up and shook his head. "Well, for a very long time. That's for sure, isn't it, Brine Amar?"

"Indeed, Potu. Your work is worn by almost everyone at the Hollow."

Potu looked at me, smiling. I was surprised by how alert he seemed to be. Why wasn't Charlie like this?

"Have you been assigned yet? I don't think so. Let me see. Something simple to start. A uniform you can build on. Do you see yourself in a militarized unit?" Potu asked me.

"Actually, what about the suits you make for the Cenots? I think that's more what I'm looking for."

Potu's smile faded, and he looked at Brine Amar, as if for guidance. From the corner of my eye, I saw Brine Amar nod gently.

"Then follow me," Potu instructed.

Potu led me to another section of his trading chamber, where there was some type of scanning machine with four pillars. Potu ask me to stand at the center of it while he adjusted each pod, raising them to my height.

"This gives me a multidimensional rendition of your exact body shape. I can make you a suit that fits better than your own skin," he boasted.

"Sounds good," I said. "Just make sure to leave my old skin where it is."

Potu chuckled as he continued to set his fitting machine. *So, Honocks understand humor,* I thought. Then Potu moved in and allowed me a closer look at the hardware attached to the base of his neck. Without asking, I pushed inside his little computer. Immediately, I found a simple interface that would allow other Space Jumpers access to Potu's mind. Not every variable was accessible. Some were password-protected. My softwire allowed me to push past that kind of simple security programming and look at the hardware in its entirety. It was fascinating—so many hardwire connections to his soft tissue, synaptic chips with chemical impulses, and electric pulse generators, all in that little construction at the back of his head.

I pulled out, and Potu was staring at me. "Don't do that," he scolded me.

How did he know? "I'm sorry," I whispered. "I just—"

"It's polite to ask first," he interrupted. "I'm more than just a machine."

Potu continued with his work and then punched at an

O-dat on the wall. A beam of green light sprouted from each of the four posts and scanned my entire body. It was over before I blinked.

"Done," he said. "Come back next cycle." The coldness in his voice was easy to detect.

"Don't I get to pick a style or anything?"

"You already mentioned you were interested in a Cenot standard. That's what you'll get."

I was embarrassed by what I had done, but I was also intrigued by how much emotion Potu displayed.

I stepped out of the fitting machine and walked toward Brine Amar. "I guess that's it," I said.

"It's just the start," he replied. "With your new suit, you can begin the next stage of your training."

I skipped my next meal and went looking for Charlie. I waited outside the ventilation grate and slipped into the shadows whenever I heard someone coming. If it was Charlie, I planned to warn him, so as not to scare him again. I didn't think I could take another blow to the head. I was convinced that Charlie's hidden O-dat setup was illegal, and I didn't want anyone tearing it down before I got a chance at it again. While I sat thinking about seeing Max again, Charlie lumbered up to the grate. I stepped out of the shadow and out of the range of his swing.

"Charlie, it's me, JT."

Charlie stood there with his head cocked to one side, as if he was trying to remember who I was. Maybe he hadn't recognized me the last time and had taken me for an intruder.

Charlie's awareness of the people around him seemed so much different from Potu's. Why? Was Charlie's brain damaged before they turned him into a Honock? I think I knew another possible reason. I was eager to find out.

"Charlie, don't you remember me?"

"Ketheria?"

"Yes, my sister. Peanut butter."

"Peanut butter!"

There was something wrong with his memory. His short-term memory was either gone or disabled.

"We're friends, remember? You showed me your screens." I pointed at the grate. "Max and Theodore. I would like to see them again."

"JT?"

"Yes!"

"My friends."

"Can we see them?"

Charlie turned and pulled the grate from the hole. I slipped inside, and Charlie followed. This time when Charlie sat at the controls, I looked at the computer circuitry behind his head. Then I remembered Potu's warning.

"Charlie, do you mind if I take a look?" I asked, pointing at the metal.

Charlie reached behind his neck and brushed his fingers across the device. Then he shrugged. That looked like a yes to me.

The interface inside Charlie's brain was just as complex

as Potu's. After a little searching, I discovered controls for memory, emotion, coordination, and bodily functions, such as metabolism and heart rate. The Space Jumpers had completely mapped Charlie's brain and applied controls to every function. Could this be done to someone who was still alive? I wondered. The thought of Citizens controlling knudniks this way sent a shiver down my spine.

When I pulled out, Charlie was leaning on his hands and staring at the green dots on the screen.

"Can you make them so I can see them? You know, see the images?"

Charlie flipped the switch, and there was Max. She was in her room with Grace and Theodore. Why was Theodore there every time I saw Max? I shook it off and looked at what they were doing. Grace and Theodore seemed to be watching the door. Max opened a panel in the wall and reached in to pull something out. It was slightly out of view, so I couldn't really see as it was. I stared at Max's face. It was so close to the secret camera that was spying on her that she was almost life-size.

When she pulled back, Theodore turned to help her. What did she have? They placed whatever it was on the floor in front of the sleeper, and Max stood up. When Max reached for her tools, I caught a full view of what they had hidden. It was a plasma rifle, and a big one, too. What was Max doing with a weapon?

Charlie reached up and flipped to another screen.

"Wait!"

But Charlie was looking at an image of Ketheria now.

"No," he replied. "Don't like guns."

"Charlie, I'm going to make a couple of adjustments, if you don't mind. You know, with that thing there on your neck."

Charlie looked back at the screens and then at me. "Sure," he said.

I pushed back into Charlie's brain and went over the controls once more. What would make Charlie a little more coherent? How much would I need to tinker in order to give him back his memory, or his old attitude? These controls weren't like dials that you set from one to ten. It was more like restricting blood flow through a vein with your fingertips. I would have to go slowly.

The first thing I did was to adjust the memory variable. Was it possible to awaken memories of his childbirth if I went too far? And which way was more? What if I cut off still more of his short-term memory? I hesitated. I bet Max would know what to do.

I made a tiny adjustment to his memory and pulled out.

"Charlie?" I said.

He turned and looked at me.

"Yes, JT?"

That was good. At least that was in the right direction.

"Charlie, where are you?"

He cocked his head and looked at me. "Here," he said, his tone slightly mocking.

"How did you get here?"

He looked around as if he was trying to remember. Maybe I needed to adjust it more if he couldn't remember how he got here.

"Forget it," I told him. "Watch your friends. I need to do a little more."

Charlie turned back to the screens, and I slipped back inside. Maybe the variables were tied together in some way. Memories can elicit strong emotions, so maybe I needed to work the two controls together. I pushed through the memories and the emotion controls, working the two of them together. I increased both a little more than before. Was that too much?

Charlie answered that for me. From inside his head, I felt his fingers clamp around my neck. I heard screaming. Was that me or was it Charlie? I pulled out and found Charlie on top of me, his hands clamped around my throat.

"Charlie!" I croaked.

"What did you do to me? Where am I?" he screamed. "Where did you go this time? I do everything for you kids and this is how you treat me?"

Spit flew from Charlie's mouth, and the blood vessels in his eyeballs beat red with fire.

"Can't . . . breathe . . ."

"Do you know what I sacrificed to take care of you? Can you even imagine what I've gone through? For what? You're nothing but a worthless, whiny punk!"

Charlie was going to kill me. At least he was trying to. I felt the familiar blackness creeping in around the edges of my vision. I pushed back into Charlie's brain controls and sloppily grabbed whatever I could find. Charlie's grip weakened, and he slumped backward. I sat up, coughing and rubbing my neck. My head throbbed from the lack of oxygen.

"Charlie?"

He said nothing. He just sat there, drooling, staring at a spot on the floor. Then he slumped over.

"Charlie!"

Nothing. He was practically catatonic. What had I done? How did I fix this? I stood up and moved him to the stool. He didn't resist. It was like pushing around a huge weather balloon. I slipped back inside his brain, looking for traces of what I had touched. Everything looked normal, the same as the first time I entered Charlie's brain. *Do I go get help?* I wondered. *But where?*

I began tweaking the variables one by one, pulling out each time to check Charlie's reaction. After a few tries, I got the drooling to stop, but he still wasn't responding to his name. *What am I going to do? I can't leave him like this. He'll never find his way out of here.* After a few more adjustments, Charlie seemed a little more alert, but he still wasn't what he had been.

"Charlie, c'mon, get up. Can you follow me?"

He just stared at me like the little ones used to do on the *Renaissance*. Once I got him up, I pushed him toward the ventilation grate. If anyone could help fix him, Quirin could.

15

"You knew he was here the whole time and you didn't tell me?" I cried. Charlie was standing next to me in Quirin's quarters.

"You are not here to make friends," Quirin said. His voice was sharp. "You are here to learn. Besides, I gathered that your emotional needs were met by the other human you so adamantly requested to participate."

"Switzer? I only wanted him here because I thought it was the right thing to do after what *you* did to him."

"I thought it was the right thing for the Honock after what *you* did to *him*."

"Me? I didn't do this! If anyone is to be blamed, it's Switzer. He had one of his wormhole pirates kill Charlie."

I cringed at the awful sound of crunching bones as Quirin shifted in his rock bed.

"This is enough," his voice boomed. "I will not tolerate insubordination. You are an instrument, controlled by us, in service to protect the Scion. Your wishes are irrelevant. I have only appeased you so far because humans are the last chance."

"Against what? Some invisible force that's eating up other universes? Sounds pretty far-fetched to me. It's just another story to oppress those stupid enough to believe it."

"Enough!"

I felt the stone walls of Quirin's room shudder as if his anger had lifted the rock. Even I knew when to shut up. I just needed to get my training over with and get back to the Rings of Orbis.

"I'm sorry," I said.

"I don't want your apologies. I want your commitment. I want you to stand up and be the man I created. Your life is filled with pathetic self-awareness that only hampers your ability to act. It is time to awaken what is in you, to awaken the Space Jumper."

The door to the room opened, and two Space Jumpers walked in and seized Charlie.

"Wait!" I cried, but I could only watch as they led Charlie, unresisting, from the room. "Quirin, what are they going to do to him?"

"Fix what you did," he spat.

"What are *you* going to do *me*?"

"Train you. I am going to turn you into the Softwire you are destined to be."

After two more Space Jumpers entered the room, the gravity of the moment settled upon me.

I just had my first argument with my father.

I did not look back as the Space Jumpers escorted me out.

I had expected to be led back to my room, but they turned in the other direction, securing me by the arms before I could resist. It wasn't necessary, though. I wasn't going to resist. As they marched me down the corridor, I thought of my sister's warning. The one where she told me that the Trust used force to awaken parts within you whether you were ready or not. Would Quirin use that force on me? I was not scared. I couldn't have been more ready.

I was taken to an area behind the labyrinth, where I was loaded into a light chute and then dumped into a part of the Hollow that I had never seen before. I looked around the huge cavernous space and couldn't see where the room ended. In the distance, I spotted a tiny light blinking through the mist on the horizon, but I could not figure out where I was. I followed the Jumpers a few meters to my left, but instead of finding solid flooring, I discovered individual platforms that seemed to float over a murky abyss. The center platform was the only one rooted to something, but I could not see what. When I looked down, the cylinder supporting the platform merely disappeared through a bluish fog. Each platform was rimmed with a cool, electric light; and a narrow railing, only wide enough to let one person pass, surrounded the entire area.

"Is this where I train?" I asked.

"This is where everyone trains," the Space Jumper to my left replied.

"Why not in the labyrinth?"

"This is where you learn to use your burak."

I wanted to shout, "I don't need a belt!" But what was the use? No one would listen, anyway.

I looked up toward the ceiling and spotted an alien descending swiftly to the center pod. The creature sprouted thick pointed tentacles from the back of his head that made him look as if he were caught in a wind tunnel. His broad shoulders were pulled back, and he carried a long staff in his right hand. The smug look on his face alone told me that I was in trouble.

Within an instant, the alien was next to me—he was a Space Jumper. He began sniffing me like an animal.

"So you're the one they speak so much of. A Tonat. How privileged are we?"

The alien circled me. Each step was a cautious gesture with a threatening glance, and I should have been scared, even terrified, but I suddenly found myself fighting the urge to laugh. I clenched my teeth and stared past the vile creature. I had an intense moment of clarity in which I saw this guy as a caricature of every alien I had ever scuffled with. Suddenly, I was outside of my body looking down at this whole absurd ceremony. All I saw was a kid—a kid from a planet called Earth. And now I was living in a comet with this animal towering over me, strutting about, as if *I* were a threat that needed to be dealt with. Maybe it was a nervous reaction, I don't know, but finally I couldn't help myself anymore, and I snickered.

"I'm sorry," I mumbled, but the alien wasn't accepting apologies.

He swung around and struck me in the stomach with his muscular left arm. The blow pushed my stomach up into my lungs, leaving no room for air. I buckled over, gasping, and the alien brought the staff up into my face. The pain exploded across my nose and I tumbled backward, slipping under the railing. At the very last moment, I reached out and caught the vertical support, but the rest of me dangled over the empty void.

"Is *that* funny?" he asked.

I couldn't breathe, let alone answer him. Blood poured down the back of my throat, and reality came crashing down upon me. Now I was scared, *really* scared.

"Is that funny?" he screamed. His voice echoed across the void.

I shook my head. That was all I could do.

"For the rest of your pitiful life, you will remember your time with me as your easiest cycles. I am your best friend now. Once you are placed in the universe, everyone will be your enemy. You will be hunted like a common cochark, and even your own family will loathe you." The alien knelt in front of me, his tone growing softer. "But *I* will love you, and so will your brethren. A Space Jumper's plea can be heard across the galaxy, and they are the only ones who will ever answer you. You have one purpose in your life now, and that is to serve the Ancients, to serve the Scion."

Then he kicked my hand and sent me falling into the abyss.

I awoke in my sleeper with all my appendages intact. Had I dreamed it? The pain in my fingers and my nose told me that everything was real, but how had I gotten here? Switzer was sitting up, putting his suit on. There seemed to be a new piece attached to it, a metal plate over his heart.

"So you met Chausau, huh? I wouldn't look in any mirrors for a few cycles."

I sat up but didn't reply. Every time I looked at Switzer now, I saw the wormhole pirate and thought about what he did to Charlie.

"Still not talking to me?" He stood up and stomped his thick boots on the floor as if they were new. "Suit yourself, but I'm gonna need your help here. I've done so much in my life, I don't know what part you want me to apologize for."

"All of it," I muttered as Switzer marched from the room, but he poked his head back in.

"You know you're not being fair," Switzer said.

"Fair? What do you call fair? Your whole life has only been about yourself. If there's not something in it for you, then forget about it. Why don't you just get out of here? Go back to whatever wormhole you were hiding in and leave me alone, *Captain Ceesar*."

"You have no idea what it was like for me. You think I roamed around the universe pillaging whatever I wanted, like it was some perpetual Birth Day celebration?"

"You certainly seemed proud of your actions."

"I wasn't even sixteen years old when I popped up onto that pirate ship! They were brutal. Simply brutal. I begged the Universe to let me be a knudnik again, but no one answered. I *fought* for my position in their world, literally.

"Life as a wormhole pirate is nothing like they whisper in

the back rooms of your cushy little school. If you've got the stomach for it, I'll tell you about the time I almost froze to death, abandoned on a mining moon with my best friend. I held him in my arms like a little one, wishing he would hurry up and die so I could gut him and then crawl inside his dead carcass to keep warm. You don't want to know what I did with his insides."

"You murdered *my* best friend."

"That was not my intention, JT. Charlie was an accident. I only wanted him out of the way for a while. How was I supposed to know he would have an allergy to the stuff? I'm sorry. I really am. Besides, he's not dead. Look at him! I think he looks pretty good."

"Get out of here."

"It was an accident."

"Get out of here!"

I fell back into my sleeper and heard the door close. Then I swung my feet around and over the edge. I didn't want to go back to Chausau. Who was I kidding? I wasn't cut out for this. Switzer should be the Tonat. It was like he relished this stuff. I couldn't stand him for what he did to Charlie, but I had to admit that the Hollow had changed him. He acted with purpose now and a sense of belonging. Why couldn't I find that?

Despite my best efforts to resist, I put my feet on the floor and stood up. I didn't have to be a softwire to imagine the consequences for missing Chausau's training. That's when I realized I hadn't taken one of those tablets for quite some time.

When I went looking for it, I found the nausea and the headache lurking inside me, but now it was more of a gauge, a tool to tell me how far away Ketheria was. The more I concentrated on the feeling, the more sick I felt. Ketheria was far away. I pushed the sickness back down, but it didn't go easily. I reached into my pocket, fished out a tablet, and popped it into my mouth. I didn't need anything getting in the way of my training. But I knew that was just an excuse.

In the food commons, I grabbed an olack, a sweet fleshy fruit Switzer had shown me, from the food wall. I also grabbed a bowl of protein grains. I ate some of it while walking, but I tossed most of it. Out of the corner of my eye, I caught Switzer with some of the other Space Jumpers. I tried to picture the old Switzer I knew popping up on that pirate ship as a kid. He had to have been scared. I couldn't even imagine trying to crawl inside another person to keep warm, let alone a friend.

When I reached Chausau's training facility, I found several other Space Jumpers, including Gora Bloom, already waiting on the outside platform. I also noticed several Honocks, but Charlie was not among them. I wondered where he was. I wanted to see him. Not just so I could look at his surveillance monitors again, but because I wanted my old friend back.

"I heard we're getting our belts," Switzer remarked as he stepped out from the light chute.

The best I could do was a grunt. When I offered Switzer no more, he walked over to Gora. Chausau entered from above, just as he had last cycle, but this time with a Honock in tow. The Honock, floating behind Chausau, concentrated on the platform below as if to make sure he wouldn't miss it. Clutched in his arms was a collection of Space Jumper belts.

"I have here your most prized possession!" Chausau shouted to us from the middle platform. "This single item has as much value as the Source used to ignite your existence. Lose this and you may as well lose your life!"

Chausau took the belts from the Honock and held them up.

"Well, what are you waiting for? Come and get them."

I looked at Gora and Switzer. They were trying to find a way across to Chausau, but there was none. His platform was too far to physically jump across the void to, and there was no craft to take them. Was I supposed to jump? I could do it without a belt, although I had only done it around Ketheria, or when I got upset. Even that little glitch had seemed to fade, however. Was this a test?

I concentrated on the center platform, trying to will myself there, but it was no use. I might as well have been trying to move the platform to me. If I was a Space Jumper who could jump without a belt, someone was going to have to show me how. I was relieved to think the burak would take that pressure off me. I was anxious to get that belt.

"Well?" Chausau called out. Then he was next to Switzer. "That's a joke. Of course you can't do it without the belt. That was the whole point."

I watched him hand a belt to Gora and then to Switzer. I could see Gora's eyes light up as he cradled the belt in his hands. Then Chausau turned to me. There were no more belts left.

"But I *was* hoping to be surprised by you," he cried. "Are the rumors false?"

"What rumors?"

"What rumors?" he said, loud enough for everyone to hear. "The rumor that you can move through space and time without a belt. That you possess an ability no other Space Jumper has ever exhibited . . . until now."

Chausau's face was centimeters from mine, and the intense air from his nostrils pushed against my skin. I didn't dare move.

"Care to demonstrate this extraordinary ability?"

"I can't," I mumbled.

"Speak up!"

"I can't!"

Chausau circled me. "You can't or you won't? I've been told that you never require a belt. That you can jump whenever you like."

"You're wrong. It's not like that," I told him. "It's tied some-how to my sister. I can't just jump when I feel like it."

"I'm *wrong*?" The other Space Jumpers standing along the railing chuckled. "I'm never wrong. Just ask any one of them. The fact that you can't jump whenever you want has to do with this," he said, and stabbed my head with his finger. "It has nothing to do with this." Chausau then stabbed at my heart. "But that's what you're here for. I will awaken that part of you that can control your gift, to make it part of you, a function as automatic as breathing. That is, if it's even true."

Chausau walked away. "Put your new belts on!" he cried.

"Look at them! Are they not beautiful? They are yours now. Take care of them as if your life depends on them—because it does."

I stood there as the other Space Jumpers cheered. I watched Switzer and Gora slip their belts around their waists and admire them. I couldn't look at the others, though. I only stared at the belts. I hated Chausau for singling me out like this. I didn't want the other Space Jumpers to look at me without a belt, naked and waiting for ridicule. Switzer looked up and ours eyes met. I expected to see that stupid smirk on his face. I assumed he would be the first to ignite my long and torturous humiliation, but he didn't. No, it was much worse than that. When I looked at Switzer, I saw pity. Pity for me. I wanted to die.

Chausau assigned a Space Jumper and a Honock to Switzer and then to Gora and instructed them to walk the new owners through their belt's interface.

"What am I supposed to do?" I asked as Chausau walked past me.

"Come with me," he said, and my nostrils immediately filled with the stench of feet.

Chausau released his grip, and I found myself standing with him on the center platform.

"Warn me next time you're going to do that, will ya?" I said.

"Hopefully there won't be a next time. Quirin has informed me of the details of your ability, and it seems quite simple. Unlike those who use a belt, you cannot jump with anyone in tow. Only a belt can create the proper time distortion for that. If you try, you will kill them. And you do not need to put coordinates in a belt as we do; you simply need to know *where* you're jumping."

"That seems pretty limiting, don't you think? Why don't you just give me a belt, like them, so I can learn this properly? Why burden me with those limitations?"

"It's not the limitations that count. It's the freedom to jump whenever you want. Imagine yourself torn apart in battle protecting the Scion. If you had a belt and it was lost or damaged you would be useless. But not you. You can still jump. It is a gift beyond comprehension. They will fill moons with stories about you."

"I don't want anyone to write anything," I spat.

"That is not up to you. Your burden is to master your gift. That is your only concern. Do you see the spot where you were just standing?" he asked, pointing back to the railing near the light chute.

"Yes," I grumbled.

"That is your goal. That is where you are going."

"How? Aren't you supposed to teach me?"

"Did someone teach you to breathe?"

"That's a stupid question."

"Really? When you concentrate on your breathing, you can block out most of the deconstructive energy that flows through you. When you concentrate on your ability, you can block out most of the Universe, as well as its physical form. You may then choose what part of the Universe will be manifested in your presence. *You* choose your own reality, Space Jumper. Whether you are here or there is up to you. Matter does not exist until it is observed; until then, it's simply waiting for you."

Then Chausau jumped, and a moment later I spotted him near the light chute where I had started.

"That doesn't make any sense!" I yelled after him, but he only turned and walked over to Switzer.

How was I going to get over there? What kind of training was this? I looked around the platform, but for what? I had no clue. Maybe I could find something to tell me what to do, but the circular markings I saw on the floor were nothing more than decorations.

You have to concentrate. But I just stood there with my arms crossed, watching the others. Gora and Switzer looked like they were swapping notes as the other Jumpers explained the workings of their new belts. Why wasn't that me? Why did I always seem to be the one like *this*? Abandoned in the middle of nowhere and left to figure things out for myself. I hated it. It wasn't fair.

"Hey, I can't do it!" I yelled. Switzer looked up as my cry echoed back to me. I cringed as my whining replayed across the void.

I sat down near the center of the platform in an attempt to concentrate, but concentrate on what? My breathing? That seemed like a bunch of nonsense to me. I closed my eyes and took in a deep breath.

Nothing.

The sound of laughter from the others across the void crept

into my mind. *Push that out. Concentrate on the spot. Picture it in your head.*

Still nothing.

"This is stupid!" I cried, standing up. No one looked across at me this time, not even Switzer. "Hey!"

I stared at the spot near the light chute. I pictured myself standing there. I clenched down on my back teeth, trying to focus harder on the location. I even bulged my eyes for effect.

"Oh, this is useless," I said, and flopped back down. This time, I sat at the edge of the platform and let my feet dangle over. I wanted to throw something down the void, to hear how long it took before it hit bottom. At that moment, I almost pushed myself off the platform. I almost threw myself down the void just to see what would happen. My arms tensed, and I even felt the rush inside my stomach just before someone does such a stupid thing. Of course it was a stupid thing. Chausau wouldn't have kicked me over if there were any chance I could die, but he wasn't here right now was he? Why even take the chance?

I looked up to see where Chausau was, but I couldn't find him. He had left. So, too, had Switzer and Gora. I watched the other Space Jumpers gather their things and leave as well.

"Hey, what about me?" I yelled.

A moment later, I was alone. Now all I *could* hear was my own breathing. Immediately I began to wonder how long Chausau would leave me here. What if I got hungry? What if I had to go to bathroom? *I could always void over the void,* I thought.

How pathetic. Look at me. What a malf.

All I had to do was jump. I had done it before. *But that was different,* I tried to reason. Ketheria was in danger. That's what triggered my jump, and the time in the food chamber I was simply angry. *Then get angry.*

I clenched my fist and snorted. Then I narrowed my eyes. I recalled every cliché I could think of to express my anger. Then I thought about Switzer and Queykay, even Odran and Weegin. I thought about the time Weegin tried to sell us, and I thought about my life on the *Renaissance.* The anger smoldered, and soon a small flame ignited all those things I wanted to say but never did. I was getting very angry now. I could feel it. I stood up and concentrated on the spot near the light chute. Oh, I was mad, really mad . . .

Nothing.

I screamed. I guess I wasn't mad enough. I lay back on the platform with my hands behind my head. My headache, the one always lurking just behind my eyes, raged against my forehead now. I reached into my pocket for one of the tablets, hoping for relief, but I paused before popping it into my mouth. These things weren't stopping me, were they? I didn't eat much or even sleep much when I took them, and it made me wonder if they were part of the problem. It seemed unlikely, but I still tossed the tablet over the edge. In fact, I turned my pocket inside out and let all of the tablets tumble into the void. I waited to hear if the tablets ever hit bottom, but I never heard a thing. *Must be too small to make a sound, anyway,* I told myself.

Then the lights went out.

• • •

I think I fell asleep shortly after the place went dark. I remember staring up at the soft blue haze in the ceiling and wondering about Max. I didn't dream about her. In fact, I don't remember dreaming about anything at all. I woke to the sound of Space Jumpers filing into the training area. I saw Switzer and Gora and then immediately looked up. Chausau should be descending upon my platform like he always did, but I saw nothing. Instead I heard him across the way. He had used the light chute, bypassing me completely. They were ignoring me, I realized.

I sat and watched Switzer make his first jump with the belt. After several tandem jumps with another Space Jumper, he moved from one platform to another. The others cheered and gathered around him, thumping him on his back. I could see him smiling even from where I sat. I hope he enjoyed the smell of stinky feet.

Gora was next. I watched him fidget with his belt as if he was checking and re-checking something, or everything, while the others waited patiently. When he did manage to jump, he found himself teetering close to the edge of the other platform. So close that he almost missed his mark entirely. Everyone remained breathless, even me, until he steadied himself and found solid footing. He turned and thrust his arms into the air, his tentacles wiping widely about, and a cheer erupted.

"Goodie for you," I said.

They made it look so easy with the belt. *Why not just give me one?* I could learn the harder way later. I wanted to be next so badly. I wanted the others to cheer as I jumped from platform to platform. I knew I could skip across every one of them if they just gave me one of those stupid belts. I sat back, concentrating on the platform they were all standing on. I would show them. I'd jump over there and demand a belt. I focused hard, willing every cell of my body away from the space I was currently occupying. I dove deep inside, looking for any exit out of my current reality. Something tingled. I was close. A little more.

Nothing.

I looked up, and Chausau was making them jump again. I couldn't hear what he said, but everyone stood still, listening carefully. I turned my back to them and started thinking about my stomach. Despite the nausea, I was starving. Right now I was so hungry, I'd even eat that slop Odran used to feed us. I tried to concentrate on the food hall. Maybe the hunger would help me. But I found nothing to grab on to. Why wouldn't they give me some sort of instruction? This was ridiculous.

I sat firmly rooted in my self-pity and continued to watch the triumphs of the Hollow's newest recruits. Switzer seemed more confident than Gora, jumping much faster and even able to pick up an object from one platform while jumping to another. I saw him for only a split second before he appeared on the platform far to my right. Gora was a little slower. I supposed he was having trouble setting the coordinates in the belt fast enough. Maybe he wasn't that attuned to working with his softwire. I wanted to jump so bad that the pain was worse than the hole now growing in my stomach.

After nearly a cycle, they all left, not a single one of them acknowledging me or even glancing in my direction. I curled up on the floor, hoping sleep would come quickly. I did try to jump once more, but it was useless. I didn't know what to do.

"Wake up," something shouted as I felt the weight of a boot push against my ribs.

I opened my eyes to find Chausau standing above me.

"I can't do it," I mumbled, and curled back up.

This time Chausau kicked me. "That's because you're weak."

"No, it's because no one has shown me how to do it. You show Switzer and Gora how to work their belts. Everyone is there helping them learn, but I'm supposed to figure it out myself. Why?"

"You were given all of the skills to perform your task. In fact, you have already done it. No one can show you because you are the only one who can do it. Yet you sit here as if someone owes you something. As if it is our responsibility to take your hand and do it for you. You are pathetic, and you are lazy."

"Yeah, well, you're ugly."

Five other Space Jumpers appeared on my platform. Each of them was carrying some sort of teal-colored piece of metal. The strain in their muscles told me that the pieces were heavy.

"On your knees, Jumper," Chausau ordered.

"What are you doing?" I asked.

"On your knees!" Chausau kicked me again, lifting me off the floor. I got on my knees. Two of the Space Jumpers moved in and placed their pieces of metal on either side of me. They pushed them together, slamming against my knees. I lifted my knees, and the pieces slid together perfectly, stopping at my waist, with barely enough room left for me. I could feel the rough iron against my legs, my hips, even my feet.

"Chausau, what are you doing?"

"Put your arms out in front of you."

"Why?"

"Do it!" Chausau screamed in my face, and my arms shot forward, a survival reflex.

The other two Jumpers placed two more pieces of the puzzle around my chest, shoulders, and arms, locking me in the metal cocoon. The only part of me that was exposed was my head. I couldn't hold the weight of the thing, and I toppled forward, slamming against the platform. The sound of metal striking metal rang across the void.

"What are you doing, Chausau?" I pleaded.

I tried to look up, but the metal was too close to the base of my skull. All I could do was stare at their feet.

"You wanted help. This is how I will help you."

"By locking me up? I already can't get off this platform."

"You're not staying here," he whispered.

I watched the feet move away from me. "Where are you going?" I screamed.

Then I heard a clink, and then another. I felt myself lift off the platform. Something was pulling me into the air. When I cleared the platform, I could see the other Jumpers watching as I pulled away. Chausau was not there.

"Chausau, where are you?"

"I'm right here," I heard him say from somewhere behind

me. He must have been standing on me as I was pulled into the air.

"Please tell me what's going on."

"Your mind is your worst enemy, Softwire. The Nagools tried to bring you through your awakening their way, but now we will do it my way."

This is what Ketheria was talking about. What were they going to do me? I could hardly see the platform below me as the mist around me grew thicker. I could feel the cold moisture against my face, but then it was gone, as if we had slipped through some atmospheric cloud. I pushed against the metal cocoon, but there was no wiggle room. The metal fit as close as my own skin. But the more I pushed, the less I began to feel the metal. I couldn't move, yet I could no longer feel anything pushing against my skin. It was maddening.

In front of me I could see the plate metal wall, scarred with hooks and bare bolts. The space closed in, tapering as I rose higher and higher. Then I passed another metal cocoon bolted to the wall. It looked identical to the pieces that were placed around me. Was he going to mount me to the wall like some trophy? My metal mold swung toward the wall. Then I heard the sound of a small motor as I rotated up, my hands and knees now pointing toward the wall in front of me. To my left was another one of the metal molds. It was empty.

My cocoon hit the wall with a clank, and Chausau was now balancing himself on my arm. I heard more whirring and clicking as I was fastened in place on the wall.

"Please, Chausau, don't do this," I begged.

"A disciplined mind is a Space Jumper's best ally."

"I don't want to be a Space Jumper, Chausau, really I don't."

"Hush now. You will thank me when it is over."

Then I felt a vibration at the back of my neck, and something began to crawl across my skull, then over my eyes, and then over my mouth. My lips brushed against the crimpled surface. It was more metal, but the sensation of something pressing against my mouth soon disappeared. Finally the thing sealed itself around my neck. I screamed out, "No!" and felt my own hot breath fall back against my skin. Chausau did not answer. All I could hear was the sound of my own breathing, and soon I was no longer able to feel the warmth of it pushing back against my face.

"Chausau!" I screamed once more, and the material covering my face spilled into my open mouth. I clenched down, pushing whatever it was out of my mouth, but then the sensation of that slipped away as well. I didn't know if the stuff had worked its way down my throat or if I had been successful in pushing all of it out.

My mind scrambled for some solution, rattling in my skull, bouncing around in my head as it searched for some way out of this. I pushed outward with my mind, looking for any sort of computer device to interface with, but there was nothing. Even the interface for my arm was no longer available to me.

I needed to move, but I felt paralyzed. I thought I was moving, but I couldn't feel it. I was panicking. *Calm down,* I told myself. Think about what Ketheria said. This is their method.

Chausau mentioned that the Nagools had tried with me, but they had failed. Failed at what? My ability to jump without a belt? What was it?

Relax. I can't!

My mind was screaming again. I hated it. I wanted out, but I couldn't think of a single thing to do. I felt like I was going crazy. I wanted out of this contraption so bad, I would rather die than spend another parsec in this thing.

Then die.

What do you mean?

Give in.

Give in to what?

Just give in.

I can't! my mind screamed.

I think I fell asleep. I'm not quite sure. Maybe my brain had simply shut down. When I awoke, the futility of my situation poured back into my metal mold, but I did not panic. I was surprisingly calm. I would not let it control me this time. I knew the only way out of here was to jump, and the only way to do that was to discipline my mind.

I noticed that even the sound of my breathing was gone. I could see nothing, hear nothing, feel nothing, and smell nothing. Every part of me was completely deprived of stimuli, and I was left with only myself to talk to. *This is how Vairocina must have felt,* I thought. *Now I understand why she searched so desperately to find a real body.* But *I* was not my body. I could still think. In fact, I was talking. Talking to myself. What was this sense of self that was left to wander about my head? As if I was talking to someone else entirely. It had no physical form, yet it demanded attention. It argued with me, influenced me, praised me, and even berated me, more often than not. But where did it come from? Who controlled it? Me?

"Hello?" I said, as if to call out that part of me, to identify it as a separate entity.

It did not respond. Or did I not respond?

Despite my lack of contact with the physical world, "I" still existed. "I" existed independently of my race, my job, my clothes, even what others thought about me. For so long, I had defined myself by those things, but here, now, they meant nothing. They served no purpose whatsoever. Suddenly, I craved to see something, feel something, or hear something. I needed to know that I still existed.

But why?

Maybe *I* didn't even exist. For all I knew, I could be dead. Was this what death felt like? I hoped not. But then it struck me. I realized something about the "I" alone with me in this mold. I realized that this was the person who loved Max, who loved Ketheria and Theodore and even the Keepers. Suddenly, despite the lack of stimuli, I felt a flood of love and warmth rush through my body. I did have a body! If I could have felt it, I know I would have felt tears against my skin. I imagined my tears rolling down my cheeks and dropping off my face. In my mind, I reached down to the puddle of tears with my fingertips and raised them to my mouth. The salty teardrops touched my tongue, and I slept again.

I awoke to a blinding white light. I closed my eyes, but the light persisted, boring through to the back of my skull. Was someone doing this, or was I hallucinating the light? I tried to will the light away, but it remained. I even imagined myself lying at the bottom of a lightless tunnel, but still the white light pierced its depths. Who was doing this? *Please stop,* I begged them.

"JT? Wake up. JT?"

"Hello?" I croaked.

The light was still there, but softer somehow, as if someone had managed to gray the edges.

"Are you all right?"

"Who is that?"

It sounded like Ketheria, or was it Brine Amar? The voice seemed to change pitch every time I recognized an inflection or the speech pattern.

"You must help yourself if you are going to leave here," the voice said. It was Brine Amar.

"Why are you doing this to me? I don't know how to jump without a belt. I can only do it around Ketheria. I think Quirin made it that way."

"Yes, you can, but you refuse to release your physical body." The voice did not belong to Brine Amar. It was Ketheria.

"Who is this?" I asked again.

"Your mind is sick, and the disease is fear."

"I'm not afraid of anything."

"You are afraid of yourself."

My mind tuned out, and I turned off.

When I woke next, I was standing on the observation deck of the *Renaissance*. The ship was orbiting a dying star, and the golden light burned away the edges of everything I saw. I shielded my eyes to look at the star. *We're too close,* I thought. *The ship will burn up.*

"Mother!" I called out, but the computer did not answer.

Of course not. The *Renaissance* was gone. Dismantled and sold for parts the moment after we arrived on the Rings of Orbis, almost four rotations ago.

Was this a dream?

"Hello, JT."

I spun around. It was Max!

"Max!"

The soft cream-colored robe she wore on Orbis 4 sparkled in the intense sunlight. The edge of her hair burned blond. She was beautiful. I rushed toward her and took her hands in mine.

"Max, I'm so sorry. I should never have left you. Can you forgive me? Please. I love you so much. I want it to be just like you said with Ketheria and Theodore. Together. We can have that!"

Max shook her head gently and held her finger to my lips. I breathed in her scent, she was so close. My mind filled with flowers and sunlight and fresh running water. I wanted to hold her.

"You've done the right thing," she whispered. "I see the importance of the task that has been placed upon you. I was so selfish to want something else. You have greatness in your future. I want you to have that. You deserve it."

"But—"

"You need to get out of here, JT," Max insisted. "You have to jump. We need you. It is time."

"Time for what?"

"Time for you."

"We can stay here, Max. Just like you wanted it. We can live here on the *Renaissance* again. We'll travel the stars, just you and me. We don't have to go."

I pulled her close to me. I could feel her warmth under her robe as she pressed against me. Was this real? I pushed my lips against hers. I could taste her.

"This *is* real, Max. I know it. Can't you feel it? I don't know how I did it, but we're together again on the *Renaissance*."

Max pulled away, gently, as if not to make a statement by her actions. She reached for my hand and led me away from the observation deck. Below deck, I took the lead, remembering each corridor, stairwell, and quarters. I had forgotten how much I missed the *Renaissance*. I pulled Max into the chow synth and saw that Mother had created all of our favorite foods, but why hadn't the computer answered me?

"Max, Mother is not responding."

But Max was gone. My hand was still outstretched, but it was empty.

"Max?"

"Hey, JT."

I turned toward the voice, a new voice. I thought I recognized it but wasn't quite sure. Out of the light stepped a young man, maybe thirty Earth-years old. I recognized something in his face, and his hair was still the same unmanageable brown nest I knew.

"Theodore?" I asked the man.

"You look well, JT."

"You look . . . older. Why are you so much older than me? We're supposed to be the exact same age."

"We still are."

I looked at my hands. They looked like they always did, and they also looked liked Theodore's — older. "I don't understand."

"That's part of the problem, JT. Everything is not meant to be understood. It is impossible for you to comprehend and control every aspect of the universe. I know you always try, but sometimes you just have to accept what is. I don't know if you noticed, but I gave up counting things. That had been my way of trying to control situations. You have to trust that no matter what comes at you, you will manage. You have to trust yourself, JT."

I felt a tinge of jealousy. "How do you know?" I said. "If anyone was always afraid, it was you. Do you know how many times I wished you had spoken up to Switzer? To defend yourself? You were the one who was afraid, Theodore."

"But I'm not anymore. This is not a competition. You can see that, can't you? Now it's your turn. I know you can do it, JT. Just let go."

"Let go of what?"

"Your mind," said a voice from behind me.

I spun around and saw Ketheria sitting on my sleeper. It was just like the first time we tried to leave the *Renaissance*. A huge sack was slumped at her feet, and in her hands she held the crude locket containing the image of our parents.

"Your entire image of yourself is based on a lie," she said, holding up the makeshift locket. "That was their only mistake. They created a false dream for you—a dream of a reality that never existed. And you are holding on to that dream in the same manner the knudniks do on the Rings of Orbis. You believe that if you allow your own domestication at the hands of the Citizens, you, too, will share in all their wealth and glory. You dream of parents who left Earth for a new life, parents who never existed. You dream of a life on the Rings of Orbis with me, Max, and Theodore living free, but no one on the rings is ever free. It has all been a lie, JT."

Ketheria squeezed the locket in her hand. When she opened it again, the locket was gone and in its place was a handful of space dust. Ketheria turned her palm over, and the shimmering particles drifted across the cabin.

"Now it is time to wake up from *that* dream and create your own dream. Humans are destined to play a marvelous role in this universe. A role that awakens oppressed cultures from their own dreams, not by war but through love and kindness. We are all that is left. You and I are standing at the event horizon, JT. You and I will lead them into the light. But you must act now. I can't wait any longer for you, JT. It is time. You must trust me. You must trust yourself."

Ketheria's eyes burned with the glow. She was standing now, reaching out to me.

"Now, JT! There is no more time!"

Her mouth hung open, ripping at the edges and consuming all the light in the room as she screamed. The sound tore me away from the *Renaissance*, and I reached out, trying to hold on, but I was swallowed by the darkness bearing down on me.

I stood up. I was alone.

I gazed out from the center platform of the training area. An alarm ripped through the silence. *Was I out of the cocoon? Was this real?* I looked up to see if I could spot the metal mold, but it was too far. If I had jumped, then I could do it again. Ketheria needed me. Whatever had happened inside that thing, I knew in my heart that Ketheria needed me.

Without thinking about my body and with complete trust that I could do it, I focused on the platform across the void. It was sort of like the pushing I did when I entered a computer. I accepted the fact that I would succeed. I did not drag my body with me, or anything else, for that matter. I simply placed the "I" inside of me on the platform, as light from the room began to pull into my eyes. I breathed deeply, welcoming the smell of stinky feet.

I stood on the platform across the void and looked back at where I had just been. I expected a rush of pride to swell up inside me, but none came. There was no need. I smiled. The alarm, which was now sounding at regular intervals, told me that something was wrong. I pictured my room in the Hollow and willed myself there.

"Where did you come from?" Switzer said as I appeared in front of him.

"I jumped here," I told him.

Switzer's eyes ignited, and a smile stretched across his face. He leaped toward me, arms outstretched, ready to thump me on my back, but he stopped.

"You still pissed at me?" he asked, his old mask slipping over his face.

"No," I said. "That was then. There's nothing I can do about it, and you've worked hard to gain my trust. Just like a friend would do."

Switzer smiled.

"What's the alarm about?" I asked.

"I was about to go look. It just started."

"I'll go with you," I said.

But before we could leave, the door to the room disappeared and one of Switzer's friends rushed in. "The Scion is gone!"

"What do you mean?" I cried.

"She's gone! Someone took her."

I pushed in front of him. "She can't be gone. She's stained. Track the staining."

"We have. There's nothing," he replied. "They're sending a team to look for her."

The Space Jumper turned to leave, and I was close behind.

"Where are you going?" Switzer cried.

"I know how to find her," I said.

"I'm coming with you."

I ran all the way to Charlie's little surveillance room. While I thumped on the grille to his hideout, I cursed at myself, thinking I could simply have jumped.

"Charlie! It's me!"

"What's a Honock going to do?" Switzer asked.

"Wait."

Charlie came to the grill and spotted Switzer. One look and he turned away.

"Charlie, it's all right. He's with me. He won't hurt you."

"I didn't hurt you the first time," Switzer added.

"Charlie, Ketheria's in trouble, We have to find her."

Charlie peeked through the grate. After an excruciatingly long moment, he hoisted the gate off it moorings. I slipped past Charlie and dashed to the monitors. They were already on. I scoured the screens for any sign of Ketheria, but there was nothing. In fact, there was no sign of Max or Theodore, either.

"They're all gone," Charlie informed me.

"What's this?" Switzer asked, looking around the room.

"There's no time to explain. We have to get assigned to that search party. Meet me back at our room." I turned to Charlie. "Keep looking for them, will you? Search everywhere you can. There must be a sign of one of them somewhere."

Then I jumped to Quirin's room. I didn't even shoot for outside; I went straight in.

"Just because you've accepted your skill does not mean you should abandon your manners," he said.

"I want to be on that search party you are sending for my sister."

"Impossible," he replied. "Tensions are too delicate on the rings. I cannot have a Space Jumper moving about freely. It will tip the scales in the Council's favor. We cannot have a war."

"But I have to go! I am the Tonat, aren't I?"

"I have sent four experienced Jumpers who will find the Scion without anyone ever seeing them. You will finish with your training."

"How will they find her? The staining doesn't work anymore," I told him.

"That is impossible. The staining is foolproof. I invented it. This is merely a glitch in the system. The staining will locate her much more easily than you can."

"You don't know about the Scion. She can do things you don't know about."

"There is no argument that will change my mind. Go back to your quarters. This will be over shortly."

"Quirin, please—"

"Go!"

I left his room, certain he was wrong. Ketheria was trying to tell me something. I knew it. When I returned to my room, I found Switzer lying on his bunk.

"Get up," I ordered him.

"Where are we going now?" he asked, sitting up.

"We're going home," I informed him.

"Have fun." Switzer flopped back onto his sleeper.

I slipped through space, compressing the distance between

us. The room blurred, and in the exact same moment, I was standing next to Switzer. Using my right arm, I grabbed him by his uniform and dragged him off his sleeper. With one clean jerk, I hoisted him high in the air, his shocked expression staring down at his feet, which were nowhere near the ground now.

"You're coming with me, and you're bringing Charlie. I don't have a belt, so I can't jump with him. It could kill him. You're bringing him back for me. You owe me that, and you owe him at least that. This is not the life he was supposed to live. Charlie doesn't deserve to live here any more than you deserved to live in that hole I rescued you from."

"Fine, enough with the melodrama. Put me down."

I let Switzer fall to the floor but he jumped in midair, reappearing soundly on his feet.

"Nice," I said, nodding at his acrobats. "Now let's get Charlie. I need to get to Max and Theodore."

16

"I don't want to go," Charlie snapped after I told him what we were doing.

"Suits me," Switzer said, turning back down the hall.

"Wait," I cried. "Charlie, look at the screens. Ketheria's gone. Max and Theodore will know where she is. We have to find them. I want you to come with me."

Charlie looked at the screens but shook his head. While he stared, I slipped into the computer device at the back of his head. With the precision of a laser drill, I adjusted the controls for memory, then pulled out.

"What did you do?" Switzer grumbled. "He's crying now."

Charlie was staring at the screens and weeping. Maybe I should have adjusted the controls for emotions when I was in there, but I didn't have time.

"Charlie? You all right?" I asked him.

He turned and said, "Let's go find them."

As Charlie stood up, Switzer said, "Wait. I can't jump without the coordinates. I'm not like you. All you have to do is bring up a memory. I'm sorry, but I can't take him to Orbis 4."

"Charlie, that surveillance system we watch—there must be some sort of coordinates link with it, right? I mean, if they're spying on people, they must know where they're looking. Can you pull up the coordinates off one of those cameras and give them to Switzer?"

Charlie parked himself in front of the O-dats without speaking. After a few moments, a stream of digits rolled across the screens.

"I only need one," Switzer scoffed.

Charlie tapped on one screen, and a single string of symbols flashed on the O-dat.

"That's JT's room," he said.

"Grab it," I told Switzer.

Switzer interfaced with the O-dat and uplinked the info Charlie had provided. "All set," he replied.

"You go first," I told him.

"Why, you don't trust me?"

"Just go first. I'll see you in my room."

"Come on, big guy," he said to Charlie. "Let's hope you stay in one piece."

"Don't say that!" I said.

But they were gone. The air rippled the moment Switzer latched on to Charlie while any light reflecting off them broke apart and scattered across the room. I envisioned my room on Orbis 4 and jumped right behind them.

Within the same breath, I was standing next to my old sleeper with Switzer and Charlie, trying to rub the smell of feet out of my nose.

"I know you were messy on the *Renaissance*," Switzer said, looking around my room, "but this is ridiculous."

Switzer nudged an errant pot with his toe, a pot I had never seen before. It rolled toward my sleeper, the lid of which hung at a reckless angle, as if someone had tried to rip the sleeper from its moorings. Someone or something had destroyed my room.

"I didn't leave my room like this," I said. "Something is wrong. Hurry, we need to find them."

Outside my room, the walls were marred with charcoal streaks, results of a plasma rifle. I maneuvered around an overturned bench and noticed that a chunk of the wall was completely missing. Switzer stepped over a discarded wall panel and crushed the remains of an uprooted plant.

"What happened here?" I asked. "And where is everyone?"

"Someone was either looking for something or just felt like trashing the place," Switzer answered.

"I saw it," Charlie murmured. "It looked like a bit of both."

"Max's room is right up here," I told them.

My stomach flipped once when I said her name and then settled at an uncomfortable angle when I paused outside her room. How would she react when she saw me? How would I react? I was so confident about finding them, but the thought of speaking to Max made me uncertain. Switzer reached past me and thumped on the door. No one answered. I pushed into the door's control panel and opened it.

"Max! Max, you here?" I called toward the bathroom without entering her room, but there was no sign of her.

Switzer whistled. "Wow, and I thought you were the messy one."

"Be quiet. It's obvious someone has trashed the place. Let's check Theodore's room."

"He's not there, either," someone said behind me.

I turned to find Queykay, flanked by four armed guards, standing at the top of the corridor. The faceless creatures, protected by long, chrome chest plates, took cautious positions around Queykay, as if ready for a fight. I had no intention of giving them one.

"They're all gone, including your sister," he said.

"Where are they?" I demanded to know.

"I was hoping that maybe you knew where they were."

"Why? Because it doesn't look good that the Trading Council doesn't know where the Scion is? Are you afraid of her power?"

"The Trading Council has far more power than you will ever have."

The four armed guards took a step toward me, their plasma rifles readied in their grips.

"Actually, I do know where one of them is," he added as an afterthought. "The one you call Theodore has been arrested for treason. I personally stopped his plot to overthrow the Council."

"That's not true!" I cried, and the guards raised their weapons at me.

"Then what *is* true?" he asked.

What had Theodore gotten himself into? Where were the others?

"Do you have something to tell us?" Queykay said.

"I don't have to tell you anything. You have no authority over me."

"That's where you are wrong. Things have changed since you left, Softwire. The Trading Council has invoked certain privileges, and I am here to enforce them. For one, strolling about the ring with a convicted wormhole pirate is definitely grounds for treason charges." Queykay pointed a long bony finger at Switzer. "Seize them!" he ordered.

"Stop!" Hach cried as he rushed into the corridor just behind the security guards. "What are you doing, Queykay? This is still *my* house," he insisted.

"The Trading Council has jurisdiction over it now."

"That's ridiculous!"

"The Chancellor has suspended all civil rights, but how could you know that, with the time you spend on Ki and Ta tending to your privileged mining rights?" Queykay turned back to us. "Arrest the enemy," Queykay growled, pointing at me. "He is a Space Jumper. The Council has clearly—"

"The Council does nothing *clearly*," Hach interrupted. He pointed at the armed guards. "Who are these men?"

"These are the Trading Council's Preservation Forces."

"Preservation Forces? I know nothing of this."

"The Council has enlisted their services, and I have been given authority to use them. I signed the order myself. If you continue to interfere, then I will have them arrest you as well."

"I will not abide by this foolish rule!" Hach cried, and reached inside his long jacket.

As Hach stepped back to remove his weapon, the four guards turned their focus on him. "Now!" Switzer hissed, and we both jumped at the same time.

I moved across the room and refocused just behind the guard on the far right of Queykay. I stepped into him, and knocked his rifle away with my strong arm. Switzer struggled with the two guards closest to Queykay, while Charlie lunged for the remaining one. I watched Charlie bend the guard's gun in half as if it were made of rubber and then fling the guard thirty meters over his head and down the hall. The guard slid along the floor and hit the wall with a thud. He did not move again.

From the corner of my eye, I watched Queykay fling back his thick cloak as he squared off against Hach. Queykay's brood, the disgusting creatures that fed off his body, launched at Hach the moment the light hit them. The squirrely creatures were at least a foot long now, and more than two dozen of them landed on Hach. He dropped his weapon, clawing at the creatures as they bit into his neck and face.

"No!" I cried.

While I watched Hach writhing under the sickening creatures, Queykay thrust a Zinovian Talon into Hach's ribs. I grabbed Queykay's arm, but when he pulled back, I saw the empty cartridge from the talon dangling from Queykay's hand. His brood must have tasted the poison now running through Hach's veins; they scurried back to their father like maggots scrambling over rotten meat. I ran to Hach's side.

"Don't fight it," Queykay whispered to Hach. "It will be over quickly. There is no room on the rings for sympathizers. The Keepers have broken their agreement, and they must be punished. Their time on the Rings of Orbis is finished, with or without the Scion."

I held Hach's head as Queykay casually reloaded his talon.

"I'm sorry," Hach breathed. "I thought I was doing good. I thought you and the Scion would be safe here. I failed."

"Do you know where they are?" I whispered.

"They disappeared after Theodore was taken. I think Ketheria knew. They are nowhere to be found. I should have been here." Hach's voice was almost a whisper.

"What did Ketheria know? Hach!" His eyes began to roll back into his head. I turned to Queykay. "Help him!" I cried, but he only smiled.

"Your Guarantor was given lucrative mining rights to new fields on the crystal moons in exchange to protect you. He made this deal with the Keepers. I have no intention of helping him."

I looked at Hach, his face and neck a bloody mess. "Is this true?"

He nodded.

"Why?"

Hach swallowed hard but did not reply.

"That's a question for the Keepers," Queykay hissed. "They have broken the treaty, and now we will take what is ours."

Switzer stepped toward Queykay as he removed a small

communication device from his robe and raised it to his mouth. "I have the Tonat," he said into the device.

"Wow, for a Trading Council member, you are one dumb alien!" Switzer cried. Then he jumped across the room and refocused next to Charlie. "We're Space Jumpers!"

As if on cue, I jumped at the same time Switzer did. I couldn't look at Hach. I knew he was dying. I didn't want to think about the deal he had made with the Keepers. I liked Hach and wanted to leave it that way, whether he was dead or alive.

I knew where Switzer was going. He only had the coordinates for one place on Orbis 4, and I jumped there. I wished it was a little farther away from Queykay, but it would have to do. I refocused back in my room, with Switzer and Charlie at my side.

"They made some pretty good improvements to you," Switzer said to Charlie, lifting his right arm and inspecting it like part of a ship's engine.

Charlie pulled his arm away. "I wish I could remember you," he said.

"No, you don't," Switzer replied.

"What do we do now?" I asked.

"I don't know; this is your plan."

"We need to get out of here, but you can't jump without coordinates. We have to walk out."

"That's not going to happen without some firepower."

"Well, whatever we do, we have to do it quickly. Vairocina?"

"JT? You're back!" her voice rang inside my head. "I'm so pleased to hear your voice."

"Well, it's not a scheduled visit, that's for sure, but listen, I'm in trouble. I need some help with burak coordinates for Orbis 4. Is there any way to uplink them from my room?"

"Why don't you—?"

"It's not for me. It's for Switzer."

"Oh."

"Vairocina?"

"Hurry up," Switzer urged.

"The only O-dat I see working near you is located inside Ketheria's chambers," she replied.

"It's not far," I told Switzer.

"JT, someone has placed a query on your whereabouts within the central computer. They are commencing a trace at this very moment," she informed me.

I remembered what they did to Ganook before I left. I assumed they had placed a trace on him and then sent some sort of explosive to finish him off. Would Queykay try to kill me?

"Can you do anything to slow them down?" I asked her.

"It will not be permanent."

"Do what you can," I told her. "And get ready with the coordinates for Switzer." I turned to Switzer and Charlie. "We have to move now. If I start turning blue, move away from me quickly."

"What does that mean?" Switzer asked.

"Just do it."

Ketheria's room was not far away, but I had no idea where Queykay and his goons had gone. I was certain that he had initiated the trace, but I was also sure he didn't think I would still be in the building. I knew that once he discovered I was still there, I would have very little time to get the coordinates into Switzer's belt. I took the lead and slipped through the debris, careful not to attract attention. Inside the main chamber, I headed straight to Ketheria's room.

"I don't remember her being the tidy one," Switzer said as all three of us filled her room. Charlie went to a table near Ketheria's bed, where some of her personal things were still arranged neatly, as if she would be right back. Charlie picked up a hairbrush and cradled it in his clumsy hands.

"You miss her, don't you?" I whispered, and he only smiled.

"Can we get on with this?" Switzer grunted.

"Vairocina, you ready?"

"Almost," she replied. "There is an O-dat in her room. Have Switzer interface with the device."

"Over there," I told Switzer, pointing to the O-dat screen on the table.

"Tell him that in the system's local memory, there is a file marked *charts*. It's big, but I just grabbed everything I had."

"Look for something called charts," I called out to him.

"Got it!" he replied.

Charlie returned the brush to its original place and looked around the room. "No one would hurt Ketheria," he said.

"That's where you are wrong," Queykay said, stepping into the room, the Talon already drawn.

"Switzer?"

"Not yet," he croaked, and I nudged Charlie to move toward him.

"It was simple. You did not want to be the Tonat. With you out of the way, the Council could control the Scion. We were in charge. Everyone feared she was not safe; we proved that. The Council would protect her, *for their Citizens*. Everything would have run smoothly, but you just couldn't play along, could you?"

"You staged her assassination attempt, didn't you? She read your mind. That's why she's not here. You can't be trusted."

"I'll make you a deal," Queykay continued, slinking into Ketheria's room. I could see the Preservation Forces moving in the shadows of the other room and Queykay's army of assassins rippling at the collar of his cloak. "You help me find her, and I'll spare your life."

"What about *her* life?" I said.

"The Scion will be very useful to the new Council. Of course we would protect her."

"Don't believe him," Switzer groaned. His voice was strange. I looked over and saw that he was swaying slightly.

"Switzer?"

His knees buckled, and Queykay raised his talon. I jumped across the room and refocused right under the weapon. I sprang straight up and knocked the weapon from Queykay's grip as it discharged, the poison spear now safely lodged in the ceiling.

"You stupid—"

But before he could finish the insult, I landed on Queykay and delivered a thunderclap to his neck.

"You really are dumb," I said as Queykay crumpled underneath me. I saw the Preservation Forces scrambling in the other room, so I pushed into Ketheria's door and jammed the energy field, preventing the others from entering. Two of Queykay's brood had escaped and sunk their teeth into my robotic arm. I already had the pain turned off. I felt nothing, but more were crawling toward my feet.

"Wrong arm, kids," I said, and flicked them off. They screamed as they splattered against the wall. The others hesitated between their father and me before choosing to retreat. They were not very brave now that he was unconscious.

"Switzer!" I turned and saw him slipping to his knees as Charlie pulled on his right arm.

"Vairocina, what did you give him?"

"I told you it was a lot of information. I didn't know what exactly to leave out or if you would have another chance to do this again. He will be fine in a moment."

"We don't have a moment!"

"Switzer! Switzer!" I yelled. I turned and saw the guards hacking their way through the wall, bypassing the energy field all together. A chunk of the wall landed on the floor. They were almost through.

"Uh . . . too much . . ." he groaned, his eyes rolling back in his head. I remembered when this happened to Theodore; he was out for a whole cycle.

"Switzer. Do you have it all? Come on. We have to go!"

Charlie helped me get Switzer to his feet. He was barely conscious. There was no way he could jump, let alone take Charlie with him.

The forces were almost through the wall.

"Take his belt," Charlie said.

"What?"

"Take his belt and jump with all three of us."

"But I've never used a belt," I told him. "I don't know—"

"The belt is only there to create the pathway for me and him. You do not even need it."

"But what if it doesn't work. What if I—"

"You'll do fine. You're a Space Jumper."

I unclipped the belt from Switzer's waist. It was warm. I slipped it around my own and let it hang down over my right thigh. There was no time to adjust it. I held up the other side with my left arm.

"Grab him and get close to me," I told Charlie. "And if this doesn't work, I'm sorry."

I pictured the city of Murat in my head and interfaced with the belt. I activated the only button on the belt that I had ever seen before—the button that I thought had once killed Switzer, back on Orbis 2. It felt like forever before the smell of stinky feet invaded my senses.

17

I half expected to find Max waiting for me. I half expected to find Charlie in little pieces at my feet and Switzer lost in some corner of the universe, but none of that came true, especially the Max part. Before I jumped, I had pictured the concert area she had shown me on Murat, recalling my amazement that she had remembered my interest in music and thinking it was one of the finest moments of my life. Standing on the stone steps with only Charlie and Switzer at my side, I looked up as the ring unrolled its shadow across the city.

"Where are you, Max?" I whispered.

"We'll find her," Charlie replied.

"Vairocina?" I called out.

"You're safe!" she cried.

"You have to tell me if anyone puts another trace on me, all right? And don't worry about Switzer. According to the central computer, he's dead, but you need to give me as much time as you can. I can't risk what they did to Ganook."

"Of course," she said.

"Can you find any sign of Theodore?"

"No, I've been looking. I cannot trace his staining unless a Citizen initiates it, and can find no record of this happening. The Keepers may have done it, but I have not been able to breach their security."

"Then you have to get ahold of Theylor for me. I need to meet with him, but be very careful. I don't know who's on what side anymore. After you establish a meeting place, check to see if a trace is placed on me. If there is, then we'll know what side Theylor is on."

"Where do you want to meet him?"

"Across from the Center for Relief and Assistance. I think I might know where they are holding Theodore."

While we waited for Theylor, Vairocina discovered two different traces placed on me.

"Can you trust him?" Switzer said.

"I want to," I replied, refusing to believe that it was Theylor who had initiated the trace. "We need to keep moving."

The more I jumped around Murat, the more obvious it seemed that war was coming to the Rings of Orbis. Vairocina had given Switzer plenty of coordinates for Murat, and this enabled us to move freely. Each time we jumped, we found barricaded streets, closed trading chambers, and barely a person to be seen. The three of us stuck out everywhere we jumped, so we glued ourselves to the shadows.

When Vairocina informed me that Theylor was waiting for us, I jumped once more to shake off anyone who might be tracing me. Switzer was walking on his own now, but not saying too much except to warn me.

"I don't trust those two-headed space monkeys," he hissed.

"I trust Theylor," I reassured him.

Across from the Keepers' aid center, I saw Theylor standing near one of those sleeper arches that Theodore had used. I watched him open a capsule and place something inside it. He closed it and slipped away.

"I'll get it," Charlie said. "You stay here."

Theylor was being careful. That worried me. How bad were things now? Charlie returned with a tap and handed it to me. I pushed in and grabbed Theylor's message.

"Wait here," I told them, and stepped out into the open courtyard. I felt naked.

On the tap were simple instructions, yet they were odd just the same. Theylor instructed me to walk across the stone plaza and jump when I reached the center. I was supposed to jump to the darkened alley directly across from the center, less than thirty meters away.

"Good," Theylor said when I had refocused in the shadow of the empty alley. "If anyone was following you, they would assume you jumped far from here. Follow me."

The Keeper turned away, his purple robe brushing against my leg. Another fifty meters down the alley and the Keeper pushed opened the dull-looking door of a lifeless building. Inside, the air felt bitter, as if trapped in a long-sealed metal container.

"How are you?" he asked, and offered me a metal crate for a seat.

"I'm good, Theylor, but I can't say the same for the Rings of Orbis."

"No, you are right. It seems the Council wants a war and the Descendants of Light are willing to oblige."

"Drapling?"

Theylor removed a small light source from the depths of his rope and placed it on the floor. The blue light exposed the veins glowing under his skin like circuits in a computer. "They feel empowered by the presence of the Scion. They believe the Ancients will return now," he confessed.

"Will they?"

"It is foolish to believe that the Ancients are still alive, Johnny. This is the reason we have worked so hard to bring you and your sister to the Rings of Orbis. Humans were the last chance for this universe. The Ancients sacrificed everything when they found your Earth, so isolated from everything else in the galaxy. Yet they feared that humans were too far along in their evolution to ever seed a Scion. To solve this, they moved backward through time, to find the precise moment to best alter the human race and seed your fate. It was almost ninety thousand rotations ago that this journey began. You were the very last component of the intricate project. But what the Ancients did is something that breaks all rules of physics. You cannot go backward in time without destroying what you leave; it is a one-way journey. However, the Ancients knew that unless they did so, someone like your sister could never be born.

"This was their sacrifice, and they have succeeded. The Scion has almost completed her enlightenment. We are so close to fulfilling the dream of the Ancients. Ketheria will have the power to enlighten every one of us and connect us all to the Source. It is our only defense against the Knull."

"How can she do this from the rings?"

Theylor did not answer.

"But she's gone now. What's going to happen?" I pressed.

Theylor shook his head. I was suddenly aware of how familiar he was now with Earth gestures.

"Why can't you find her?" I said. "That's why you agreed to the staining in the first place, isn't it? How else could you keep track of her? You knew back then."

"We do not understand how she's doing it. Drapling is livid. Somehow she has cloaked her staining. She is nowhere to be found. In our defense, we had never stained a Scion before."

"You never stained my sister before," I reminded him.

"You must find her and bring her to us."

"I don't think she'll come."

"Why do you say that?"

"Because if she trusted you, she would have gone to you already."

"It is the Descendants of Light who cannot be trusted. They want to *use* the Scion just as the Council would use a weapon. They believe she can unite the knudniks and the new Citizens against the Council and the First Families. The DOL have never forgotten the humiliation and loss caused by the War of Ten

Thousand Rotations. They are convinced that the Scion can bring them revenge."

"Can she?"

"She is the Scion. Of course she can."

"I have no idea where she is," I told him.

Both of Theylor's heads stared at me, each one creased with anxiety.

"But—"

I interrupted him. "Do you know where Theodore is? Is he where they held Switzer?" If anyone knew Ketheria's whereabouts, it was Theodore. I was certain of it.

Theylor shook his head and said, "We have been trying, all of us."

"Trying what?" I asked.

"To keep him alive. The Trading Council has charged him with treason. The penalty is death, even for a Citizen."

"You have to stop them!"

"The Council has convinced the Citizens that unless the Scion is controlled, she is a threat to their well-being. The Citizens have granted the Council control over every aspect of life on the rings, and they have banned the Keepers from participating in any decisions. This in itself is grounds for war, but the Trust does not want to attack until the Scion is located. I am afraid that Theodore, as he has been so close to you and Ketheria, is merely being used as a pawn in all of this. They are using him as an example of the Council's ability to deal with the growing rebellion of knudniks and to convince the Citizens that they can use force over the Scion's power."

"How can I get to him?"

"I am afraid it's impossible. He is guarded more carefully than the Ancients' Treasure."

"I already got through that defense," I reminded him.

As I feared, Theodore was being held in the same facility that Switzer had called home for so many phases. Theylor could not provide entry, as the Keepers had been banned from entering the holding area, and he was convinced that the Trading Council would carry out Theodore's sentence, with or without a war.

I first thought about simply jumping into Theodore's holding cell, but I didn't know which one it was, nor did Theylor. In fact, he believed they were using Theodore as bait to lure me into a trap. But if they were, why wouldn't they simply declare his location to me?

"Oh, this is ridiculous," Switzer said, bolting to his feet, as Charlie and I were discussing an assortment of strategies. "Why can't we just walk into the Keepers' building, use the light chute, and jump our way through? That's what we do. We're Space Jumpers! How many times do I have to remind you of that important fact?"

"He might be right," Charlie agreed.

"And remember: we have the Hulking Honock here. He's a regular superhero, if you ask me. I'm sure he could crack a few heads if they overwhelm us."

"You can't do that," I told him. "We don't have any weapons, and we don't have a clue what their defenses are. For all we know, they could have changed the path of the chute and directed it right into a holding cell that we can't jump out of. We may be Space Jumpers, but you seem to have forgotten most of what we learned at the Hollow."

"Well, my way has worked a million times before," he said, almost pouting.

"You're not a wormhole pirate anymore, Switzer. Look, I'm going to do this myself. I'm going to jump in there and grab Theodore and then jump out. You don't have any coordinates, and at least I know how to get inside."

"How are you going to bring him out? You don't even have a belt!"

"I'll use yours."

"And leave me here with nothing? Did you pop a chip? What if you get caught? No way. You're not taking my belt."

"Switzer. There's no other way!"

"JT, another trace has been placed on you," Vairocina whispered in my ear.

"How long do we have?" I asked her.

"They're close, maybe a fraction of a diam. If you jump now, you might be able to shake the trace."

"Thanks," I told her, and turned to Switzer. "Come on. We can't stay here."

We jumped to the far side of Murat, near the restaurant I went to with Max and Theodore. My whole life seemed marked by moments with them. I had to find them.

"Look, Switzer, do you have a better solution?" I asked, pushing Charlie into the shadows of a trading chamber.

"Of course. We can all go. You jump with me. My belt will

store the coordinates. We jump back out and then grab circuit-man here."

"You really don't trust me, do you?"

"It's not that I don't trust you; it's that I don't trust them. I've got a good thing here. I lose this belt and I have nothing. There's no way I could get back to the Hollow, and I don't even want to think about what the Council will do to me. I really thank you for getting me out of that hole, but I cannot risk going back in there. If you want your little friend, then we do it my way. I'm not letting this belt out of my sight."

"What if we jump right into *them* and give our plan away? Then we lose the element of surprise."

"I'm afraid there ain't much to give away," he said.

"Let's do it, JT," Charlie urged. "I don't think we have much time."

A clatter was seeping through the stillness. I peeked out of the shadows and glanced up the empty alley. On the horizon, a jagged line of darkness was gobbling up the sky.

"Who are they?" I whispered.

"You want to stick around here and find out?"

"Fine! Give me the belt. Charlie, we'll be right back. And stay hidden!"

Charlie nodded as Switzer unlocked his belt and moved next to me. I slipped the belt around my waist and grabbed Switzer. I was so angry with him, I wanted to throw him through the jump.

I remembered the corridor Drapling had taken me to in order to see Switzer. That's where we jumped. As we refocused,

Switzer and I crouched with our backs to each other. It was a standard position we learned using SEMs at the Hollow when jumping tandem into a hostile environment. I had never tried it before, but I needed it.

Four armed guards from the Council's Preservation Forces were marching straight toward the spot where we had materialized.

"Again!" Switzer shouted, and I jumped behind the four guards as they readied their plasma rifles.

Before they could spin around, Switzer and I dropped to the floor and swept their feet out from under them. The four guards collided into one another as Switzer and I each secured a plasma rifle. Since I had the belt, I knew Switzer was unable to jump again, so I refocused back to my original position. My hope was to keep the guards disoriented.

"Hey!" I screamed. I greeted the first guard with my right foot. I spun around and planted my new plasma rifle in the belly of the second guard. Then I turned to help Switzer.

"Could you take longer," he said. Switzer stood triumphantly over the remaining guards, who were unconscious, with both of their rifles slung over his shoulder.

"Show off," I muttered under my breath. Switzer was a natural.

I stared down the corridor. No one else was coming.

"What's wrong?" Switzer asked.

"I don't know. It seems too easy."

"I tell ya, we're Space Jumpers!"

"Still."

"Think they contacted anyone?"

"I don't think they had time," I told him.

"Your guys might have."

"Funny."

"So where's split-screen?"

"Don't call him that."

"Fine, any idea where we might locate *Theodore*?"

"He has to be in one of these rooms. You never had any guards watching your cell. I guess they weren't as afraid of you."

"Now, *that's* funny," Switzer said.

I found Theodore in the third cell down from Switzer's. He sprang from the floor when he saw me.

"JT! How—?"

"Don't worry about that. We have to get out of here."

"You want to go get circuit-man first?" Switzer asked.

"What's he doing here?" Theodore asked.

"Don't worry—he's on our side," I said.

Theodore only snorted.

"We could leave you in there, you know," Switzer said with a sneer.

"No, we won't," I argued.

I jumped to the other side of the energy field and refocused next to Theodore.

"Golden!" he cried.

"Grab on to me," I instructed.

Outside of the cell, both of us refocused next to Switzer. "Now you," I told him.

"Give me my belt. I can take both of you," Switzer protested.

"You're ridiculous," I said, unlatching the belt and handing it to Switzer. He slipped it lovingly around his waist and then held his arms out to both of us.

"Come to Papa!"

"Oh, shut up," I snapped.

Back on the surface, Charlie was waiting patiently, shrouded by the shadows. The angry mob I had seen in the distance now spilled through the streets of Murat. I had to shout in order for Charlie to hear me.

"Who are they?"

"Knudniks, Citizens, all of them angry," Charlie replied. "Very angry."

"Charlie?" Theodore said, his voice almost cracking.

"Hi, Theodore," he said. "I missed you."

"But . . . I thought . . . he . . ." Theodore was gawking at Charlie, then Switzer, then me.

"It's hard to explain, but, yes, that's Charlie."

"Part of me," he corrected me.

"The best part," I pointed out, and Charlie smiled.

"Enough with the family reunion," Switzer butted in. "I don't like hanging out here in the middle of their party."

I looked down the alley and saw that the mob was blocking the entrance. I watched hundreds of aliens file past, some with metal pipes, some with sticks, a few even with real weapons. Zinovian claws were popular, but I also saw a Fedaado blade and even a Choi cril.

"They mean business," I said.

"They're everywhere," Theodore remarked. "Ever since the Council began adding more and more restrictions on our way of life, people have been rallying. They want a war."

"So does the Council," I replied.

Suddenly I felt a horrible rumble that dampened the sound of the crowd. The shock stretched down the alley and called up the stone beneath my feet.

"What was that?" Theodore cried.

The crowd was turning. I watched a Honine backtrack and then fall. Another retreating alien stomped on his chest, and the Honine screamed in vain. I jumped to the end of the alley.

"JT!"

Panic. The crowd was rushing from something, but I could not see what that was. Another explosion. I jumped to the top of the building across the street to get a better look.

"What do you see?" Theodore called out.

I didn't speak at first. Not because I couldn't see what was coming, but because I couldn't believe it. An army of Neewalkers was marching, rolling, and flying through Murat. One machine, or monster (there wasn't much difference), rolled over anything in its path while firing at anything above it. A Neewalker, strapped to the controls, artfully maneuvered the rolling tank against the outmatched aliens. I counted more than a dozen of the machines before I jumped back into the alley.

"It's bad," I told them.

"What do we do?" Switzer asked.

"We should help them," I said.

"Let's do it."

Neewalker defense strategies were a vital part of a Space Jumper's training. These nefarious creatures were often at the heart of conflicts in this star sector. At least this is what we were taught at the Hollow, and it happened to be the norm on the Rings of Orbis.

"Are you thinking what I'm thinking?" Switzer asked. His faced brightened with anticipation.

"Remember: I can push into those stilts and disable them once you knock them out. It will take you too long to decipher the interface."

"Always trying to show off," he muttered.

"And I'll handle those rollers as well."

"Why do you get all the fun? *Those* I can handle."

"Fine," I agreed. "But let's get the guys on the ground first. Those machines look like they'll take forever to turn around."

"Got it."

"I'll be right back," I told Theodore, and turned to Charlie. "Make sure—"

"I will."

Switzer and I jumped behind the center roller. We refocused next to a Neewalker. We dropped fast, swiping out the stilts with our legs. My good arm was far more effective, and I grabbed the first Neewalker and snapped its stilt. As it fell, I pushed inside the stilt chips and trashed anything I could find. Switzer and I took out more than a dozen Neewalkers before they even knew what had hit them, and even then they couldn't find us. When one spotted us, we jumped to the other side of the battalion, working in unison. I jumped a nanosecond behind Switzer, waiting for the Neewalker to fall before taking out its computer. I began to see glimpses of Switzer as he broke through time and space and refocused next to the unprepared Neewalker, as if a ghost image of him revealed his whereabouts between dimensions. I found the effect extremely useful in trying to stay close to him.

Soon Neewalkers began to abandon their broken stilts, but their fins were useless on the streets of Murat. The rollers crushed many of them as they frantically searched the skies for Switzer and me.

"JT!" Switzer called.

I turned to Switzer, who was strapped into one of the rollers, firing on our enemy. I watched the Neewalkers turn and run while the crowd of angry aliens moved in on them.

"Get out of there!" I shouted at him.

"I couldn't resist!"

One of the other rollers saw Switzer and returned fire with a direct hit.

"Switzer!"

I jumped next to the attacking machine and pushed into the controls. The machine was useless by the time it tried to fire again. I jumped to Switzer's machine and found it pitched wildly on its side. Switzer was coughing and swiping at the smoke as a small fire licked at the cockpit, but he was still alive.

"Get out of there, Switzer!" I grabbed him by the collar with my good arm and hoisted him out, and we both jumped to the ground.

"The Tonat!" I heard someone cry from the crowd, and a group of aliens near the front line rushed in and smothered me. "The Tonat! The Tonat is helping us!"

The words echoed through the crowd.

"It's time to go, Switzer!" I cried out.

The aliens were trying to lift me up. Hands grabbed at me from all sides, like kids reaching for a pouch of toonbas.

"Tonat! Tonat! Tonat!"

"Now, Switzer!" I shouted.

We both refocused in the alley.

"That was amazing," Theodore cried.

"Dazzling would be a better word," Switzer argued. "Maybe even stunning, but we can't stay here. There'll be more."

"Come on, this way," Theodore instructed.

We followed Theodore through the streets. My blood was pumping; I was filled with pride in our victory.

"That was golden," I told Switzer.

"I gotta tell ya, you're fast," he complimented me.

"Did you see the looks on their faces?"

"They didn't have a clue what was happening to them."

Switzer followed Theodore up another street, and I fell behind.

"You were amazing, JT. The way you and Switzer worked in unison, those Neewalkers didn't have a chance," Charlie said.

"Thanks, Charlie."

It seemed obvious to me why Space Jumpers worked in tandem. Switzer and I had performed like a single machine connected by some kind of cosmic cable as we sliced through space, refocusing in the exact position required to chop down our enemy. I wondered if I could work with Switzer, as in permanently. When Space Jumpers were teamed together by the Trust, the only thing that separated them was death. What would that be like? What would Max say?

Theodore stopped outside a building draped in permanent shadow. The plastic structure was the color of despair, and if you didn't have a reason to be here, you would never even see it.

"Where are we?" I asked.

"The hideout," he whispered as he pushed the door open and stepped inside. "This is where Max and Ketheria are. Hey, everyone," he called out into the darkness, "look who I found!"

"Theodore! No!" I cried.

But it was too late. Switzer and Charlie had followed Theodore inside. My cry was muffled by Ketheria's scream as she caught sight of Charlie. I stayed back as she jumped up from her metal crate and charged at her old friend. Gone was the Scion, the person who had the weight of the Universe placed on her shoulders. Instead, I saw the little girl I knew as my sister, the little girl who loved the man once called Charlie.

The Honock scooped her up in his clumsy arms and hoisted her into the air like a piece of solar paper. She dripped tears of joy on his face.

"Charlie! How! Oh, Charlie," she cried.

Max walked up behind her. She was looking at Charlie, but she saw me as well. She moved slowly, and then, as if everything that had happened between us recently melted away, as if the Rings of Orbis had melted away, she rushed toward me. That was my signal, and I flung myself at her. We collided in the middle of the room, and I gulped her in. How long had I dreamed about this moment? With my face in her hair, I felt her tears on my neck. I squeezed her tighter.

"I'm sorry," she said.

"I love you," I whispered back, and she held me tighter.

We were all together again. Despite what had happened and who we had become, it was still us—just the kids from the *Renaissance*. This is what Max had always wanted. This is what *I* had wanted. It should have been a wonderful reunion, but it lasted only a nanosecond.

"JT, a trace has been placed on Theodore," Vairocina whispered in my mind. "It was triggered the moment you left his cell. A mobile force has picked up the signal. They have you as well, I'm afraid."

"I know," I replied silently with Max in my arms. It crushed me to let the outside in during that moment. I knew we were in trouble as soon as Theodore found this place. That was why they just let me take Theodore. They knew we would come here. "How long do we have?"

"Not long. Not long at all."

It was the most difficult thing I ever had to do, but I unlocked from Max's embrace.

"Listen, everyone!" I called out. There must have been thirty people or more spread out across the dusky rooms. When I spoke, more kids stepped out from their hiding places. "Do you have any weapons?"

"What's wrong, JT?" Max asked.

I looked over at Theodore. He knew. "They're coming," I whispered.

Those sitting on crates jumped up. Someone cried out, but Max took control.

"We planned for this! Everyone get ready!" she ordered. "Grace! The windows. Theodore, raise the barricade." Then she turned to me. "We have weapons."

"Good," Switzer cried. "We're going to need them."

He tossed a plasma rifle to Theodore, who caught it in mid-air and came closer to me.

"JT, I'm sorry. I wasn't thinking —"

"Stop," I interrupted him. "It's all right. This moment was inevitable. We had to take a stand eventually." I turned to my sister. "Ketheria!"

She was still in Charlie's grip. Seated on his crossed forearms, she was gently examining the metal and wires exposed in his neck. She was smiling, but her eyes were close to unloading their payload of regret. I let her have another moment. It was an expensive gesture, but I let them have it.

Then I spoke again. "Ketheria!"

She turned to me slowly, as if forcing herself to come back to this moment.

"How are you blocking the staining?"

"It's easy," she replied. "I sort of let my mind drift around it, and then it's not there anymore."

"Can you do it for everyone?"

She nodded.

"Then do it now, please." I turned inside. "Vairocina, how long—?"

The wall behind Charlie blew apart. Shards of plastic and stone rained down on him and Ketheria.

"They're here!" Vairocina said.

"Move!"

I jumped outside and refocused for a nanosecond. I was gone again before I could swallow my surprise. "I think they sent an entire battalion," I whispered to Switzer.

"That just means more fun for us," he gloated. "Theodore, you ready?"

"Ready!"

"JT! Can you create a distraction, give us more time?" Max called out. She was tossing weapons to anyone within range. Four other people piled crates and other pieces of metal into a makeshift barricade. It wouldn't be enough. Not even close. We were dead.

"Yes!" I told her, and turned to Charlie. I pointed at Ketheria, still in his arms. "Protect her!"

He nodded.

"Switzer, this time we have to take the big machines out first. There are four of them. I don't know if we can confuse them like the Neewalkers. These guys are going to be ready for us."

"No one is ever ready for *me*," Switzer said, and looked back at Max and the others. "You think these guys can hold while we go out there?"

"They have no choice," I whispered.

"Down the street, then on the backside. Go," he ordered, and we refocused behind the battalion of Preservation Forces.

In front of us, hovering on the flanks of the battalion, I could see four of the metal monsters—two on each side.

"Take the one on the far left and fire across the battalion. You get one shot," Switzer said.

I refocused inside the weapon's cockpit.

They were waiting for me.

Two guards from the Preservation Forces tossed a net at me the moment I refocused. The mesh burned my skin as it touched me. The net was weighted with some sort of electrical spheres that were moving together, trying to close the loop. Something told me that if they touched, I would never get out of this net. I jumped back.

Switzer was already waiting.

"What was that?" he cried, rubbing at his skin.

"They know we're here."

"So much for that plan. Time to show you what I learned during my missing years. Wait here."

Before I could protest, Switzer jumped. A few moments later, he was standing next to me again holding two plasma cannons. There was a trickle of blood running down his forehead.

"Where did you get those?" I exclaimed.

"Up my ass, where do you think? From out there! Here."

Switzer tossed me a fist-size object. It was spiked like a space mine.

"Explosive?" I asked.

He nodded as one of the huge metal tanks blasted another

hole in the hideout. "Get out of the way after you toss that thing," he ordered. "And toss it hard. It blows on contact. They'll know what's happening after the first one. I figure we jump as we toss. We have to do this together. You ready?"

"Absolutely."

"You take the two on the left; I've got these two. On three."

"One . . ."

"Switzer?"

"What?"

"Thanks."

"Shut up and go blow stuff up."

I nodded and smiled.

"Three!"

I jumped within a meter of the first hover tank and felt the burn from its turbine reaching for my skin. No one saw me as I wound up and drilled the explosive into the rear-mounted engine. I jumped before it hit the tank. I refocused behind the next tank and felt the pressure from the first explosion race me to the next tank. Even the air was trying to get away, knocking over everything in its path. As I felt myself fall, the explosive slipped from my fingers.

It blows on contact.

I watched the spiked device roll over in the air as debris from my first strike pelted my skin. I refused to close my eyes in fear the explosive would speed up. I pushed myself through the empty space, reaching for the explosive before I even refocused. I stretched out and grabbed the prickly metal from some other dimension, refocusing on my back. I hurled the hunk of metal at the belly of my target. When I looked up, I saw the butt of a plasma rifle coming down from the sky, guided by a Preservation guard. The rifle and the guard both disappeared with the exploding hover tank. Obviously things standing straight up were ripped away first. I jumped before I was forced to follow them.

Back behind the action, I watched the last hover tank rip apart and the bulk of the beast land lopsided on the ground. Several troops were crushed after being knocked down by the explosion and unable to get out of the way. Switzer was next to me before they even cried out.

"Now for the messy part," he said, and hoisted the cannon onto his shoulder. He looked at me before firing into the crowd. "Why don't you go see if they need help inside?"

"You all right here?"

"Perfect," he said, grinning.

As I refocused inside, I heard the first cannon blast from outside. Grace cried out as the walls of the building echoed the explosion.

"Don't worry," I told her. "That's us. We got the tanks, too. It's almost over."

Every one of the kids in the room was armed and ready, hidden by a crate or a wall or some sort of makeshift barricade, most of the items just hunks of garbage. One blast from a cannon out there would blow all of this apart. Maybe they should know the Scion was in here. It would probably save a few lives.

"I'll be back," I whispered to Max, and she nodded.

I jumped outside and refocused away from the fight. I

searched the mayhem for Switzer and found him to my left, jumping through the troops. I watched one guard turn where Switzer had refocused and fire. The errant round sailed past Switzer as he jumped again. After the guard watched one of his comrades fall from his own gun, he dropped his weapon and ran. Others followed his lead, but as the guards began to scatter, I heard a roar rushing up behind me. I turned to witness thousands and thousands of knudniks and Citizens marching to join the battle. The Preservation Forces were about to be unmatched.

I jumped next to Switzer. "Having fun?"

"More than you can imagine," he replied.

"It's time to go," I told him. "That mob is even larger than before, and they're headed this way. We need to leave before more troops arrive."

"I'm right behind ya."

We refocused inside.

"Theodore, come here!" I called to him, and then found my sister. "Ketheria, we are going to leave, but we'll be back. When we return, can you do that thing you do and cloak us in your staining? Both me and Theodore. You have to be fast. Can you do that?"

"Sure," she said. "Is Charlie staying here?"

"For now," I told her, and turned to Switzer.

"Let's jump back to Hach's and wait for the trace to be picked up there. The moment they have us, we'll jump back here and slip under Ketheria's cloak."

"Then what?" he said.

"I haven't thought that far ahead, but I know we can't stay here."

Suddenly, the door behind Switzer swung open. Everyone turned and readied their weapons in the direction of the door as Drapling strolled into our hideout with three other Keepers following.

"The Scion can handle all of this," Drapling announced. "She can take care of this fighting. She is coming with us. The Descendants of Light will show her how to use her powers. The Scion will restore order. Our order."

"That's not going to happen," I told him.

Max stood next to me. "How did you find us?"

"I imagine everyone on the rings is converging upon this point," he said, and then raised his hand toward Ketheria. "Come, my child. Now is the time for you to fulfill your destiny."

A surge of kids jumped up and surrounded Ketheria. We made an imposing posse of plasma-toting teenagers.

Drapling stepped back, his arms still reaching out to Ketheria. "This is ridiculous. She is the Scion! You have to let the prophecy fulfill itself. You must not intervene in these matters."

"Like you, Drapling?" I said.

Drapling would not look at me. He wouldn't take his eyes off Ketheria, and she wouldn't leave Charlie's side. I could see the yearning in Drapling's eyes. His prize was right in front of him! I looked at Charlie. "Don't let him touch her," I whispered, and he nodded. I might as well have locked Ketheria in a safe.

"C'mon, guys," I said to Switzer and Theodore. "Be ready, Ketheria. We'll come right back here. Max, please make sure everyone is ready."

"For what?"

"To leave," I told her.

"To leave where?"

"To leave the Rings of Orbis."

We jumped back to Hach's and hid in an empty room down the corridor from Theodore's room. The stillness of the air made the building feel empty and lifeless.

"I don't think there's anyone here," Theodore whispered.

"What do we do now?" Switzer asked.

"We wait. Vairocina, let me know when a trace has been placed on one of us, will you, please?"

"Already waiting for it," she replied.

"I'm sorry about back there, JT. I wasn't thinking," Theodore mumbled.

"It was my fault. I should have told you."

"That's enough, girls," Switzer scoffed. "Look, we found them, can we get back to the Hollow now? Pick your favorites and let's jump back. I'm hungry."

"I'm not leaving any of them," I argued. "In fact, I'm not going back to the Hollow."

"What—?"

"JT." Vairocina materialized in front of us. "The trace has been placed. The Trading Council has mobilized an even larger force, and they're heading in your direction."

"Perfect. Now—"

"JT, they have no intentions of capturing you. The Trading Council has given orders for you to be killed on sight."

"JT!" Theodore cried.

"It's all right," I assured him. "If they wanted me dead, they could have done it already. They could have killed me like they did Ganook." I turned to Vairocina. "Thanks. One last thing."

"Don't say it like that," she replied.

"Don't worry. I have no intention of dying this cycle," I told her. "Listen, can you jam the signal from the staining? I don't know how, but is there some way of thinking I'm still here after I leave?"

"I don't know if it's possible, but I could try some sort of echo. I might need a little time, and it certainly won't last. I'm sure they'll figure it out."

"That's all I can ask." I turned to Switzer and Theodore. "Switzer, straight back to Ketheria. Let her put Theodore under the cloak."

"What about you? You're not staying here by yourself."

"Just until Vairocina's ready. It's me they want. Not you two."

He nodded. "Then what?"

"Then it will be time to go. We're not wanted here anymore," I said.

18

I sat alone in my old room and waited for Vairocina's cue. It wasn't much of a room now, but that did not matter anymore. I wasn't scared, either. In fact, I was quite excited by what was coming next. We would all leave the rings together, I thought, including the Scion. And better yet, I would have Max with me. With her and Switzer at my side, we were an invincible force.

"It's ready," Vairocina said.

"How much time do I have?"

"Fraction of a diam, not much more."

"I'll take it. Thank you."

What am I going to do without Vairocina? I suddenly wondered. I didn't even know how I was going to say good-bye.

The moment I returned, Ketheria confirmed that we were now protected from any attempts to trace our genetic stain. I did not question her methods. I simply trusted them.

Outside the hideout, I could hear the war cries from knud-niks charging the Preservation Forces.

"They're pushing them back," I said to Switzer.

He nodded. "I figure the rebels are getting squashed or being forced back into the city. Either way, I don't think we have much time. "

"I know you have a plan," Max whispered, slipping next to me and wrapping her arm in mine. I took a moment to enjoy her touch.

"I always knew you two had a thing," Switzer added, and Max smiled.

"I do," I told her. "But it wasn't my idea. This idea was presented to me a long time ago, but I refused to listen."

"Tell me! Don't be so cryptic," she begged.

Theodore, Grace, and a few other kids from the *Renaissance* had gathered around me. I looked over at Switzer. "It was really his idea," I told them, thumbing in his direction. "Before we ever arrived on the Rings of Orbis, all I ever thought about was coming here and starting a new life with my sister. Remember our observation deck?"

"Of course," Grace answered.

"Well, I would lie there dreaming about what my life on the Rings of Orbis would be like."

"We all did that."

"Yeah, but I had imagined a utopia. A place where they handed out chits and no one went sick or hungry. It was childish. In my imagination, this was a perfect place. I gobbled up every story they planted in Mother and wished away every moment so I could get here sooner. Even when Theylor told us about our fate, I refused to let go of my dream. I would not even consider that the Rings of Orbis might be a cruel place, motivated by greed, a place where success was achieved only by sacrificing others."

"It wasn't always like that," Drapling cried out. "The Rings of Orbis were different. The Trading Council changed everything. This is why the Scion is here."

"Shut up!" Switzer growled. "Or I will come over there and do it for you, you two-headed space freak."

"I should have listened when Switzer convinced you guys to take the *Renaissance*."

"No!" Max said.

"Let him talk," Switzer argued.

"If I had known back then that I was a Softwire, I could have pushed into the ship's computer, or at least I should have tried. You don't know how many times I have thought about that moment, over and over and over again. I know now that I should have listened. We *should* have taken the *Renaissance* and never looked backed."

"What are you saying?" Theodore asked.

"I say we do that now."

"The *Renaissance* is gone, split-screen," Switzer reminded me.

"No, he wants to steal a new starship and leave the rings," Max said, smiling.

"Have you flipped a chip?" Theodore cried. "We can't steal a starship. Who's going to fly it?"

Switzer's face sparkled with surprise, quite a feat for such a scarred mug. He put his hand up and grinned sheepishly. "Captain Ceesar, at your service," he gloated.

"And Switzer and I have been versed on a zillion different spacecraft in our training," I added.

"It's still crazy," someone else complained.

I turned to Max. "Isn't this what you always wanted? We can be together, all of us, away from here. No Scion, no Tonat, no Space Jumpers. Just *us*. We can find a new world to live on, and we'll never look at the Rings of Orbis again."

"Where did the Keepers go?" someone asked.

I turned and they were gone. "Drapling?" No answer.

"I don't think Twin-Top ran off to book us a seat on the shuttle," Switzer said.

"If we're going to go, then we go now," I told the group.

"Wait!" Grace cried. "Can we think about this?"

"What for?" Switzer said, throwing his arms up and stomping to the back of the room.

"We don't have time," I argued.

"Just wait!" Grace said.

Grace and two other kids broke into their own group, then four other kids did the same. Theodore glanced at them.

"It will be all right," I told him.

"I know it will." He stepped toward me. "Of course I'm with you."

"I think it's perfect," Max said. "Especially the part about us being together. Not just you and me. I mean, of course I love that, but I want all of us to be together, even Switzer."

I looked over at Switzer, who was now perched on a metal shipping crate. Ketheria was next to him. They were whispering about something, and I could only assume she was forgiving him for everything he had done in their past. Inside, I smiled (I wouldn't dare let Switzer see me). Their reconciliation was necessary if we were going to live together on a starship again. I could not even guess how long it would take to find a new home.

"They have a lot to discuss," Max whispered.

"He's different now," I told her. "He's not the Switzer we used to know."

Max took my hands and turned me to face her. She was intoxicatingly close to me. It took everything to keep my eyes open.

"I'm sorry," she whispered.

"Don't," I said.

"No, I want to. I wasn't fair to you. I ignored the pressures they placed on you. I did not want to admit what they had done to you, *to us*. I'm so sorry. I love you, and I don't ever want us to be apart again. It just hurts too much."

"We won't. I promise."

"All right!" Grace said. "We'll go. But Switzer cannot be in charge. It has to be Ketheria."

I looked over at Switzer, knowing he would protest, but Switzer was staring over Ketheria's shoulder. His faced showed no sign that he had heard the group's objection.

"Switzer?" I called out to him.

"What's wrong with him?" Max whispered.

"Switzer!"

"What?" he grunted, shaking off his trance.

"They won't let you be captain. They want Ketheria," I told him.

"What?" Switzer protested. "I'm the captain."

"Then no deal," Grace said.

I glared at Switzer.

"Fine," he grumbled, although his protest was unusually weak. "But I'm not calling her Captain Ketheria."

Ketheria glanced at Switzer. "I'm ready," she said.

"There's still a war going on out there," I warned them, "and Switzer's right: Drapling didn't leave to reserve a seat for us. It's a long way to the spaceport, maybe four kilometers."

Just then I heard a *WHUMP*. In fact, I felt it. Even the air pushed against me.

"What was that?" Grace cried.

"We better hurry," Max whispered.

"Can't you jump there and take us?" Theodore asked.

"First, there are too many of you to jump at once with Switzer, and I don't have a belt to help."

"I don't know how far my cloaking works, either," Ketheria said.

"We can't risk it. We need to stay together and move as a group."

The building shivered from another blast, coaxing the dust and debris from the ceiling.

"Can we go?" Grace demanded.

"I will take the lead and Switzer will follow last. Everyone else pair up and keep Ketheria protected. Charlie, you stay with her, in the middle. Don't talk to anyone, and keep your head down!" I yelled.

People began pairing off, moving Ketheria to the middle. Max came up behind me. "I'm with you," she whispered.

"Stay close," I said, and kissed her on the cheek. I thought of Vairocina's warning. "But not too close. Give yourself some running room."

I'm not dying this cycle.

Once outside the building, I could see intense fighting still raging to my left. The knudniks appeared to be holding their own as the Preservation Forces hunkered down into a building at the edge of Murat.

"Don't look," I whispered to Max as I stepped around the aftermath of Switzer's cannon.

"Oh, that's disgusting!" Grace cried.

My plan was to race around the far side of Murat in order to reach the spaceport. The military aircraft (and there were a lot of them) were converging over the center of the city, so most of the conflict was happening there. The detour added a kilometer to our run, but there were too many of us to risk getting caught in the skirmish. I was certain that once we reached the spaceport, operations would be so chaotic on the landing pads that Switzer and I could jump inside a ship and leave orbit before anyone even knew we were there.

"Ketheria, what's the range on that ability of yours?"

"I don't know," she called out.

"Then stay close, everyone!"

I treated the city as nothing more than an obstacle course. To me, it was just another map in a game of Quest-Nest, and my bait was the spaceport. Actually, my bait was a shiny new spaceship ready to take me to my new home, far away from here.

As we raced past the busted buildings and abandoned trading chambers, I concentrated on the prospects of a new life and it sparked an excitement in me. The energy moved my legs forward unconsciously, and I occasionally glanced behind to make sure everyone was keeping close.

We moved as one group over barricaded alleys and crumbled buildings, slowing only when a quick climb seemed faster than finding a new way around a fallen structure or mountain of garbage.

"I didn't know things had gotten so bad here," I called out to Max.

"The Trading Council really wants the rings."

"They won't go without a fight."

"You weren't the only knudnik who thought the Rings of Orbis should have been their utopia."

We had run about a kilometer when I was forced to pull up.

"Stop!" I cried out.

In front of us was an enormous hole in the ring. Some sort of bomb or missile had destroyed an entire city block, preventing us from going any farther. I couldn't tell what had caused the damage, but whatever it was, it was big. Scary big.

"I hope they ran out of whatever did that," Theodore remarked.

The guts of Orbis 4 lay open at our feet, like some kind of busted space shuttle abandoned by its mechanic.

"This just happened," I said. "The dust has hardly settled and parts are still burning. That must have been the sound we heard back at the hideout."

"We can't cross this," Max said.

She was right. To my right I could see rows of factories turned into mountains of rubble by the explosion.

"Just go around it," Switzer ordered.

"We can't," Max said. "I've been here before, handing out taps in the city. Those factories go on forever. That would be a very long detour."

"It looks like someone knows what they're doing," I said.

"They're cutting off access, keeping everyone in the center," Switzer pointed out.

"Or they're making it very difficult for anyone to leave," I added.

"There's only one person who knows what we're trying to do," Max whispered.

"Think Double-Dome would risk baby-malf's life like that?" Switzer asked.

I frowned at him.

"Sorry," he mumbled.

I looked to my left. The long street still sparkled, a reminder of the city that once was. Only now it led directly into the conflict, a route I wasn't prepared to take, but I saw no other choice.

"We don't have to go all the way in," I told Switzer. "We could work our way in just a little, to cut back over and up."

"I know this street, too," Theodore said. "Every alley dumps into the center of Murat."

"Maybe we should send a reconnaissance group out and map a route to avoid that," I offered.

"No, JT," Max said. "If one goes, we all go. We stay together now. You said so yourself. Think of the staining."

"I agree," someone else called out.

I looked back up toward the factories.

"We could jump—" I started to say, but Max cut in.

"No," she snapped. "Look!"

Far down the street, I spotted two enormous hover tanks as they rounded the corner. Behind them was a wave of Preservation Forces. I couldn't tell if they were retreating or moving toward us. Circular fliers spun overhead, firing into the crowds.

"Look! Knudniks!" Max cried. They were fighting the Preservation Forces hand to hand. "We're trapped."

"Let's move!" I cried. "Everyone into the alley!" I pointed to an opening in the building between the hole and the fighting moving toward us.

"Vairocina," I called out. "I'm stuck in the city, trying to make my way around Murat's industrial core. Can you see where I am and find me the shortest route around it?"

"I am unable to locate your whereabouts, JT. The manner in which you are blocking the staining is very effective. More than three dozen attempts to trace your location have been attempted—unsuccessfully, I might add. If you give me a bearing, I can pull up a schematic to help you navigate," she offered.

A small speck tumbled toward us like an extinguished star giving up its spot in the night sky. The speck grew larger, and for a moment, I didn't comprehend what it was. In fact, I was mesmerized by the curve of its trajectory as it sailed past my head. Only when the thing disappeared inside the factories next to us, did I realize.

"No!" I cried, but a deafening *WHUMP* rolled over me, flinging me backward as the air seemed to disappear, as if it was being sucked into outer space.

The ground vomited as I hit it, tossing me back up and mixing me into the debris. The blast from the explosion refused to subside, as if it were taunting me. I couldn't get a bearing on anything, or anyone, and it felt as if someone had set the ring spinning out of control. Suddenly, I slammed to a stop. A large hunk of factory followed me to the ground and crushed my robotic arm. I pulled my arm out and watched my fingers curl back, almost touching my wrist. The pain shot up my arm before my fingers snapped back into place, lifeless.

"Switzer!" I cried out. Even I was surprised that this was my first word.

I turned into the swirling debris. "Max!"

I tried to focus on something—anything to make my world settle, but everything was in motion.

Charlie slumped, lifeless, on the ground.

Theodore crawled on his knees.

Grace wandered, bleeding.

Switzer was nowhere to be seen.

"Max!"

I jumped out of the chaos, to a place just beyond the explosion. I refocused and saw another gaping hole in the center of the street as debris swirled about the opening as if some vortex had been ripped open by the blast. I could see some people standing; some were lying on the ground. Some I could hardly see at all.

"Ketheria!"

The Preservation Forces were now at my heels, but they were too busy fighting the knudniks. I jumped back to the highest point of the rubble and refocused atop the aftermath and inside the growing tornado. I tried to flex my crushed arm again, but it would not respond. It flopped at my side, useless.

"Max!"

Still no answer.

"Max!"

In the hole, about twenty meters below me, I could see the purple stream of a light chute, untethered and flailing about like a broken gas line. The stream crackled and hissed across the black void. Another uprooted chute intersected with the first one, igniting a light storm whenever they touched.

"Max!"

"JT," my sister called out.

"Ketheria! Where are you?"

"Down here," she cried. "I have Max."

I fell on my belly and peered over the edge. Ketheria's crimson hands clung to a utility pipe sprouting from the rubble and over the hole in the ring. Max, her hair matted with blood, was lying unconscious on a chunk of concrete just above Ketheria's head and slightly to my right.

"Ketheria! Are you all right? Is Max alive?"

"I don't know. Be careful. I think everything is really loose."

"Hold on!"

I jumped to the far side of the hole so I could get a better look. Max was barely on the rock, and there was no way to jump to Ketheria. *Where was Switzer?*

I refocused on a small metal girder just above the girls. I struggled to keep my footing as the girder tilted severely toward my sister. My right arm was now switching between functioning and useless as I looked for a way to secure myself. I jammed my legs between the girder and a slab of concrete. As I reached over the edge, another explosion set the world in motion yet again.

"Ketheria!"

The blast heaved Max into the air while the rock underneath her tumbled into the void. The busted light chute gobbled it up. Ketheria reached out and caught hold of Max's shirt while my left hand clamped onto Ketheria's right wrist. My other hand, the bad one, snagged Max's shirt. It wasn't much, but it was holding.

"JT, help me!" Ketheria begged.

Ketheria's plea for help ignited some part of me that found strength I never knew I had. My mind focused on my contact with Ketheria while I shifted my weight to help Max. She was heavy.

"Max!" I pleaded.

"I have to let go of her, JT!" Ketheria said. A red trail grew on Max's shirt as she slipped through Ketheria's bloody fingers.

"Wait! I don't have her!"

I concentrated hard to maintain what little hold I had. I interfaced with my arm, but there was only a patchwork of controls at my disposal now, and most of those were unresponsive. I only managed to squeeze a little more strength out from it.

"JT!"

"All right! I have her."

Ketheria grabbed the pole again as Max's shirt ripped.

"You don't have her, JT. Use both hands!"

Ketheria was holding on to the metal pipe sticking out of the concrete, but my hand would not release her wrist.

"I can't!"

"Yes, you can. I'm fine!"

"No. I can't." I stared at my left hand clamped around Ketheria's wrist. "My mind won't let me."

As much as I wanted to let go of Ketheria and use both hands to pull Max to safety, something inside of me refused to let go of my sister, to let go of the Scion.

"That's not you, JT! That's what they did to you! That's the coding working. The coding the Trust put inside of you. You love her, JT. Fight it! Let go of me!"

Max's shirt ripped again.

"JT!" Ketheria screamed.

I tried. I tried so hard to let go of Ketheria, but my mind refused the logic.

"Max, wake up, please," I whispered.

Everything in my vision now began to swim together in the purple light. Tears fell from my face and sparked against the chute.

"JT, it's not you! Let go of me and grab Max, please!"

I thought of every moment I'd ever had with Max. The first time she helped me with the hidden files on the *Renaissance*, the first time she held my hand, even our first kiss. My hand wriggled on Ketheria's wrist, but it was not enough. I could not let go.

Max's shirt ripped again—a final time.

Ketheria grabbed at Max as she fell, and I like to think I tried as well. My left hand stayed on Ketheria while my right hand scratched at the air.

I didn't scream. I didn't cry out. Instead, I told Max I loved her as her body plunged into the purple light chute.

"I'm so sorry, JT," Ketheria whispered through her sobs. "I'm so sorry for this."

I stared at the purple chute for a while. *This couldn't be happening. Max? Max! This isn't real,* I tried to tell myself, but I knew Max was gone. I could hear Ketheria sobbing, and I could hear the war raging over my head, but I could also hear my breathing over it all, for some weird reason.

As I stared at the purple light chute, waiting for time to reverse itself, I felt my hate for the Rings of Orbis burn my insides. I hated everything they had done to me. I hated them for everything I had lost and everything I'd never had.

"It's not your fault, JT."

"Yes, it is," I whispered.

"It's not. It's this place, these people."

"I know that, but it won't bring Max back."

"I'm so sorry," Ketheria whispered again as she stood up. I was still staring down the hole where Max fell. "They did this to you, JT, and they'll do it again. I have to stop them."

Without looking, I said, "What do you mean?"

"It's my destiny."

"What is?"

"To save them."

"Save who?"

"Save everyone."

I finally turned toward my sister and away from where Max had fallen. In the back of my mind, I was aware that my life was still moving forward. "Ketheria, what are you talking about? Here, grab on to me. Can you pull yourself up at all?"

"JT?" It was Switzer.

"Where were you?" I screamed. "I needed you! You could have helped me."

Switzer was kneeling on the far side of the hole. I could see blood gushing from a nasty cut over his right eye, and his left arm was clearly busted.

"Switzer!" my sister cried, trying to look over her shoulder. "Is that you? I'm ready."

"Ready for what?" I said.

Max is gone.

"JT, I must suffer this," she said. "It will not happen if I do not do this. It is the last thing I must do before I can truly awaken."

"Ketheria, tell me what you are going to do," I demanded.

"I have to do this, and I have to do it without you. I see that now. I'm sorry."

Then Ketheria bit down on my hand. "Ow!" My fingers loosened just enough for her to slip from my grip, and she let go of the bar.

She tumbled into the hole.

"Ketheria!"

Switzer was next to her in an instant and plucked her out of the purple air. He refocused on the far side of the hole, just as he had practiced at the Hollow. I did the same, surfacing in the center of the battle. Preservation Forces were fighting hand to hand with knudniks and Citizens alike. I couldn't help but think that Switzer, with Ketheria in his arms, was a far better Space Jumper than me.

Max is gone.

"What are you doing, Switzer?" I said.

"Getting a little payback. Something you should have done a long time ago."

"Put her down!"

"No. I'm not like you, buddy. Things are black or white for me. You spend too much time in here," he said, pointing at his head. "*This* is a good deal, and I'm going to take it."

"Deal? What deal?"

"It was my idea," Ketheria said. "Don't blame him."

"What are you doing?"

"Put me down, Switzer, but don't let go until I say."

"Ketheria. I don't understand. Tell me, please," I pleaded with her.

Max is gone.

Ketheria did not reply. She stood perfectly still with her feet together and lifted her arms to the side. Then the glow within her eyes seemed to expand. The golden luminescence flowed from her eyes and formed a radiant coronet around her head before dropping to her feet. When the light hit the ground, it exploded outward like the birth of a new galaxy. The circle of light engulfed everyone in its path. Citizen, knudnik, and soldier alike dropped their weapons and bathed in the stream of light now flooding Murat. I could not tell how far the light was going, but soon it flowed as far as I could see.

Everyone just stood there and stared at the people next to them with this perplexed look on their faces, as if they were trying to understand how they had gotten here. Soon some people were tending to the fallen and no one was fighting anymore. I gawked as Preservation Forces stepped down from their tanks and pulled knudniks from the rubble. Was Ketheria doing this? I turned toward my sister as the stream of light faded and eventually stopped flowing. Then she turned toward me slowly. There was something different about her. I didn't know if it was her eyes or her smile. She looked as if she was capable of understanding anything.

Then she smiled at me and said, "Good-bye, JT."

"Are you sure you want to do this?" I asked Charlie.

"I have a few debts to repay," he replied.

Charlie and I were seated in the spaceport on Orbis 4. His shuttle was about to leave, and he had asked me to visit him before he left.

"Your real name isn't Charlie, is it?"

He shook his head and said, "Harlan. Harlan Admunsen."

"I like *Charlie* better."

"Then let's leave it like that."

"I'm going to mi—" I started to say, but he interrupted me.

"Don't get me crying. Something might start to rust. You never did turn down those emotion levels, either," he complained. "But thanks for making me feel like myself again. You know, with the . . ." Charlie pointed at the metal around the back of his skull.

"No problem," I said.

I stared at the floor, swallowing the lump in my throat.

Then he said, "They still might find her."

I shook my head, unable to talk.

"*The shuttle for Orbis 2 is now boarding.*"

Finally, I croaked out, "No." I looked up at him. "I wish I could feel what everyone has been feeling since the awakening. Theylor said I was designed to not experience it. The enlightenment had no effect on me. Just another gift from the Trust to ensure that their fighting machine stays true to its mission. I don't mind, though. . . ."

"I'm sorry."

"No, I think it's helped a little, with Max, you know, to fill that hole up a little bit."

"You're going to be all right," he said, and clamped his hand on my shoulder. It was a painful blow.

"Ouch! You may act like the old Charlie, but you have super-human strength now."

"Sorry."

"*The shuttle for Orbis 2 is now boarding.*"

"I gotta go," he said, standing up. "Give me a hug and then go and get on with your life."

I laughed.

"Hey! None of that. You know what you have to do. You are a Space Jumper. They're going to write stories about you one cycle, JT."

I stood and smiled. Then I gave Charlie a hug. "Come find me," I whispered.

"I will," he croaked.

"The shuttle for Orbis 2 is now boarding."

Charlie broke away. "Go on, go say good-bye to Theodore," he ordered.

"Good-bye. Charlie."

"Good luck, kid."

Charlie picked up his bag and joined the line for the shuttle. He didn't turn back to look at me again, but I waited until he disappeared through the loading door. Even after everything that had happened, Charlie still managed to avoid most of my questions. I wondered where he was off to. I wondered if I would ever know.

I set out to find the New Arrival Processing Center, to say good-bye to Theodore. Theodore was now helping the new knudniks arriving on the Rings of Orbis. He had wanted to take this cycle off work, but I told him not to. I figured it would be easier to say good-bye that way.

No one referred to the new arrivals on the rings as knudniks anymore, and they were no longer indentured to the Citizens, either. Ketheria's enlightenment had spread fast through the rings, even reaching the Trading Council, who structured a new power deal with the Keepers.

Watching everyone file through the spaceport, I couldn't help but feel that they looked a little happier in their home. But the Rings of Orbis were no longer home for me. For so long I had thought that this is where my life would end up, but now I realized that it was only the starting point. My home was always where my friends were. I had had a home on the *Renaissance,* and I had had a home on the rings when we were all together, despite the conditions. I just didn't see it.

I missed Max terribly. I hoped for so long that the light chute had transported her to another place on the ring, but after a long and fruitless search, the Keepers were unable to locate her. Phase after phase, I blamed myself for that moment. I was unable to turn off the creature inside of me long enough to help the girl I loved. I could still get angry thinking about it, but at least the awakening had created enough space for me to move on with my life.

I stopped outside the entrance to the New Arrival Processing Center. I watched Theodore talking with each alien, directing them to the R5s and then helping them uplink information for their adjustment period on the rings. He moved from alien to alien, more confident than I had ever seen him. Theylor said it was from the enlightenment, but I couldn't get a sense of that. In fact, I think Theodore's change had nothing to do with Ketheria. I think he'd simply found his passion.

"JT!" Theodore called out when he finally saw me.

I waved at him and walked into the room. "I wouldn't have guessed in a billion rotations that we would have ended up like this," I said.

Theodore looked back at the aliens huddled near the R5s.

"I know! It's crazy, isn't it? But you know, I feel so empowered. It's hard to explain. I just want to help. I want to make the rings a better place, and it's not just me. The sentiment is spreading through every ring."

"It's almost as if the Ancients have come home," I replied.

"That's what Theylor said!"

"I guess we did what they needed."

"But what does it mean? You know, for us? What will happen when Ketheria goes around the universe waking everyone up?"

I looked at Theodore and shrugged. "I don't know. Like this, I suppose."

"Then it's going to be great."

"You can still change your mind."

Theodore shook his head. "No. My place is here now. You know, *you* could stay. Switzer can take care of Ketheria. Even you said he's changed."

"I don't think so. Switzer saw a good deal and he took it. He will always be looking for what's best for him. Ketheria will have no effect on him. One of those deals is going to hurt Ketheria some cycle, and I can't have that. Besides, I think she expects me to find her. It was something she said. You know . . . after . . ."

Theodore looked at his feet, and I did the same. It was a routine we went through whenever there was nothing left to discuss but Max. Theodore had helped me the most after the accident, and I was grateful for that. I hoped he knew.

"Thanks," I whispered just in case he didn't.

He nodded and smiled. "Will I ever see you again?"

"I'm going to make it a promise," I said. "One that I will keep."

"Then I'll see you soon, my friend. Stay safe," he said, and hugged me.

"You too."

Theodore broke away and waved as he returned to the new arrivals. I watched him slip back into his work, and then I turned for the door. I spotted two Keepers walking through the spaceport and wondered if Theylor had arrived yet. He had personally disbanded the Descendants of Light after it was discovered that they were the ones who bombed the exit points from Murat. I wondered if Drapling even knew what he had done. Theylor never mentioned what happened to him.

My instructions stated that I meet Theylor at the wormhole launch located at Gate 5 on the far side of the Spaceport 1. Whenever a knudnik's work rule had expired, the knudnik was offered the choice to stay and petition for citizenship or take a free trip through the wormhole. Not once had I ever thought about taking that trip. I always saw the rings as my final destination, yet here I was, ready to leave the place I had so wanted to call home.

The cycle's traffic was sparse near the gate. I figured few knudniks opted for the wormhole option anymore. I spotted Theylor waiting near the gate. Both his heads were smiling.

"I have a present for you," he said.

"That sounds intriguing. Is it something to eat?"

"You must be hungry, but you can eat on the other side. It's best to travel through the wormhole on an empty stomach."

"So what is it?"

"Come, I'll show you."

I followed Theylor through the gate. He was the first person I had ever met from the Rings of Orbis. It was appropriate that he be the last I see. Throughout everything, Theylor had never changed. He was the same alien as he was the first time I met him.

I stepped through the gate and onto a curved platform. Theylor moved toward the huge windows that arched up and over our heads. On the other side of the glass was a small space-craft docked at the portal. The slick flier glistened under the warm floods that spilled down on the ship.

"That's mine?" I asked.

"Well, you certainly cannot walk through the wormhole. Did you ever wonder why the trip was so expensive? You need a vessel."

"And you're giving this one to me?"

"It is our gift. A token of our gratitude for everything you have done for the Rings of Orbis. I took it upon myself to make a few upgrades and enhancements," he said. "I see you've done the same." He glanced at my right arm.

"You know?" I said.

"Of course. She was worried that we might still need her, but I assured her that we could cope in her absence. Besides, I believe she would have missed you more than she will miss us."

I held up my right arm and fiddled with a thick piece of jewelry made of silver metal and black bands of rubber that now clung to my wrist. It looked like a bracelet, but it was one that I could never take off, for it was actually attached to my arm.

"Vairocina made the addition," I whispered.

"A girl needs a little room," she teased inside my head,

"especially if I'm going to traipse around the universe locked inside your arm."

"It looks nice," Theylor remarked. "No one will ever know. Would you like to see your new ship?"

"You know I have to do this, right, Theylor?" I said.

"Of course I do."

"And I have to do it alone."

"As you have always stated."

"Vairocina gave Switzer the coordinates of every place she had ever visited in the galaxy when she uploaded those coordinates in Ketheria's room. Switzer can only jump to those star systems. I figure I'll simply do the same thing. I'm certain I can pick up his trail somewhere along the line."

Theylor reached into his robe and removed a Space Jumper's belt.

"Then you'll need this when you find her," he said.

I took the belt in my hands. All my thoughts and emotions for Max ignited inside my chest. If only I hadn't been so stubborn, if only I had accepted my fate sooner, then I would have had one of these stupid things. I could have jumped to Max after she fell and then jumped to safety. It was the most costly mistake of my life, but one I would never make again.

"Thanks," I mumbled, and slipped the belt around my waist. "I still don't understand why Ketheria had to leave without me. Switzer is not the most trustworthy person."

"She had to. It was part of her awakening. The fourteenth and final step required her to let go of the thing she cherished most in this universe. That, I am afraid, was you. Only when she released you from your duties could she truly be the Scion. The results were immediate, as you remember."

I nodded.

"When you emerged from the cocoon on the Hollow, you, too, completed the final step of your awakening. Without it, you would never have become a Space Jumper and Ketheria would be on her own forever."

"I'll find her soon," I told him.

"I know you will."

"Ready, Vairocina?"

"Absolutely," she said.

"Good-bye, Theylor. Thank you for everything."

The Keeper smiled, and both heads nodded. "Drink deep from the Source, my friend," he said.

I looked back at the spaceport before stepping onto the ship. The tallest spire was reaching for the eclipse as the ring laid its shadow across the city. *I will never miss this place,* I told myself. As I hesitated outside the bay, I felt a deep pain in my stomach and a wave of nausea rose up in my throat. I smiled, not because I was leaving but because I knew that Ketheria was still within my reach.

ACKNOWLEDGMENTS

You always hear about writers locked away, toiling over their manuscripts for years, before unleashing them on the world. It sounds like a solitary process, but it's far from that. I would personally like to acknowledge those who have namelessly helped me bring the Softwire series to life. Thank you so much. I really mean it.

To Eddie, for getting the ball rolling in the first place.

To Liz, Lynne, and Michael for finding the Softwire books a home at Candlewick.

To Sarah for putting up with me and making me a better writer.

To Laura, for your patience and always taking my phone calls. :)

To Lisa, for your big bookstore support when others were silent.

To Denise and the girls at KNTR—your support has never wavered. Thank you. Ninjaritas for everyone!

To Jim, thank you for your insight and encouragement.

To Faith for living up to your name and helping me carry the torch.

To Nard—the keeper of the case. Thank you for always being there.

To Michelle, for your amazing novel studies.

To Alan, for your encouragement and friendship. And your voice.

To Nathan, for your relentless support and unwavering friendship. Thank you.

To my fans for your great letters and e-mails. They really kept me writing.

To the Citizens of Orbis for helping me create an unbelievable place to hang out online at the ringsoforbis.com

To teachers and librarians who invited me into your schools and placed books in the hands of kids who might never have heard of them.

To all of the independent bookstores that love the Softwire series and hand-sell my books. I can't thank you enough and tell you how important that is.

To Frank, the best friend I could ever have in my corner. Thank you so much.

To Sky, for being patient with Daddy and loving me no matter how often I had to go away to promote the Softwire books.

And to Marisa, for your love, your understanding, and for sticking it out with me. You're amazing. I love you.